KV-107-873

UNITY

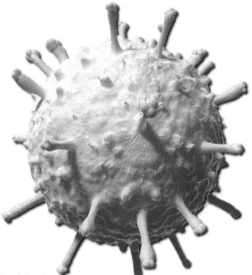

Leabharlanna Poiblí Chathair Baile Átha Cliath
Dublin City Public Libraries

JOHN LEAHY

NECRO PUBLICATIONS
–2016 –

UNITY

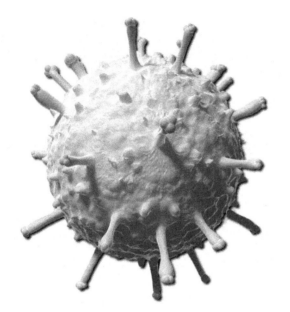

Brainse Ráth Maonais
Rathmines Branch
Fón / Tel. 4973539

JOHN LEAHY

FIRST EDITION TRADE PAPERBACK

UNITY © 2016 by John Leahy
Cover art © 2016 Andrea Cavaletto

This edition 2016 © Necro Publications

LCCN: 2015915581
ISBN: 978-1-939065-88-9

Book design & typesetting:
David G. Barnett
www.fatcatgraphicdesign.com

Assistant editors:
Amanda Baird

Necro Publications
5139 Maxon Terrace, Sanford, FL 32771
necropublications.com

All rights reserved. No part of this book may be reproduced or transmitted in any form or by any means, electronic or mechanical, including photocopy, recording, or any information storage and retrieval system, without permission in writing from the author, or his agent, except by a reviewer who may quote brief passages in a critical article or review to be printed in a magazine or newspaper, or electronically transmitted on radio or television.

All persons in this book are fictitious, and any resemblance that may seem to exist to actual persons living or dead is purely coincidental. This is a work of fiction.

Printed in the United States of America

10 9 8 7 6 5 4 3 2 1

For Noah

To patience

PART 1

LOVE
RISING

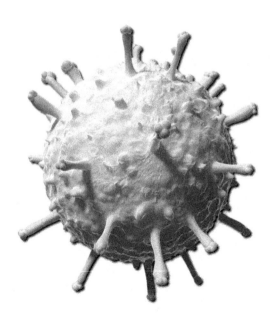

CHAPTER ONE

The connection that resulted in the crippling of the world thirty four years later was forged at a late night sing-along around a fire on Westward Beach in Malibu. Chuck Gates gazed over the flames at the pretty girl singing Joni Mitchell's *River*. Her voice was simple but beautiful, soft and melodious. A breeze had blown up and the waves thundered in the distance but Chuck had filtered out these distractions, all his concentration focused on the dream swimming in the heat-haze across from him.

She sang mostly with her eyes closed or fixed on some point in the distance. Every now and then she would cast a fleeting look around the group and would smile before closing her eyes again, losing herself to the song. When once her eyes met Chuck's, they lingered. Brave with beer, Chuck didn't look away. They held each other's gaze until she blinked and smiled. He smiled back and she turned her head before closing her eyes again.

《《—》》

During the day she busked with members of her caravan and sold jewelry and clothes from a stall. He worked with a painting contractor. In the evenings they surfed (she sucked), smoked weed, had sex. She brought her guitar with her everywhere and always ended up serenading him. She had some of her own songs, most of which he liked. She also painted, and showed him some of her work at the campsite one evening. He said he thought it was good, which was a lie. It was like that guy Van Gogh, whose stuff he thought was childish and crap (He though nearly all art to be crap, except Meatloaf album covers. They were cool.).

Her group usually stayed no longer than a fortnight in any one place, but because they were doing well financially in Malibu they decided to stay on for another two weeks. Chuck was delighted when he heard this from her. He had two more weeks to make sure this girl didn't leave.

«««—»»»

And she didn't. Their arms around each other's waists, they watched as the vans tooled along the dirt road toward the northbound side of the busy PCH. She waved at the straggly-haired and bearded faces smiling at her from the back windows of the vans as they drifted toward the roaring highway. She had tears in her eyes while Chuck himself waved, smiling not in farewell at the hippies, but in ecstasy.

«««—»»»

Kara Englen was a long way from home.

A Pittsburgh native, she had hooked up with the hippies a year and a half earlier at Myrtle Beach in South Carolina during Spring break. She'd been in her second year studying business at the University of Maryland at the time. She and a few friends were ambling drunkenly along the beach late one night and came across a group of longhairs having a round-the-fire singsong. They were invited to join and did. Kara's friends didn't stay long but she remained with the group until dawn, singing, drinking and smoking joints. Completely bored with her life and utterly disinterested in what she was doing in college, she soaked up the hippies' go-with-the-flow, let-the-wind-carry-us-where-it-will philosophies.

Two days later when the caravan left town headed south towards Charleston, she was with them. Her parents' reaction consisted of three phases as she'd expected: shock, anger, and pleading. They loved her and she loved them but no amount of sweet-talking and cajoling from them was going to get her back into college. When they finally abandoned their attempts they said they'd send her money every month to keep her going while she was on the road. It'll be hard they said, mark our words, you'll need it. At first she was put out by this. She was determined and optimistic of making a living for herself independent of her parents for the first time in her life. Busking and selling the group's various trinkets and clothing would provide her with a modest income. She told her parents she wouldn't need their cash, she'd make it on her own.

Three weeks later in Savannah, her stomach rumbling, she gave in and made the call. The money was in her account the following day and hit it the same date every month after that. Not much, she was hell-bent on not being too reliant on her parents. She didn't want to have to swallow all her pride. They said they'd visit her on her travels every now and again. She said ok—she was their only child after all.

And so it went. The first time they met was in Jacksonville. Olivia Englen smiled through her tears at the encounter, happy to see her daughter and devastated at witnessing her new state, a woman of the road. Her father Ronald betrayed no extremes of emotion as he sweated in the vicious Florida heat over the two-day visit until he hugged her goodbye and she felt his chest hitch a little against hers. When they parted he had a weak smile on his lips and he was blinking, trying to eliminate the glistening in his eyes.

They visited her again six weeks later in Tallahassee, after the caravan had gone all around the peninsula and was now headed west. Roughly a month and a half after that it was New Orleans. When she told them that the group would be heading into Mexico and deep into Central America, perhaps even as far as Panama, they became very distressed.

Were they mad? her father had asked incredulously. They could be killed! Worse could befall the women! There was no law and order in places down there. As he railed on about the dangers that faced the caravan south of the border her mother started crying. Eventually Ronald went quiet. He looked Kara in the eye and asked her to come home with them the next time they were due to meet, at Corpus Christi. She said no.

Her father met her unaccompanied in Corpus Christi. Olivia could not bear to see her daughter for what she thought could possibly be the last time. Kara couldn't believe her parents' melodrama and her amazement was lifted even further when on the second day of his visit her father sat her into his rental car and took her out of the city, saying he had a little surprise for her. When they pulled into the parking lot of a firing range he presented her with a small Ruger handgun. Before she could say anything he went to leave the car, saying come on, he'd show her how to use it. And he did. As she fired at the targets before her she felt surreal. Only a few hours before she'd been singing Neil Young songs looking out at the tranquil Gulf of Mexico and now here she was, blasting holes in cardboard cut-outs.

During the group's ten months south of the States she twice ended up being relieved that she had the gun. The first time was in Honduras when she woke in the middle of the night upon hearing some clattering outside. She'd heard that Honduran thieves could be pretty determined and vicious so she exited the caravan with the Ruger in her hand. When the three young men saw the weapon they froze but didn't run until she pointed it at them. The second time was in San Salvador when her and a few of the women in the group were followed home by a gang of drunken Indians who'd been eyeing them all night long in a bar. When they wouldn't go after being ordered to, Kara had brandished the gun. When they laughed at this Kara fired it in the air. The men, thinking that they'd find easier pickings, went away.

Despite these incidents (and numerous others of lesser seriousness) and a few run-ins with ridiculously corrupt police officers, Kara felt her heart aching as they crossed the border back into the U.S.. Memories of sights of incredible beauty filled her mind as they headed north on the I5 toward San Diego, as did images of the smiling faces of some of the amazing people they had met.

But it had been incredibly hard at times to make ends meet down there. Most of the people had been much poorer than themselves (and that was saying a lot). As they made their way up along the Californian coast, her belly (relatively) full, the comforts and affluence of the American way began to get to her. The thought of getting off the road never entered her head but after she'd fallen for the good-looking, charming, surfer-boy Chuck, it hadn't taken much cajoling from him to get her to do just that.

«««—»»»

Chuck had moved to California from Denver the previous year for the surf. He lived in a tiny apartment with two other guys and worked six days a week with a painting contractor to make the exorbitant rent on the place. On the day Kara told him that she was leaving the caravan to stay in Malibu with him they went looking for their own place. With nothing affordable Kara called her parents. They were so ecstatic to hear she was off the road that they wired her some money there and then. The following day she and Chuck put down a deposit on a dusty little mouse-hole off Latigo Canyon road. She got a job in a florist's and a two-night-a week gig singing and playing guitar in a restaurant.

When Kara's parents called out to visit they were despondent to see her living in a pokey drifter-dive and weren't uplifted upon meeting her partner. But still they were enthusiastic enough in their dealings with Chuck as they saw him as a savior of sorts. After all he had taken their daughter off the road.

Three months to the day after they'd first met, they got married. A month later Kara was pregnant. Her parents were overjoyed (and relieved—she was well-rooted now, off the road for good). Insisting that the place they were in wasn't suitable for the rearing of a child, the Englens bought the expectant couple a slightly larger apartment.

The following summer twins Mark and Kelsey presented themselves to the world. Those early days were hard but happy. Chuck would come home in the evening, exhausted after the longer day he'd taken on upon Kara's becoming pregnant and would let her head off to do her gig in the restaurant. He would take the babies out onto their tiny balcony and would watch the sunset with the boys asleep on his lap. Sometimes his tired eyes would track the surfers flitting along the waves in the fading light and a faint stab of longing would slice his gut—he'd always loved to hit the water for a set after work. But he had responsibilities now. He'd look down at his two children and kiss them softly on their heads. He'd look back out at the darkening ocean, knowing that one day the three of them would be out there together.

«‹‹—››»

And they were. Graceful and athletic, Mark and Kelsey loved surfing from the off, becoming skillful on the waves in no time. One day, worn out after a hard hour-and-a-half long session in the water with the boys Chuck watched them from the shore as they called, shouted and gesticulated to each other, tanned and handsome beneath their rich heads of blonde hair. Good at school, plenty of friends, good-looking, excellent at every sport they tried…the world was their oyster.

And then two months after the boys' eighth birthday, along came Jonah.

«‹‹—››»

From the very beginning Chuck knew there was something different with his third son. The boy didn't cry much. Didn't produce much sound at all, in fact. Chuck often found himself approaching Jonah's cot with a knot of concern in his gut. He would look down in relief to see the boy alive and well. The relief would slowly dissolve as Chuck found himself drawn to Jonah's eyes. Sometimes he stared for long periods into them. At times it felt to Chuck like his son's eyes were more…*empty* than alive. Thinking himself ridiculous, Chuck would muster a smile for the boy and walk away.

«‹‹—››»

As his father suspected Jonah grew up to be a quiet boy. Good-looking like his brothers, he shared none of their other traits. He wasn't outgoing like them and his school grades were on the weaker side of average. He had virtually no interest in sports. Sometimes he'd go surfing with his brothers when they invited him along but would never go on his own initiative. Instead of going off playing with friends after he'd done his homework he'd usually spend his evenings in front of the TV. One evening Chuck came into the living room after work and observed the boy gazing at the screen before him. Jonah's eyes were fixed on the images flickering in front of him but to Chuck they looked blank, as though what lay behind them had no interest in what they were watching.

《《——》》

A little bit after his eighth birthday, in an attempt to get him out of his shell, Kara got Jonah to come down to her flower shop (she had her own place now) after his homework was done and help her out there. To Chuck's surprise Jonah took to the work. He talked a little with the customers. Chuck was hopeful that this was the first step, maybe soon he would be talking more to kids his own age. One evening after work Kara mentioned to Chuck that takings were up in the shop. She pulled Jonah to her side and smiling, ruffled his hair. Grinning down at him she said it was probably because her handsome little helper was such a big hit with the ladies of Malibu. Jonah smiled back up at her and it lifted Chuck's spirits no end to see it. The boy smiled so seldom.

Then the hippies returned.

《《——》》

Seventeen years later and they were still on the road. When they walked into the shop, Kara, her assistant Lori and Jonah were busy preparing bouquets for an upcoming wedding. Jonah watched his mother stop speaking mid-sentence when she saw the worn-looking, long-haired troupe approaching the counter. The man leading them smiled at her and after a few seconds she managed a weak smile in return. Her lips quickly began to quiver and she burst into tears. She went quickly to the man and they embraced.

After hugging a few more of them she introduced them to Jonah and Lori, telling her son and helper that these were friends from a long time ago. The hippies informed her that they wouldn't be staying in Malibu, they were just passing through and had decided to stop and pay her a visit. She said that she'd go for a coffee with them. She turned toward Lori and Jonah and told them she'd be back in half an hour. Then she left with the group.

An hour later Jonah looked out toward the front of the shop for the umpteenth time. There was no sign of his mother approaching the door. After an hour and a half had passed he went down the street to the coffee shop his mother usually frequented and looked in the window. His mother and her friends weren't there.

«««—»»»

A little over an hour later he returned to the flower shop having checked eight more coffee shops, all to no avail. Relief flooding her features, Lori scolded him for being gone so long. Paying her no heed Jonah went past her to the phone and called his mother's cell. It was off. He called his father who was working on a job in Calabasas. Jonah told him what had happened. Chuck asked his son what his mother's friends had looked like. After Jonah described the group there was no sound from his father's end of the phone for a long time. When Chuck spoke again Jonah could hear real fear there, something he had never heard in his father's tone before.

«««—»»»

They searched Malibu from one end to the other. They tried her cell every fifteen minutes or so but it remained off. A little after one a.m. with the boys having gone to bed a half an hour before, Chuck was sitting at the kitchen table, his cell by his elbow. Suddenly it buzzed. He looked down at it. His stomach rolled when he saw that it was a voicemail from Kara. His heart pounding, he lifted the phone to his ear and played the message. Through tears, sobs, and coughing, Kara told him she was sorry. She loved him and always would. She told him to tell the boys that she loved them. After blurting out a shuddery goodbye she hung up. Chuck stared blankly at the table, the cell remaining at his ear.

"That was Mom, wasn't it."

Chuck turned to see Jonah standing in the kitchen doorway. With tears threatening, Chuck coughed away the lump in his throat.

"Yeah" he said.

"She's not coming back, is she?"

His resolve cracking, Chuck let out a shuddery breath. "No son, she's not."

Jonah watched his father's face crumple before turning and going back to his room. Chuck turned back to the table and cried softly for a few minutes. When he stopped he went to the press over the sink and took a bottle of whiskey from it. He drank half of it and went to bed. This was a ritual he would complete every night from then on.

«««—»»»

Mark and Kelsey were devastated. Broken-hearted, shocked and bitter at their mother's departure, they were in no mood to return to school in the fall. But they were resilient and this was their final high-school year. As the weeks ticked by and to their father's relief they got back into the swing of things, their usual focus and determination returning.

Jonah however was a different story. The little bit of promise he had shown before his mother's leaving evaporated and he lapsed into his old, vacant self, this time even more so than before. He engaged in even less activities with his brothers. He hardly talked to his grandparents when they visited. With Kara gone and not in contact with any of them, the despondent Englens and Chuck had become closer. Ronald and Olivia flew out to their son-in-law and grandchildren once a month. Late one evening, with Mark and Kelsey having gone off to play football with some friends and with Olivia having gone to bed early with a migraine, Ronald came out to the kitchen where Chuck was sitting at the table drinking a beer and reading the sports pages. Ronald had been in the living room with Jonah for a while where the boy was gazing tepidly at the TV. Ronald went to the fridge and took a beer from it. He sat across from Chuck and cracked his can open.

"It's like that boy is drifting in space, Chuck" he said, and took a drink of his beer. "He needs something to pull him back to earth."

A month later Jonah found exactly that.

《《—》》

For the twins' birthday Chuck took them and Jonah on a weekend camping trip to Yosemite. On their second night they were eating sausages around a fire they had made when they heard a rather odd chattering noise coming from the trees nearby. Looking in the direction of the sound they saw a raccoon ambling slowly toward them. It continued approaching them, chattering away. Kelsey threw the remainder of his sausage to the raccoon and it gobbled it up. When it finished eating it looked at Kelsey as though seeking more food. Kelsey told it to scram, he had no more. The raccoon began chattering again. Suddenly it made a dash at Kelsey and bit him on the arm. Then it scuttled off into the gloom. They didn't see it falling drunkenly twice on its dash for the trees. And they didn't know that raccoons didn't normally make a chattering sound.

With the bite not looking bad, Chuck got some antiseptic from his tent and poured it on Kelsey's arm. Then he covered the small wound with a plaster.

《《—》》

About six weeks later Kelsey complained of a tingling sensation in his arm in the vicinity of where he'd been bitten. A week after that before being ushered away down a hospital corridor, a nurse's arm around his shoulders, Jonah caught a glimpse of his older brother lying in a bed trembling uncontrollably, his eyes rolling dementedly in his head, drool flowing from both sides of his saliva-flooded mouth.

The shock and sadness Jonah felt at Kelsey having contracted a terrible disease was quickly washed away by Jonah's research into his brother's affliction. There were a lot of big words but he didn't let that stop him. His nine-year old brain, having never felt such fascination and focus until now dusted itself off and warmed to the challenge.

Rabies. Of the *Lyssavirus* genus of the *Rhabdoviridae* family. Wow! What cool names for something so *small*! But of course small was nothing here. These small things (*virions*—also very cool) *deserved* cool names because they were so *powerful*. So *deadly*. He knew the flu was a *virus,* he'd had it a couple of times, but it was nothing like *this*. This *rabies*. This...*destroyer.*

Jonah gazed at the rabies virion on the laptop screen before him, his heart pounding with excitement. It was hard to believe that this tiny, microscopic organism was killing his brother. An odd-looking thing, essentially a bullet with hairs (these hairs were actually *glycoprotein spikes*—he'd always thought that protein was good for you, obviously not all of it was), Kelsey had gotten it from the raccoon and it had lain silent for a while, quietly multiplying inside his own cells (*incredible!*) before destroying these cells and bursting out of them to cause havoc. Over the last few weeks it had travelled from Kelsey's arm all the way to his central nervous system. And there was no cure. *No cure.*

Wow.

«««—»»»

With Kelsey having been very popular in school and in the Malibu sports community, his funeral was a large one. There was a huge outpouring of grief at the terrible passing of such a likeable, promising young man. Standing at his brother's graveside, Jonah was oblivious to it all. As Kelsey's coffin was lowered into the ground he focused on a droplet of rain that splashed on the timber. Gazing at the water, Jonah's mind's eye conjured up images of the virus particles he knew were floating in the liquid, dormant, just waiting for something to invade.

«‹‹—»››

In the weeks following Kelsey's death Jonah became an expert on viruses. After school he would spend hours on his father's laptop, reading voraciously on the subject. He watched every video clip and documentary on viruses he came across. He even ordered DVDs from online stores using his father's credit card. Often, on school nights, it would be after one a.m. before he would go to bed and during his early-morning classes his teacher would have to call his name to snap him out of a doze. On one occasion when he was supposed to be reading a passage in English class, his book on the desk before him, his teacher caught him with another book concealed beneath the table on his lap. When she looked at its cover and saw what its subject matter was (virology) she blinked and quietly told him to put it in his bag.

The ocean, which had never held much appeal for him before, became a source of fascination to Jonah. With his new knowledge of what its depths contained, Jonah would often stop off at the beach on his way home from school. He would sit down on the sand, rest his arms on his knees and look out over them at the blue expanse before him. One evening he diverted his gaze from it and observed a couple walking along the shore. After a few seconds he shifted his eyes to a family not far away from him on the sand, where a father was helping his little daughter dress herself while the child's mother read a book. Further off to Jonah's right a few people were playing volleyball. Jonah wondered if any of these people knew that there were five million virus particles in a tablespoon of seawater. Did they know that if all the viruses in the ocean were placed in a straight line, the line would stretch two hundred million miles into space? Did they know that if all the ocean's viruses were placed on a scale, they would equal the weight of seventy-five million blue whales? Jonah turned away from the volleyball game, his eyes returning to the water just in time to see a surfer wipe out badly and disappear into the white of a wave as it broke. Did this surfer know that right now he was being inundated with trillions (probably more—Jonah didn't know what the next number up from a trillion was, he'd have to find out) of viruses?

The amazing thing about it, was that all these viruses swirling in and about the surfer's body were for the sea's organisms only—its fish, plankton, coral and whatnot. They couldn't infect humans. One of the most fascinating things that Jonah had come across so far in the virus world was the way viruses suddenly changed, developing the ability to spread from one organism to another. That was how humans could catch viruses from creatures that were closely related to them on the evolutionary scale, like apes, pigs and chickens. But water-dwelling organisms were very different from humans so the viruses that infected them would be completely incompatible with human cells. Jonah found the prospect of a fish virus infecting humans a scary, but compelling thought. He'd spent a while reading up on viruses that infected fish and had come across some downright nasty ones.

IHNV was the pleasingly shorter form of saying Infectious Hematopoietic Necrosis Virus. This unpleasant customer caused bulging of the eyes, skin darkening and hemorrhaging in several areas including the mouth, behind the head and near the anus. Unfortunate diseased fish ended up floating belly-up on the surface of the water. It caused necrosis (another horrendous, incredible word) in the kidney, liver and spleen. The virus killed ninety percent of the young fish it infected.

Even more dreadful was the Betanodavirus. Capable of causing mass mortality in outbreaks, some of its more sinister symptoms included spiral swimming and fast, erratic movement. It also caused cannibalism. A few hours after reading about this virus Jonah had woken up in the middle of the night, his breath coming hard and fast, his heart pounding in his chest. He'd dreamed that he'd been walking down the short road between his apartment and the PCH. Not far from where the road met the highway was a bus-stop. There was a woman sitting on the bench there. A few feet from the bench a man was walking around and around in rapid circles. The woman appeared not to notice, her eyes fixed at some point on the other side of the highway. Suddenly the man launched himself at the woman on the bench, grabbing her shoulders and flinging her up against the corner of the bus-stop. The man's body obscured what was going on from Jonah's view until the man let the woman go and turned around. The man's face around his mouth was bathed in blood, as were his neck, chest and hands. Paying no attention to Jonah he turned and began walking away from him along the shoulder of the highway. Jonah looked at the woman, now slumped in the corner of the bus stop. Except she was more of a carcass now than a woman. Chunks of flesh from her cheekbones were missing. Jonah could see the white of bone amidst red. The bottom of her nose was gone. She appeared to be grimacing, her teeth bared, but this was a result of her no longer having lips. There was a ragged, gaping hole in one side of her face through which Jonah could see almost a full line of teeth. Her neck was a torn ruin. From her chest upward she was drenched in blood. Jonah looked up the highway. The man was still walking there, his back to him, his scarlet hands the only trace of his feasting upon the woman. Every now and then he would dart erratically out onto the road before zipping back into the shoulder again, causing cars to swerve out of his way. At that point Jonah had woken up.

Watching another wave crash into foam, Jonah knew what he had dreamed to be virtually impossible. There was almost a zero chance of something like the Betanodavirus crossing the species gulf between fish and humans. But those were the key words, weren't they? *Virtually. Almost.* Neither of them meant *definitely.* Because with nature nothing was definite. Nothing was completely impossible.

Jonah let out a long breath, a contented one. He felt happy. He was happy because he knew what he wanted to do with his future. Nine-year old Jonah Gates would be devoting the rest of his life to viruses. He wanted to be a *virologist.* A shiver of pure excitement flashed in his gut. *Virologist.* It had to be the coolest word of all in virus-world. And he was going to *be* one! Already he couldn't wait.

He looked to his right at the family he had been observing earlier. The little girl, fully-dressed now, met his eyes and waved at him. She smiled at Jonah and he returned her wave. She was pretty in a yellow summer dress, her long blonde hair hanging loose.

Suddenly her smile was crimson, her face, neck and the top of her dress soaked in blood. Little bits of what Jonah presumed to be shredded flesh hung around her mouth and from her chin. She began running around in a demented circle before rushing off down the beach, zigzagging erratically in the same manner as the man in Jonah's dream. Jonah watched her fall and pick herself up twice in her bizarre gallop before he turned his attention to the little girl's parents, lying motionless on their beach rug. Except it wasn't her parents that lay on the rug, it was Jonah's mother and the leader of the hippy group that had called into the flower shop the previous summer. Their dead eyes stared upward from mutilated faces that were just about identifiable.

(Bitch, fucker)

A second later the girl's parents were before Jonah again, the woman still reading her book and the man now applying tanning lotion to his arm, his daughter beside him holding a beach-ball. Jonah watched them for a little while longer before picking up his schoolbag and heading home.

«««—»»»

While Kelsey's death had brought his younger brother to life, it had gutted his twin and his father. With Kelsey's passing happening so close to his year's graduation, the school had postponed the event for two weeks. During that period Mark hardly ventured beyond the apartment door, barely speaking to his father and Jonah. He would stay up late watching TV and listening to music. Sometimes he would sit out on the balcony late into the night, staring at the ocean. A couple of mornings before heading off to work his father found him asleep in his chair.

On his graduation night Mark ended up getting badly drunk and he and a few of his friends got involved in a nasty fight with some out-of-town kids. Mark ended up doing the worst of the damage, smashing a beer bottle over a guy's head and tearing another guy's neck with the broken remains. Both of the victims needed a large number of stitches and it looked like they'd possibly be scarred for life. Their parents wanted to press charges but Chuck begged them not to, pleading with them that his son was in a very bad place at the moment, he'd lost so much in less than a year. The parents softened and agreed to let the matter rest.

Mark's mood lifted as the summer wore on, but only by a little. He got a job waiting tables in a restaurant but was fired after two weeks for being consistently late. He lasted a week in a supermarket before he quit, saying that his boss was too much of an asshole. He told his father that he didn't want to get another job, he'd make up for it the following summer. He wanted to relax before college. Chuck said there was no way he was going to spend six weeks on his ass sleeping and watching TV (which was all he did now, he'd more or less given up meeting his friends for football or surfing) and demanded that Mark come and work for his painting company. After much protest, Mark agreed. During the remainder of that summer Jonah frequently woke to hear his father in Mark's room, telling his son to get his lazy ass out of bed, they were going to be late. It was a far cry from only six months before when his brother would be out of bed after the first buzz of his alarm clock.

«« — »»

In the fall Mark began studying at the University of Kansas for a degree in health fitness instruction (he hoped to open his own gym in Malibu one day). He scraped through his first semester exams and failed most of his summer ones. After failing in the repeat session he ended up repeating the year but dropped out just before Christmas. He returned to Malibu and got a job in a bar frequented by some question-able characters. After a month of rows and unpleasant silences with his father he moved out and got his own place. Jonah didn't see his brother again for a full three months, with Mark ignoring all of his father's phone-calls. When the lines of communication were eventually re-opened, one early summer's evening, Jonah arrived back at the apart-ment to see Mark talking to his father in the living room. To Jonah it was like a changeling had taken his brother's place. Gone was the well-groomed, solidly-built brother he'd previously known—in his stead was a greasy-haired, pale, skinny creature.

Mark visited his brother and father maybe twice a week after that, each time his appearance seeming a little worse to Jonah. As the visits went on Chuck began to plead with his son to consider giving college another try. Mark said no, his college days were done. One day Chuck tag-teamed with Ronald and Olivia, the three of them trying to get Mark to see sense, at the very least to get out of that dive he was working in. Mark (who had two large tattoos by now, one on each arm) flipped his lid, telling them to shut the fuck up, he wasn't going to college to keep them happy and he enjoyed working in the bar. So fuck them all. He stormed out of the apartment and the next time Jonah saw his brother was at Mark's funeral service. Mark had been found dead in his apartment after a cocaine overdose. He'd been dead for two days.

«««—»»»

Chuck, who'd been drinking half a bottle of vodka more or less every night since Kara left, ratcheted his alcohol intake up in incremental phases with the passing of each of his sons. With Mark gone, he was downing a full bottle of vodka every day. His personality began to deteriorate. He became gruff and morose in his dealings with customers and his employees which resulted in the painting company he had built up over fifteen years slowly falling apart. As the months went by, Gates Painting Contractors received less and less work orders. The employees began to leave. A year and a half after Mark's death, Chuck closed the business and went to work for a former rival who he'd worked with back in the days before they'd ventured out on their own.

«««—»»»

As Jonah advanced through puberty he grew tall and broad like his brothers had been, but because he had no involvement in sports he remained skinny-limbed. And even though he was quiet and friendless in high school, his physical traits combined with a thick head of sandy hair drew some interest from girls. And he was becoming interested in them.

«««—»»»

He had his first date a few months before his fifteenth birthday. A pretty, popular and intelligent girl, Charlene Schossing was on the school's junior cheerleader team. She'd become more and more intrigued by the cute silent boy who was nearly always reading some thick, academic-looking book whenever she saw him. So much so that she asked him if he'd like to hang out sometime. Jonah said yeah, and suggested they go for a walk on the beach some evening after school. Charlene said she'd like that.

When they met at the beach they greeted each other and began walking along the sand. With Jonah venturing nothing by way of conversation, Charlene asked him what kind of music he liked. Jonah said he didn't know, he didn't listen to much music. Oh, Charlene said and they walked on in silence for a while. She asked him what kind of TV shows he was into. He said he didn't watch much TV. Silence again. He said that he watched stuff on YouTube. She asked him what kind of stuff. Documentaries, he said. Documentaries on what, she asked. Viruses, he said. Oh. Silence. She asked him if that was what his book was about. What book, he asked. The book he was always reading around school, she answered. Oh, yeah, he said.

As they strolled on wordlessly Jonah looked sideways at his companion. Charlene was blinking, her eyes fixed on the ground a little ahead of her. Dully aware that she was uncomfortable, Jonah wondered what to say to her. After a few more seconds of silence he turned toward the ocean and began talking about the only thing in the world he really cared about.

«««—»»»

to interrupt his reading and research. A couple of weeks before he left for college (he'd made it onto a biology degree at the University of Michigan) he came home from work to find his father in a crumpled heap at the bottom of the stairs, dead. He'd broken his neck.

«««—»»»

During his first year in Ann Arbor, Ronald and Olivia told Jonah that he should spend the summer with them in Pittsburgh instead of heading back to Malibu, which he'd intended on doing. It wouldn't be good for him to be in that apartment all by himself. Jonah said ok.

A week after arriving in Pittsburgh he got a job working nights as a car-park attendant. He worked every hour he could get, and when he wasn't there or sleeping he was reading or online in his room. The Englens hardly ever saw him. By the end of the summer they were a little spooked by his silent, solitary behavior.

During his second year in college they visited him and he them, but no invitation to spend the summer in Pittsburgh came. That suited Jonah fine. He missed the ocean.

«««—»»»

A little after Christmas in his third year Jonah was studying in the library one evening when movement at the corner of his eye caught his attention. Four booths to his left, where a few minutes earlier there had been no one, there now sat a very attractive girl. He watched her as she placed her books and folders on the desk before her. As she bent to take some more items from her bag she saw Jonah looking at her and gave him a polite smile.

«««—»»»

Her name was Bethany Polarian and she gave Jonah more of a chance than her predecessors. She went on two dates with him before giving him the flick. The post-rejection process of phone calls, flowers, anonymous texts and voicemails ensued as it had done with Louise nearly four and a half years before. When Bethany threatened on two occasions to inform the police and didn't follow through, Jonah pushed the boat out further.

She worked three nights a week in a bar. On her way home one night she caught Jonah following her. She told him that this time she'd definitely be calling the police and she did. Upon finding out that Jonah had pestered a girl before, the cops took the matter seriously. They checked the street CCTV of various businesses on Bethany's route from work to her accommodation. Jonah had been following her home for over a month.

«««—»»»

The Englens flew to Ann Arbor to intercede for him where they were shown the CCTV footage by the police. Ronald and Olivia gazed at the screen while an officer informed them that this was not the first time Jonah had harassed a female, he'd done it in Malibu too. His face pale, Ronald stared at the darkened figure of his grandson skulking about in the late-night shadows. Half a minute into the footage Olivia raised her hand to her forehead, shielded her eyes, and began crying softly.

«««—»»»

Using Jonah's troubled life in his defense, the Englens managed to get Bethany to drop the charges and the university not to expel him. Bethany had one condition, and that was that Jonah should seek counseling, which he did. After his first session his counsellor rang the police and told them that Jonah was someone they should keep a close eye on for a while.

«««—»»»

.

Realizing that he was probably very lucky to still be on course for his goal in life, Jonah knuckled down even harder at his studies as a means of preventing women from distracting him. It was difficult—he saw a lot of beautiful women every day—but he succeeded, and his discipline paid off when he graduated a year and a half later, top of his class.

《《《—》》》

The following fall saw him begin his microbiology masters at Columbia. He found it much easier to focus on his studies here—there had been a lot of filler on his undergraduate degree. The masters program was much closer to the core. Here again he finished top of his class before returning to California to study for his doctorate in virology at Stanford.

He completed the three-year program in two. He was hot property, with the private sector wanting him very badly. Pharmaceutical and bio-tech companies made him lucrative offers.

Then General Alec Soranor from Vandenberg Air Force Base paid him a visit.

CHAPTER TWO

Jonah's doctoral research had been on virophages. Shortly after beginning his doctoral program at Stanford he'd become obsessed with these viruses that hijacked other viruses, and for two years he lived and breathed them. The result was a brilliant dissertation on the possible future of these unusual entities: the types of virophages that were likely to emerge in the years ahead, how they would possibly respond to various selective pressures they were likely to encounter and how they were likely to impact on the viral world as a whole going forward. The dissertation received coverage in scientific and medical journals the world over, making a veritable celebrity of its writer in these circles and cementing Jonah's position as the leading young talent at the cutting-edge of future virology.

As he looked through Jonah's file one last time, General Alec Soranor knew that the young Doctor Gates was the right guy for his project. Sure, the kid was far from perfect (he had a copy of the police report from Ann Arbor—"borderline sociopath" it had read) but his transgressions had been committed over five years previous. And they'd obviously stemmed from his awful family catastrophes. Soranor had had some of his own—his father and brother had been killed in a car accident just after Soranor had turned fifteen—he'd gone off the rails and obsessed a bit for a while himself, not with women, but with alcohol. But he'd reined himself in and gotten himself back in line, and it looked like this kid had too.

To Soranor it would have taken a lot more than the few incidents in Jonah's record to even come close to outweighing the reason he wanted the young man at Vandenberg: Jonah Gates lived for viruses. He had no friends or social networks. Outside of his grandparents in Pittsburgh he had no family. Viruses were all he had.

Perfect.

Soranor didn't doubt that Jonah would be fascinated by what his scientists had found on the launch pads at Vandenberg. He closed Jonah's file and smiled. Shit, the kid would cream his *pants*.

《《————》》》

"It's quite something, isn't it?" Soranor asked.

They were in Jonah's apartment in Stanford, the contents of the Vandenvirus file spread out on Jonah's study desk. The kid had been silent for nearly five minutes as he'd made his way through the photos, diagrams and electron microscope images. No expression had crept into his face during his examination of the classified material (Soranor had a feeling emotion rarely showed there), but his fingers betrayed his excitement. Soranor could see them quivering slightly as Jonah analyzed the documentation.

"Yes" Jonah said eventually, not lifting his eyes from an image he was holding. Soranor watched him put the image down before picking up two more, one in each hand.

Soranor had already informed Jonah of the nature of the discovery of the Vandenvirus, or the Vandenvirus virophage to be more accurate. A few months before, the Air Force had begun launch-testing of the new Delta VI series rocket at Vandenberg. They'd used a revolutionary fuel—a much more powerful substance than anything previously used before—in the process. A scientific analysis of the exhaust powder left behind after the first Delta VI launch revealed the presence of a previously undiscovered species of bacteria that was somehow feeding on the rocket's exhaust products. Spreading in the bacterial colony was an infection that was killing it—a bacteriophage virus. And capping off this incredible parasitical chain was a virophage which was using the machinery of the bacteriophage virus to replicate itself, killing the bacteriophage in the process, and very quickly too.

Soranor had done some research on virophages himself. It turned out that these viruses-of-viruses (he had to admit he was a little bit fascinated by the whole thing) were more or less virgin territory in the virological field. Not many people knew much about them and only a few had been discovered. There were some important features that distinguished the Vandenvirus (a lab technician had come up with the name) from the others of its species. Whereas other virophages merely hindered the replication apparatus of their viral hosts, the Vandenvirus killed them in the process of making more of itself. Another distinguishing characteristic was the speed at which it operated. The scientists at Vandenberg had monitored the process after the launch of the second Delta rocket. From the time the Vandenvirus made its appearance in the replication factory of the bacteriophage to its obliteration of the entire bacteriophage outbreak in the bacterial colony, only four hours had passed. And what had also been quite fascinating to discover had been the fact that the Vandenvirus wasn't restricted to parasitizing that particular bacteriophage—the scientists had placed it in other bacteriophages and it had hijacked their replication machineries and killed them with equal functionality and speed. The Pentagon brass had become interested and moved the project to more suitable facilities at the Point Mugu Naval Complex. One of them had asked a question that was the reason Soranor was now sitting opposite Jonah.

"So what do you want *me* for?" Jonah asked, putting down a photo and picking up another.

Soranor didn't answer immediately.

"I'm looking for someone to modify the Vandenvirus's genetic makeup," he eventually said. "Turn it into a killer of human viruses."

Jonah's eyes flicked up to meet Soranor's, his hand, which had been in the process of placing a photo back down on the desk, froze. He blinked.

"You're *serious*" he said flatly.

"How long do you think it would take?" Soranor asked.

Jonah blinked a couple of times and snorted. There was a look on his face which suggested slight irritation at the question.

"Well first of all, some of the equipment you'd need hasn't even been invented yet."

"Design it. We'll build it for you."

"It'll cost a lot of money."

"I've a big checkbook."

Silence.

"So" Soranor said. "How long?"

"Ten years" Jonah said after a few seconds.

"Great. You want the job?"

"You talk to any of the other guys before me?" Jonah asked. "Fragian...McDougall?"

These were the names of the main authorities in virophage research, both of them more than twice Jonah's age.

"Yeah" Soranor answered. "Washington wanted to stick to the proven entities. Fragian said it couldn't be done at all. McDougall said maybe in twenty-years, probably twenty-five. But I knew you were the guy to go with from the beginning." Soranor grinned slightly. "Looks like I've been proven right."

A small smile appeared on Jonah's face. Soranor wasn't sure he liked the look of it.

"So" Soranor said. "You up for it?"

Jonah's eyes dropped to the paraphernalia spread about on the desk. His eyes moving around on the material, he said "Yeah. I'm in."

"Good." Soranor extended his hand. "Glad to have you on board, son."

Jonah took his hand and they shook.

《《——》》

With his first high-paying job secured Jonah decided to leave the old apartment in Malibu to his grandparents for whenever they wanted to come on holiday, and took out a mortgage on a small house on the western outskirts of the town. He commuted to Point Mugu every day where he usually ended up working at least ten hours a day, more often than not six days a week.

Security was very tight on the program. Although the research was being carried out for the benefit of humanity the Pentagon did not want the Vandenvirus falling into the wrong hands for fear its destructive power might be harnessed for more nefarious purposes.

Whenever Jonah's grandparents were in town he would spend some time with them. They would ask how work was going and he would say "fine," and that would be it. He had told them shortly after beginning at Point Mugu that he did "lab work" and that he couldn't say any more, it was classified. They'd been content with that, happy that things had turned out so well for their unsettling grandson.

And then, a little into his fourth year on the project, Jonah's eyes fell on Mary Leydon.

«««——»»»

A few months after Jonah had begun the second year of his doctorate program at Stanford, Mary Leydon moved to Los Angeles from Sheridan, Wyoming. Armed with a high school diploma and a six-week acting course from her local community college she was set on conquering Hollywood. Her scant resume proved no hindrance. Arriving on the scene in the middle of a glut of girls whose effusive desperation to be famous made itself apparent in embarrassing on-screen performances, her calm, assured demeanor, allied with significant ability was a breath of fresh air to casting directors. Also in her favor were her looks. Slim-figured with a rich mane of auburn hair and striking pale-green eyes, she drew attention wherever she went.

As she made her way up Tinseltown's greasy ladder she received plenty of proposals for sex in exchange for helping her to the next rung, some to even bypass a couple altogether. She politely turned them all down. When the director of an intended big-budget cable-TV show offered her a prominent part in his project but that involved occasional nudity, she'd turned him down. As she rose to leave his office he turned dark at the rejection, saying that her Walton's mountain morality would only get her so far in the business. She thanked him for his time and left.

A little over a year after that meeting she landed her first for-cinema-release part. A modestly-budgeted movie outlining the trials and tribulations of a female journalist reporting from Rwanda during the nineteen-ninety-four genocide, it was a moderate success at the box office.

Then came her big break. She landed the lead role in *The War Beneath*, a big-budget action thriller in which she would play the commander of a submarine who had to contend with an underwater terrorist threat while keeping in check a sly, misogynistic executive officer. A few hours after she got the part she and some friends headed to Malibu for a celebratory meal.

«««—»»»

Jonah and the Englens were nearly finished with their dinner when Jonah's eyes fell upon the four women being ushered to a table nearby. They were all attractive but the stunner with the auburn hair and strong, confident smile stood out from the rest. It was all Jonah could do to keep his gaze from her, restricting himself to furtive glances in her direction lest his grandparents spot him and something uncomfortable ensue. The group were celebrating some good fortune that the auburn-haired woman had enjoyed—she was the center of attention at the table.

When Ronald and Olivia announced they were leaving, Jonah bade them goodnight and said he'd stay on for another glass of wine before heading off himself. As soon as the Englens had their backs to him Jonah's eyes flicked to the beauty nearby. As he sipped a glass of wine he alternated his gaze between the woman and the ocean darkening on his right. Eventually their eyes met. Almost instantly hers switched their attention back to her friends. A minute later she looked at Jonah again. This time she held his gaze a little longer before turning away.

«««—»»»

When they were finished Jonah watched them leave. When they'd gone out the front door he rose from his table and did likewise. Standing outside he looked to his right, his eyes combing each side of the street. He didn't see them. Looking to his left he saw them heading into a bar. Jonah walked down the street and went in after them.

The place was reasonably busy, with Aerosmith playing loudly on the speaker system. Jonah went to the counter and ordered a beer. While he was waiting for his drink he scanned the area. He saw the women at a table at the far end of the bar. His beer arrived and he drank some of it. He held the bottle in his hand, savoring the feel of the cold glass against his palm. He gazed at the woman by the back of the bar.

She was *amazing*.

«««—»»»

He was in the process of paying for his second beer when something caught the corner of his eye. He looked to his left and saw, talking to a barmaid by the other end of the counter, the auburn-haired woman. When the barmaid turned away Jonah picked up his beer and walked over to the woman.

"You stalking me?" she asked without looking at him as he approached. Jonah could see traces of a smile on her lips.

"Maybe," he said, resting his beer on the counter. "You enjoying your evening?"

"Yeah," the woman said. She turned to face him. A knot tightened in Jonah's gut, his heart instantly speeding up a notch. The most beautiful face he'd ever seen was only two feet away from him. Looking directly at him. "You?" she asked.

"Yeah, I'm having a good time."

The woman's drinks arrived before her and she paid for them.

"So are you guys celebrating something?" Jonah asked.

"Yeah. I got some really good news today."

Jonah nodded. "Congratulations."

"Thanks."

The barmaid returned and gave the woman her change. "Could I get a tray for these please?" the woman asked. "Sure" the barmaid said and went off to get one. A silence fell.

"You're running out of time" the woman said, her eyes on the barmaid.

"For what?" Jonah asked.

"For asking for my number."

The waitress returned with a tray. The woman began loading the drinks into it.

"Ok" Jonah said. "Can I have it?"

"No. But you can give me yours." She lifted the tray of drinks and faced him. "You got a card?"

"Yeah."

She lowered her eyes to the tray before lifting them again. "Then drop it in."

Jonah took a business card from his wallet and put it into the tray. The woman looked at it.

"Hmm" she said in a thoughtful tone, her eyes still on the card. She looked up at Jonah. "Well, Mr. Virologist" she said, a playful look on her features. Jonah found it hard to breathe looking at her. "Enjoy the rest of your night." As she walked past him he said "You too."

He watched her make her way past a few tables and then he left.

«««—»»»

He found it difficult to focus at Point Mugu the following day. What he was working on was a beautiful, perfect thing (being made even more so by him) but the woman he had met the previous night was even more flawless.

She didn't call that day, evening, or night. He slept poorly and the following day Henry Kintaro, his lead assistant, asked him if he was alright, he seemed a little distracted. Jonah said he was fine, he just had a little bit of a headache.

Late that evening he sat vacantly eating a sandwich in his kitchen, his cell on the table beside his elbow, an unanswered call from Ronald Englen on the screen (Ronald and Olivia were heading back to Pittsburgh the following morning). Suddenly the phone began ringing. Jonah's heart immediately began beating faster. It was her, he knew. The screen told him that the number was withheld. Yeah, definitely her. He took the call.

"Hello?" he said.

And then relief and ecstasy flooded through him.

«««—»»»

They met that weekend at a bar in Westwood. She filled him in on her acting career and about the big role she'd just landed. He talked about his life with viruses and shared with her the few scraps of information he could about his job at Point Mugu.

Afterward he walked her to her car. When they reached it she took her keys from her handbag and looked at him. "Listen, Jonah" she said. "I had a nice time tonight…but I don't think there's much *spark* between us." She watched him blink. "I'm sorry, but…I don't see any real point in us meeting up again."

Jonah looked across the boulevard.

"Well" she continued. "Good night."

He looked back at her. "Good night."

"Take care."

He nodded but said nothing.

She turned and got into her car. He watched her drive down the road for a few seconds. Then he turned and went to his own car.

《《—》》

Not having her phone number, the following day Jonah called in sick (it was the first day he'd ever missed on the job) at Point Mugu and went to the DMV. He started off at one hundred dollars with the counter-attendant, saying that he'd seen this beautiful woman in a nightclub who'd left before he'd had a chance to approach her and get her number. He'd followed her out of the club and had gotten her car registration as she'd driven away. Now he was begging the woman before him to give a guy a break, had she ever fallen in love at first sight?

The attendant blinked a few times, her eyes dropping a little. A small, embarrassed smile appeared on her reddening face. Jonah pushed a third fifty under the glass.

"Sir-

"All I want is to send her some flowers."

Another fifty made its way into the attendant's side of the divider.

Not moving a muscle, the attendant looked down at the money for a few seconds. Suddenly her eyes darted up to meet Jonah's for a split second before falling again. In a swift smooth movement that told Jonah she'd done this type of thing before, the cash disappeared under the attendant's computer keyboard. Her fingers danced on the keypad.

"Apartment four, twelve-twenty six Shoriston Avenue, Hancock Park."

"Thanks" Jonah said. He turned and left.

«‹—›»

Thirty minutes later Jonah killed his engine a little way down the street from the address he'd been given. He had to *check*. He folded his arms and waited.

A little over three hours later a shade-wearing, lycra-clad Mary Leydon and a blonde-haired woman that Jonah recognized from the night in Malibu emerged from the apartment block onto the street. They jogged off down the sidewalk.

Jonah watched them until they disappeared around a corner and then he drove away.

«‹—›»

She called him the following night.

"Jonah…how did you get my address?"

"I found it on a star map."

She said nothing for a while, as though she were pondering the likelihood of this. Eventually she exhaled loudly. "Jonah, the flowers are beautiful, they really are. But…you're wasting your *time. And* your money."

Jonah didn't respond.

"Are you listening, Jonah?"

Jonah remained silent for a while before eventually mouthing flatly "yeah."

"Ok. Now don't send me any more flowers, alright?"

Again Jonah waited a while before speaking. "Ok."

"Good. Goodbye, Jonah. Take care of yourself."

Jonah said nothing. Eventually the line went dead.

《《—》》

He sent her flowers twice a week, the deliveries getting larger each time until she softened and agreed to give him another chance. They met in a hotel bar in Pacific Palisades. At one point Mary excused herself and went to the ladies', leaving her cell on the table. When she was out of sight Jonah picked it up and turned off the hide number option on her call settings. He dialed his own number from her phone and when Mary's number appeared on his screen he ended the call. He reactivated the hide number option on Mary's cell and put it down. Then he saved Mary's number on his own phone.

A little bit after she returned from the bathroom Mary remarked that the conversation between them was too forced, even more so than on their previous date. She said that there was simply no click between them at all. When Jonah stared mutely at the table by way of reply Mary exhaled loudly and put her cell into her handbag.

"Bye, Jonah" she said and stood. "And don't send any more flowers. I mean it this time."

Jonah remained silent.

Mary turned and walked toward the door. Jonah watched her leave.

《《—》》

The cell-phone harassment began the following night and continued until Mary threatened him with the police if he contacted her again. A few hours after that warning phone call from her Jonah sat in his living room, his thumb poised over the SEND icon on his cell, a blank message ready to go to Mary.

His thumb moved lower until it was a hair's breadth from the screen-glass. There it remained. Jonah gazed at the screen, the only thing penetrating the silence being the faint sound of traffic on the PCH in the distance.

He withdrew his thumb a little and put the phone down. He went to his bedroom, undressed and got into bed. It being not yet seven-thirty it was still bright outside. Jonah stared upward at the ceiling, not taking his eyes from it as it grew progressively darker. He fell asleep a little before midnight.

«««—»»»

The following morning he called in sick and did the same the three days after that. During that time he didn't change his clothes, remaining in the boxers that he'd gone to bed wearing after having been threatened by Mary. He ate little and didn't shave. No water touched his body. He only left his living-room sofa to go to the kitchen, the bathroom, and to bed. The night before Alec Soranor paid him a visit he didn't bother going to bed, opting to simply change his position on the couch from sitting to horizontal.

When the doorbell rang a little before midday the following day Jonah ignored it. It rang twice more and still Jonah did not move a muscle on the sofa, where he sat gazing out the window at the ribbon of ocean he could see beyond the highway. When his phone began ringing on the table before him Jonah stared at its screen for a while before rising to his feet and going to the door. He opened it and was greeted with the sight of his superior at Point Mugu replacing his cell in the breast-pocket of his uniform. Soranor's eyes flicked down along Jonah's scantily-clad form before returning to his pale, stubbly face.

"Can I come in?" the General asked.

It took a while for Jonah to nod, after which he turned and went into the living room. He sat back in the spot he'd left to go and answer the door, re-commencing his staring out at the ocean. The General sat in an armchair beside him. No words passed between them for a while.

"Is it a girl?"

Jonah turned slowly to look at Soranor. He could see from the General's face that the man knew his…history. Jonah looked back out the window.

"Try to put her out of your mind, son" Soranor said. "It's never easy, but…dig deep. You'll find the strength."

Jonah said nothing, his eyes fixed on the blue beyond the highway. When he heard Soranor's voice again there was authority in it.

"Look at me, Jonah."

Jonah faced his superior.

"Let it *go*" Soranor said. "Move *on*. Focus on your work. It'll clear your mind."

Silence descended again.

Soranor rose from the armchair. "Take tomorrow off as well" Jonah heard him say. "I'll see you on Monday."

The General left the room. Gazing at the shimmering water, Jonah heard the front door open and close. He remained where he was for a few more hours then he dressed and went for a walk.

«««—»»»

Over the weekend Jonah dragged himself out of his emptiness. He ate properly, maintained himself, and got some exercise. By the time Sunday evening came he was looking forward to returning to Point Mugu.

He flung himself back into his work with vigor, confident that he could purge Mary from his thoughts. He'd done it with Louise and Bethany, he could do it again. But with the passing of the days Mary did not grow fainter in his mind. He lasted a little over three months before succumbing. The day after he left the silent voicemail for Mary the police came for him at Point Mugu.

«««—»»»

A week later Soranor called Jonah into his office.

"I've just been to see Mary Leydon" the General said when Jonah was seated before him. "She's agreed to drop the charges."

Jonah blinked. "That's good. Thank you, Gen-."

"I told her that I would personally see to it that you do not bother her again."

Jonah nodded slightly. "Yes, General."

Soranor leaned forward on his desk. "We're getting close here, Jonah. Close to something very special. We need to keep our *eyes on the prize*. Especially *you*."

Jonah breathed deeply and nodded. "Yes."

"Good. That's all."

Jonah rose and left.

CHAPTER THREE

For two years Jonah held back. There was no phone harassment. But he still kept the dark fire well-stoked. Every evening after work he spent some time keeping tabs on Mary online. He filled folder after folder with links, images, newspaper articles, interviews and videos that had anything to do with her. Every couple of months he braved a vigil close to her house in Hancock Park. After three long stakeouts (they'd gotten longer each time) and not having seen her once he went to the DMV again. After parting company with four hundred dollars he was given her new address in Glendale.

Upon first seeing her here he drew a deep breath, his heart beginning to race. He gazed at her as she walked her dog down the street. God, but she was so *beautiful*. A burning sensation in the pit of his stomach, he watched as she entered a shop. He stared at the shop door, hardly blinking until she re-emerged and continued along the sidewalk, now carrying a bag in her hand. When she came to a pedestrian crossing she pressed the button there and waited. A few seconds later she made her way across the road. She continued onward, the road slowly swallowing her figure as she made her way down along a dip. Eventually she was gone. Jonah stared at the point where she'd disappeared for a few minutes. Then he started his car and drove away.

He went to Glendale on two more occasions. And then her new movie was released.

«« — »»

On its opening weekend Jonah went to every viewing of *The War Beneath* that he could make. The Englens were in town that weekend and on the Saturday night went to the eight p.m. showing with him (he'd already been to the early and late afternoon ones). They'd made plans to go for dinner afterward but as they left the cinema Jonah said he felt a little under the weather and cried off. Half an hour after parting company with his grandparents Jonah came back into the cinema and bought a ticket for the late screening. By this stage a few of the staff were giving him strange looks but he was completely oblivious of them as he made his way toward the theatre for his sixth viewing of the film.

The following night, having seen the film three more times, Jonah sat in his kitchen clad only in his boxers. He was drinking a glass of water before going to bed. But he knew he wouldn't sleep in the state he was in. He felt stressed, agitated. He *had* to reach out to Mary. He *had* to let the woman that he had spent so much time watching over the weekend know that he was still alive. He stared at his cell before him on the table.

He picked it up and dialed, intending to leave her a voice message congratulating her on the success of *The War Beneath* which was having a great opening weekend. The number was no longer in service. Of course, she had changed it.

He'd send her flowers. Yes.

Jonah's agitation began to dissipate. A little while after deciding on his course of action he felt calm enough to go to bed. He was asleep in minutes.

«‹‹—››»

Two days later he was summoned to Soranor's office.

"I've just had a call from Mary Leydon" the General said. "Seems she spent an hour handing out unwanted flower bouquets to her neighbors this morning."

Jonah's eyes dropped to a point on Soranor's desk.

"Lucky for you I managed to talk her out of going to the police" Soranor said. He paused before adding in a lower tone, "I practically had to fucking *plead* with her."

Jonah felt a knot tighten in his stomach. On the few occasions he had seen the General angry over the years he had never heard him swear. Jonah cleared his throat. "I apologize, General" he said. "I had a little lapse."

Soranor snorted. "Well, you certainly lapsed in style. Fifty flower bouquets!" He released a long breath. "Do you get a *kick* out of this kinda' shit, Jonah? Do you *enjoy* having your commanding officer begging for you? Do you enjoy watching me break my word?"

He paused, causing Jonah to wonder if maybe he should venture something. "Because that's what *really* pisses me off with this sad situation" the General said, rising from his chair. "I made a promise to that woman" he said, walking toward the front of his desk. When he arrived there he sat against the edge of it and stared down at Jonah, his arms folded. "I assured her that you would leave her alone. Now I've failed in that assurance."

"It was just a gift, General. Nothing more. A congratulatory present on the opening of her new movie-."

"NO-CONTACT!" Soranor almost shouted. "You are not to engage with this woman in ANY WAY, be it ever so slight, while you are working here. Do you understand?"

"Yes, Sir."

Silence.

"Do not cross me again, Jonah," Soranor said quietly. "Is that clear?"

"Yes, Sir."

Soranor kept his eyes on Jonah for a few more seconds before returning to his chair.

"Go," the General said as he picked up a pen. He began studying a document on his desk.

Jonah got up and left.

«««—»»»

Jonah began working even harder than before, rarely leaving the base before having spent at least the round of the clock there. Mary rarely left his mind but pushing onward at Point Mugu was better than being in Malibu and keeping tabs on her on his laptop.

During this period Mary moved again, this time to Studio City. With her stock rising high after the huge success of *The War Beneath* and her much-lauded performance in it she had her pick of roles. She opted for the lead female part in *The Lower Ones*, a medium-budget movie which would be directed by Lowell Bach, a much-revered rising talent in the directorial world. It would be a far cry from the glamor of her character in her previous venture—set in a poor El Paso suburb, in *The Lower Ones* she would play an impoverished, abused housewife and mother of four. She'd been very impressed with the script and when she'd heard that Lowell Bach had been drafted in for the project she saw the role as possible Oscar material for her. Late on the night before she was due to sign the contract for the part, Paul Zeller, her agent rang her. She'd been offered the role of Cleopatra in what would be a lavish biopic of the Egyptian queen's life. A nine-figure budget had been sanctioned for its production. It would blow the 1963 film of the same name out of the water in size and spectacle.

"Who's the scriptwriter?" Mary asked.

"Still tba" Zeller answered.

"Who's directing?"

"Carter Hornsby."

Mary smiled. Carter Hornsby was a bit too Michael Bay-ish for her liking—an action-first, story-second guy.

"Wish them the best of luck for me," she said.

"Look, Mary, I know you like your deep characters and strong plot-lines but if this movie is a hit…it'll *make* you."

"Gee, I don't know, Paul," Mary said, smiling. "I'm kinda' thinking it'll *break* me."

Zeller sighed. "Well will you at least sleep on it?"

"Sure, Paul."

"I guess I shouldn't really be holding out much hope here, should I?"

"Nope."

Zeller knew how resolute Mary was when her mind was made up. "You principled ones," he said. "You're not good for my ulcers."

"Sorry, Paul."

"Yeah well, I'm still going to stop at a church on the way home and pray that you wake up a completely different person."

Mary laughed. "Ok."

"Good night, Mary."

"Good night, Paul."

The line went dead.

The following morning she drove to Burbank and signed her contract for *The Lower Ones*.

«««—»»»

She felt the spark between her and Lowell Bach the second they were introduced. As they shook hands their eyes lingered on each other's. Tall and handsome, Bach had intelligence, charisma and a great work ethic to boot. Her agent had a lot of time for him too. "A male version of you" was Zeller's opinion of Bach.

Even though she knew the attraction was mutual, Bach kept his interest under wraps during the four months of filming and Mary respected him for it. If he had asked her out during their period of work she would have said no. Not that she expected him to do so—from the off she knew he was a consummate professional and that was exactly what proved to be the case.

When she wasn't being filmed she liked to watch him work. He controlled the set with a quiet confidence. Everything ran smoothly. On the odd occasion when things weren't going to his liking he pulled on the reins with diplomacy, getting the ship skillfully back on course.

The day after they finished shooting he asked her out and she accepted. They met for drinks at a bar in West Hollywood. When she arrived she found him sitting at the counter, sipping a beer and picking casually at a bowl of peanuts. Looking calm and collected as per usual (something that she found very attractive about him) he looked incredibly sexy in a simple black shirt and jeans.

"Hey," she said as she neared him.

"Hey."

She sat beside him.

"Aren't you going to compliment me on how I look?" she asked, smiling expectantly as she placed her handbag on the counter. She'd put a lot of effort into her appearance for the night. His mouth stopped working on the peanuts and he gave her a quick once-over. He nodded.

"Yeah, you look ok."

She looked at him in mock-shock. "Just *ok*?"

"A little bit better than Norma, anyway."

She elbowed him playfully, laughing. He began smiling too. Norma was the character she'd played in *The Lower Ones* and Mary had spent most of the time she'd been in Lowell's company wearing worn, old-looking clothes, her hair and face made-up to look shiny and greasy, and her teeth discolored. She'd often sported black eyes and swollen lips.

"Get me a drink, smartass" she said.

He did.

«‹‹—››»

After his second reprimand by Soranor Jonah had held himself in check quite well. He'd found out that Mary had moved to Studio City (he'd always want to know where she was based—there was *no* way he'd be able to survive without that) but had only driven to the address and seen her there once. He'd restricted himself to one night a week of keeping tabs on her online.

When he became aware of Lowell Bach's existence it happened quite by chance. He was driving on Ocean Avenue in Santa Monica one Sunday afternoon when he saw a woman that looked very like Mary coming toward him on the far sidewalk with a tall, shade-wearing man (there was no way Mary would be with another man—that was why it was a woman who looked like her). But as he slowed down and maintained his gaze at the woman she began to look more and more like Mary. Suddenly the woman smiled broadly and that sealed it. It was the smile Jonah had been captured by nearly three years before when he'd first laid eyes on it in the restaurant in Malibu. Mary tilted her head sideways and leaned it against the man's shoulder. A bomb went off in Jonah's gut.

There was a loud bang and the sound of glass breaking and Jonah pitched forward against the steering wheel. He faced forward and saw uncaringly that he'd drifted off the road into the back of a parked car. A stocky balding man was emerging from the driver's side of the car, a truculent look on his face. Jonah got out of his car and turned his attention once more to across the street. He barely heard the balding man's obscenities as he gazed at the couple getting farther and farther away from him.

«««—»»»

It took him a few hours that evening to find out that the new man in Mary's life had been the director of her most recent film. There was nothing on the celeb gossip sites about them being an item so they were obviously keeping it low-key. Jonah stayed on his laptop all that night. By the time he switched it off at seven a.m. the following morning to headed off to Point Mugu he knew practically everything there was to know about Mr. Lowell Bach.

«««—»»»

He began to go to Studio City more regularly. On the occasions he saw Mary leaving or heading toward the apartment Bach was rarely with her. One time when they were together Jonah watched them stroll down the sidewalk until they came to a pedestrian crossing. As they waited for the traffic to stop they chatted. Suddenly Bach smiled and a second later leaned forward and kissed Mary on the mouth. A knot tightened in Jonah's stomach and a horrible heat began to swell upward to his chest. Breathing deeply, he started his car and drove away.

As he drove, the heat made its way to his head and he felt his face redden. Beginning to feel nauseous and weak he pulled over and got out of the car. He leaned against a tree and vomited.

«««—»»»

The night he found out about their engagement Jonah lifted his laptop from his legs and placed it on the coffee-table before him. He looked out the window at the moonlit ocean, not moving from the couch all night. When he needed to urinate he did it where he was. In the morning he didn't go to Point Mugu and didn't call in sick.

When his cell rang in the kitchen at some point he didn't answer it. A little over an hour later he heard a knock on his front door. He didn't rise to go to it.

"Jonah?" he heard Soranor call.

Jonah blinked once.

Soranor knocked again, louder this time. "Jonah."

Jonah remained inert.

He heard the front door opening, not having bothered to lock it the previous night. A few seconds later Soranor appeared at the corner of his vision. He heard the General sniff and he became dully aware again of the dampness beneath his thighs. Soranor sat in the chair he'd occupied on his previous visit. The two men remained silent and unmoving in each other's company for a while. Eventually Soranor leaned forward and turned the laptop toward him. Upon reading the headline about Mary's and engagement and seeing a photo of the couple looking very happy in each other's company he exhaled loudly.

"I'd say you're one hell of a guy to carry a torch except it's not a torch you're carrying. It's a goddamn *cancer*."

Jonah turned to face the General.

"It's obsession, Jonah" Soranor continued, his face hard. "And it *kills*. You've got to kill *it*. Or at the very least *bury* it. Once and for all." He sat forward in his chair. "You're on course to make possibly the greatest contribution to human medicine in the history of mankind Jonah, and you're letting this—" he gesticulated contemptuously at the laptop, "-*shit* get in the way." He sat back in the chair blinking, a look of frustration on his face at having momentarily lost his composure. "I'm sorry to use that kind of language. I know you probably feel something for this woman beneath this fixation you have with her but it's over now. *This* is it" he said, gesturing at the laptop. "She's going to marry this guy and they're going to live happily ever after." He paused, his face softening and some sympathy appearing there. "It's *over*."

Jonah turned back to the window.

"We're only a year and a half away from testing the virophage on human flu virus" Soranor said. "If it's successful…you'll be able to have any woman you want. Let this one go. For good."

Soranor went quiet and joined Jonah looking out the window. "It's a beautiful day" he said. "You should get some air."

After a few more seconds of silence he rose to his feet. "See you at base tomorrow," Soranor said. Then he turned and left.

«««—»»»

Jonah remained where he was until late afternoon. He rose, showered and changed his clothes and then he walked to the beach. Upon arriving there he sat down not far from the shoreline and gazed out at the water, his arms folded on his upturned knees. The tide was coming in. He remained where he was until the breakers were thundering only a few yards below him down the steep sand-slope. A few passers-by cast glances at the fully-clothed, shoe-wearing man sitting motionless near the water's edge as the hissing foam crept closer to him. When it finally came past Jonah's shoes and stopped shy of his buttocks he rose and walked away.

He had dinner at the restaurant he'd first seen Mary at three and a half years before. As he ate he gazed at the seat she'd occupied that night.

«««—»»»

A few months later *The Lower Ones* was released. It was a box-office hit and received a lot of critical acclaim. Mary was nominated for a Best Actress Oscar and Lowell received a Best Director nomination. Ironically Mary lost out to Simone Walker, the actress who had played the part of *Cleopatra* in the film that Mary had turned down. Mary had seen the movie; she'd had to agree when the critics lauded her competitor's stunning performance in "an otherwise very mediocre, overdone film."

Jonah gazed at his TV screen as he watched Lowell walk in triumph to the podium on Oscar night to collect his Best Director award. The heat in the pit of Jonah's stomach almost painful, he listened as Lowell thanked all who'd been involved in the film, especially his amazingly talented wife-to-be Mary who'd made life so easy for him during its making. Smiling at her in the crowd, he began applauding. The rest of the crowd joined in and the camera focused on Mary as she beamed at her fiancé on the stage. After she blew a kiss at him the camera switched back to Lowell in time to catch him blowing one back in return. As the clapping for Mary continued, Jonah went to the TV and turned it off. Then he went to bed.

«««—»»»

In the ensuing months Jonah got to know all of the most conscience-less paparazzi in Los Angeles. None of them could tell him where the wedding festivities would be held. Jonah hired one of their more cash-strapped members as his own private investigator and six weeks before the ceremony was scheduled to take place, he got his information.

«««—»»»

With both Mary and Lowell having a lot of friends and coming from large families the dance-floor of the function room in the Tribune hotel in Santa Monica was a pretty lively place once the band got into their stride. Mary was dancing with her agent when the glasses-wearing, mustachioed man appeared beside them.

"Can I cut in?" the man asked Zeller.

"Sure," Zeller said, making way for the man to dance with Mary. "Gotta' get me a fresh one," Zeller said to Mary. He put his hand to his mouth in a taking-a-drink gesture. "You want anything?"

Mary shook her head and smiled. "No thanks."

Zeller looked at the man. "Want a drink?"

"I'm ok, thanks."

Zeller nodded and head off in the direction of the bar.

"I'm sorry, but I'm not sure I know you…" Mary said to her new dancing partner, an enquiring smile on her face.

"You look beautiful" the man said.

Blinking, Mary studied the eyes that were gazing into hers. Eventually her smile began to fade. She stopped moving.

"Jonah?"

Jonah said nothing, maintaining his stare. Mary snatched the black wig from Jonah's head and flung it to the ground. A few people in their immediate vicinity stopped dancing, concern on their faces. Next, Mary took Jonah's glasses. She stared at him, fury in her eyes. A lot of people were watching the goings-on at this stage.

"How *dare* you," Mary said. "How *dare* you show up at my wedding. You…*loser*."

The band faded out.

"Look at you" Mary continued as Jonah removed the moustache. "In your pathetic disguise." When she spoke again it was in the tone of an adult talking to a child. "Can you not get it, Jonah? Can you not get it into that sad, sick little head of yours that you can't have me? You never COULD HAVE. I'm married now. To a *man*. Not a freak, or a weirdo, like *you*. A man." She paused. "Something you can never be."

Lowell appeared at her side and slipped an arm around her waist. She softened a little at his touch, her lower lip trembling a little. She blinked a few times, raising her head a little in an effort not to lose her composure.

"Is this the guy you were telling me about?" Lowell asked, his eyes fixed coldly upon Jonah.

"Yeah."

"Get out," Lowell said. "Before we call the cops."

Jonah turned and walked away, the crowd parting before him as though he were a leper.

«《——》»

Detective Eddie Nemvicius had no time for stalkers. He'd handled plenty of cases before, calling them the "saddest scum on earth." He was not happy with Soranor's interceding with Mary on Jonah's behalf. Soranor pleaded yet again with Mary not to press charges, going all out in his efforts this time. He told her that they were at a crucial stage in the project—pivotal tests were only six months away, the results of which could significantly enhance the quality of human life on earth. Jonah was the key man in the whole thing—at the moment he was simply too important to compromise. To Nemvicius's frustration Mary agreed to drop the charges. But she was not prepared to let Jonah off scot free this time. There would have to be a compromise. At a meeting in his office with Mary, Lowell and Soranor, Nemvicius insisted that at the very least Jonah should have to wear a GPS ankle bracelet.

"I'll do you one better" Soranor said.

«《——》»

Jonah stared at the inch-and-a-half by one inch bio-chip in Soranor's hand.

"You want to put that thing in my *leg*?"

Soranor made no reply.

Jonah shook his head. "No fucking way."

"Fine," Soranor said. "Then I call Mary and tell her you're being un-cooperative and that she has my full blessing to go ahead and press charges. Which Detective Nemvicius will be *delighted* to hear. He seems to think you're a right piece of work," he paused before adding, "and that he can get you jail time."

Soranor watched Jonah closely as he absorbed this information. He smiled inwardly as Jonah's chest rose and fell visibly, his reddening face a mask of barely suppressed frustration.

"You're enjoying this," Jonah said.

"Just letting you know the exact state of play."

"You can't DO this without me. You KNOW it."

"My friend, at this stage that's a risk I'm willing to take. I'm *through* with cleaning up after you, Jonah. So if you don't agree to wear this chip and I lose you because of that…then so be it. We'll move on without you."

Soranor let this sink in.

"So," he resumed, toggling the chip between his fingers. He was enjoying this *immensely*. "What's it going to be?"

Jonah looked to be on the verge of melting with frustration.

"Will I have a limp?" he asked.

"During healing, yes."

"What about after?"

Soranor shook his head. "I don't know."

"Has it not been tried out on anyone?"

"No. It's a prototype."

"So I'm the guinea pig."

This time Soranor had to smile outwardly.

"You're about to become a hero, Jonah," he said. "Not only are you about to rid your country of an illness that has plagued it since time immemorial but you're also doing your bit for its security."

《《《—》》》

Four days after his surgery Jonah returned to Point Mugu. His limp was pronounced but not as bad as he'd feared. Upon arriving at the base he was informed that Soranor wanted to speak with him.

"Good morning," Soranor said when Jonah walked into his office. "How's the leg?"

"Bearable," Jonah replied, limping toward the chair in front of Soranor's desk.

"Stay standing," Soranor said and got to his feet. He went to one of the windows and began closing the blind. "I need to show you something."

Jonah stopped walking toward the chair and looked at Soranor. He watched as the General moved to his second window and closed the blinds there too. Soranor went back to his desk and opened a drawer. He took out what looked like a cell phone. He showed the screen to Jonah. On the screen was a satellite map showing Point Mugu and its environs. There was an arrow pointing at Point Mugu and at the bottom of the screen were latitude and longitude co-ordinates.

"This is your tracker," Soranor said. "It's keyed to the chip in your leg. The arrow is pointing at you. Detective Nemvicius has one of these as does Mary Leydon. We will know exactly where you are at all times, day or night. Detective Nemvicius and I will be keeping in regular contact with each other. If we see any remotely suspicious movement on your part on this map, one of our people will be calling you to inform us of your intentions. If you do not answer the call, either Detective Nemvicius or I will dispatch units to intercept you."

Soranor observed Jonah silently for a few seconds, letting what he had said sink in. Then he turned the screen-side of the tracker back around toward him. His thumb went to the screen and Jonah screamed as his right leg became a log of agony from groin to knee, spasming uncontrollably. His hand flew to the aggrieved thigh and he automatically transferred his weight to his left leg. He clasped the back of the nearby chair for support but with the awkwardness of his position it went from under him and he collapsed to the ground. Gripping his thigh with both hands now, he writhed about on the floor, his face a rictus of pain. Suddenly the agony stopped as abruptly as it had begun. Breathing hard, Jonah moaned with relief. He looked up to see Soranor standing over him, the tracker still in the General's hand.

"I had that feature installed myself," Soranor said. "But don't worry. Nemvicius and Mary don't have it. It's just on mine." He lifted the tracker a little for emphasis.

"You...*fucking* asshole," Jonah gasped.

Soranor tut-tutted, shaking his head. "Such unbecoming language, Doctor," he said, and turned his attention back to the tracker's screen. "I'll just increase the voltage a little."

"No, NO!" Jonah begged, a pleading arm flying in the General's direction. "A-A-A-A-A-A-A-HHHHHH!!!!!!!!" he shrieked in a type of trembling jitter as the horrible, buzzing pain burst into life in his thigh again, only this time more intense. This time his lower torso spasmed in sync with his leg. His abdomen was so tightly tensed it was almost unbearable. And then the nightmare vanished again.

"Any more disrespectful comments?" Soranor asked.

Panting, Jonah closed his eyes.

"Good."

Savoring the bliss of painlessness, Jonah heard the sound of footsteps and other movement. When the noise stopped Jonah opened his eyes and found himself looking at Soranor's shin. The General was sitting in a chair, his feet not far from his face.

"There will be no more *shit*, Jonah," he heard Soranor say quietly. "From now on, you will keep your head down, work your ass off and *deliver*. You'll collect your Nobel Prize and I'll get the top seat at the Pentagon. After that I don't give a fuck what you do."

When Soranor spoke again, his voice was lower and much closer.

"But mark my words, if you so much as put a foot wrong between now and then I'll crank up the voltage and keep my thumb on the button until your leg cooks itself from the inside out and your muscles and bones *snap*. Are we clear?"

Still panting a little, Jonah said nothing.

"I said are we clear?"

Now the General sounded as though he were only a few inches from Jonah's ear.

Jonah nodded. "Yes." He heard Soranor pull back.

"Good. I'm going to go and get a cup of coffee. I'll be back in a couple of minutes. If you're still here when I get back…then we go for round three."

Jonah listened to him get up and leave.

«««—»»»

Jonah found the phone calls from Soranor's and Nemvicius's people very demeaning. At the start his cell rang practically every time he headed east from Malibu and he had to give a detailed outline of what his intentions were. One time he left for Los Angeles with very little charge in his phone and it died a few minutes after he set out. As he pulled into the car-park of a shopping mall in Beverly Hills he saw a police car flashing behind him. Upon showing the officers his dead cell they escorted him to a cell phone shop where he had to buy a charged phone. After watching him transfer his sim card into the new phone they left.

After three months the calls had only eased up a tiny bit in frequency. When driving he constantly felt like he was being followed (which he was being, technically) and the feeling abated only slightly when he was out of the car. Even when he walked to the beach or into the center of Malibu he felt unpleasantly "accompanied."

Worried that his phone was possibly bugged he'd bought a second one for his correspondence with Zarrani. When Zarrani called to say that he'd be coming to meet him in a week's time Jonah told him to come to his house in Malibu. They'd always previously met in Los Angeles but this time Jonah figured the safest place was probably right at home.

CHAPTER FOUR

uring his fourth year at Point Mugu an Islamist militant group called Hammer of Fire had approached Jonah with an offer: fifty million dollars for a deadly human virus derived from the Vandenvirus. Ten in advance and forty on delivery of the completed, tested product and its antivirus. After shaking hands on the deal, Jonah said he'd have the items for them in four years max.

After the ten million had been lodged in his Swiss bank account he'd had an underground lab built as an extension to his cellar. This he stocked with medical and computing equipment purchased on the black market. During a retrofitting of the lab at Point Mugu, with security a little lax, he smuggled out a sample of the Vandenvirus.

Before he went to work, Najib Zarrani, a senior in the Hammer of Fire ranks met Jonah in Los Angeles. Zarrani and his fellow warriors wanted a virus that killed viciously, taking an undignified toll on the bodies it occupied as it dragged them towards the grave. The Retribution virus, as it would be called from then on, would be Zarrani's people's deadly drone strike on the nation that had brought so much wreckage and dishonor to their land.

Every six months after that Zarrani met with Jonah in Los Angeles for progress updates. After four years lapsed and with Jonah informing him that he was still some way from completion, Zarrani increased the meetings to once every four months. After the expiration of the fifth year Zarrani was visibly impatient. Jonah assured him he was close, very close. Zarrani increased the frequency of meetings to once every three months. At the first meeting of year six Jonah said he'd definitely have the items the next time they saw each other.

‹‹‹—›››

When Jonah heard the car coming to rest outside his window he took a deep breath. A few seconds later there was a knock on his door and he went to it. He opened it and let Zarrani in.

"Hello, Doctor," Zarrani said and went past Jonah.

His heart speeding a little, Jonah closed the door and followed Zarrani into the living room. Standing by the coffee table Zarrani turned and looked at Jonah.

"So. Is it ready?"

Standing just inside the doorway Jonah waited before answering.

"Three more months," he said, trying not to sound frightened. "I *promise* you'll have it then."

Zarani stared at him for what seemed like an age before buttoning his blazer and walking toward him. He arrived before Jonah, his face deadly serious.

"You have six weeks, Doctor. If you do not have our property ready then…we take your grandparents."

Zarrani brushed past him and left.

«««—»»»

The following four weeks saw Jonah putting himself through a gruelling regime. After coming home from a twelve-hour day (at least) at Point Mugu he would go straight down to his lab and work on Zarrani's virus until he could no longer keep his eyes open. He would snatch a few hours sleep at his workbench before waking and repeating the process.

And then at two-thirty a.m. on a Saturday morning, Jonah found himself looking at a vial of completed Retribution in his hand. He snorted contemptuously at the name Zarrani had given it. The vulgarity of it. Jonah twisted the vial one way and then the other, gazing at the clear liquid inside. The fruits of five years labor. All that remained now was to test it on a human being. A mixture of relief and elation coursed through him. He didn't feel in the least bit tired.

"Want to take a walk?" he said to the colorless fluid. He paused, then nodded. "Let's take a walk."

He left the lab, vial in hand. He took a small remote control unit from his pocket and pressed a button on it. The six-inch thick door of the lab thudded closed and a sham brick wall rose from the cellar floor to conceal it.

He put on a light jacket, slipped the vial into an inside breast pocket and left the house. It was a beautiful moonlit night. Upon reaching the PCH he found it strange to see it so quiet. In a few hours it would fill up again as people went about the Californian way, endlessly driving from here to there. He crossed the westbound lanes and stopped at the divider to let a convertible full of late-night revelers whizz by him on the esstbound side.

"Wooooo!!" a girl cheered at him from the backseat, beer-bottle in hand. "Cheers, man!" she shouted, extending the bottle toward Jonah. He watched her put the bottle to her mouth and then he crossed the road. When he reached the sand on the beach he removed his shoes and socks and carried them in his hand. He walked toward the water, the waves growing louder as he drew closer. He watched them swell quickly in the half-light from thin lines to thick, dark powerful strips that boomed to their end, their replacements growing behind them, rushing to the same suicide.

He turned left and began walking in the direction of Malibu. He was walking for ten minutes without having met anyone before he encountered a group of young people playing volleyball. A few couples were watching, drinking beer by a fire. There was a lot of laughing going on amongst the players and the movement of some of them was sluggish and un-coordinated. As he walked past the game one of the drunker players made poor contact with the ball and it flew toward Jonah, brushing his shoulder before continuing on its way to the ocean. A dart of heat flared in his stomach.

Close one.

His heart beating faster Jonah kept walking, the game receding behind him. A few minutes later he passed a couple grunting and moaning as they made love on the sand. About a quarter-mile on he stopped, a circle of people up ahead of him. They were singing around a fire. One of them, a woman, had a guitar. She was smiling as she sang. Jonah knew his parents had met in a beach sing-along. His father had told him. His mother had been playing the guitar and smiling like this woman before Jonah now.

Jonah stared at the woman. Eventually the happiness left her features and Jonah found himself gazing at a coughing, hacking woman, her hair hanging in her shiny, sweating face as her body responded to Retribution's initial assault, the virus's real horror yet to begin for her. Suddenly the woman's face became that of his mother's. Jonah watched Kara Englen spluttering and coughing for a few seconds and then the smiling, guitar-playing woman returned.

Jonah lifted his eyes and saw that up ahead the sky was brightening with artificial light. He wasn't far from the center of Malibu. He turned and headed for home.

《《—》》

Two days later the Englens flew in from Pittsburgh. Jonah met them after work for dinner and invited them over to his house the following evening. He'd cook for them. Ronald and Olivia smiled and accepted. It was something Jonah had never offered before.

《《—》》

Dead on six weeks from the day he'd issued Jonah with his ultimatum, Zarrani returned. After closing the front door behind his guest Jonah nodded at Zarrani. The hard look in Zarrani's eyes softened a fraction.

"Show me."

"Follow me," Jonah said and walked past his guest in the direction of the cellar.

In his lab Jonah went to a refrigerator beside his workbench. He pressed a few digits on a keypad set into the refrigerator's door and it opened. He took two vials from a holder on the top shelf inside and turned to Zarrani.

"Virus" Jonah said, raising the vial in his right hand. "Antivirus" he said, raising his left.

"And the human testing?" Zarrani asked.

Jonah replaced the vials and closed the refrigerator. He picked up a plastic case from his workbench and opened it. He turned it toward Zarrani so he could see the four DVDs inside.

"Show me now," Zarrani said.

Jonah blinked. "Certainly."

Zarrani watched Jonah turn and go to the wall beyond the refrigerator from which hung a TV. Beneath the TV a DVD player sat on a shelf. While Jonah busied himself with preparations for viewing Zarrani looked around the lab. His eyes came to rest on the large glass structure beyond the workbench. A four-sided unit not unlike a small greenhouse, with two narrow single bed-frames inside, yet no bedding on either. Zarrani walked around the workbench to get a closer look and saw that there was a door on one of the structure's sides. In the corner of the structure furthest from him was a toilet. On the ceiling over the toilet was a dome camera. There was another camera over the beds. To the left of the door at floor-level, was a small rectangular pane of glass, cut into the side of the chamber. A food-slot, Zarrani supposed. Looking back into the cell again Zarrani found his gaze drawn to a faint, almost unnoticeable red stain on the floor by one of the bed-legs. There was another similar, smaller stain on the under-part of the toilet bowl.

"There's four full days of recording here…" Jonah said.

"Show me the main parts," Zarrani said, still analyzing the cell.

No words passed between the two men for a while.

"Ok," Jonah eventually called. "It's ready to go. You, ah…want something to drink?"

"Iced tea."

"Sure."

Zarrani heard Jonah heading off. A few seconds later he turned from his examination of the cell and walked back around the workbench. He looked at the TV screen. On it was footage from the camera over the cell-toilet. It showed two people, an elderly man and woman, lying either asleep or unconscious on the beds. He looked at the two figures for a few seconds before moving closer to the screen. While he was studying the faces of the individuals Jonah came back into the lab.

"These are your grandparents," Zarrani said, his eyes remaining on the screen as Jonah approached him.

"Yes," Jonah said, arriving by his side.

Zarrani turned sideways to see Jonah holding a glass of iced tea toward him, a bottle of Budweiser in his other hand. Zarrani held Jonah's eyes for a few seconds before letting them drop to the iced tea, which he took. He watched Jonah place his beer on the workbench and go to the back of the lab. By the wall there was a sofa-chair which Jonah wheeled closer to the TV. When he was just a few feet from Zarrani Jonah stopped and gestured at the chair.

"Please."

Zarrani didn't move immediately. Eventually he walked forward and sat down.

Jonah lifted his beer from the workbench and drank some of it. He faced Zarrani.

"Retribution is a two-pronged virus," he said. "It replicates in the respiratory and nervous systems. From introduction to the body to death it takes ninety-six hours to run its course. After initial infection via the respiratory tract, the incubation period lasts for twenty-four hours. During roughly the first twelve hours of this period the carrier is not contagious. After that, they are. Symptoms appear after twenty-four hours. They're basically those of the common flu—runny nose, sneezing, coughing, sore throat, muscle aches, temperature rise. They escalate in severity until the patient is bed-ridden by forty-eight hours. A peak in severity is reached and the patient's condition does not deteriorate any further. From approximately the sixtieth hour onward the symptoms begin to abate—the patient is able to walk around, appetite increases. By this stage the virus has become active in the nervous system and by approximately the seventy-second hour has begun replicating in the amygdala region of the brain."

Jonah drank some more beer.

"The viral replication in the amygdala gives rise to Kluver-Bucy syndrome and Pica. Symptoms of Kluver-Bucy include docility, overeating, hyperorality—"

"What's that?" Zarrani asked.

"The examination of objects by mouth. What you and I would examine by touch, a hyperorality sufferer would examine by taste, or by placing in the mouth."

Zarrani nodded and took a sip of iced tea.

"Then there's hypersexuality, visual agnosia, memory loss and emotional changes. The patient has a heightened sex drive and can seek sexual stimulation from inappropriate or unusual objects. With visual agnosia there is an inability to recognize familiar objects or faces."

"What are the emotional changes?"

"Apathy...indifference, lack of facial expression."

"And what is this other thing you speak of...besides this Kluver Bucy syndrome—

"Pica."

"What is that?"

"The eating of inappropriate objects."

Nodding, Zarrani turned his attention to the screen where Kara and Ronald Englen were still lying on their cell-beds, the footage paused.

"The amygdala," he said. "Something I didn't even know existed before today. And its destruction can cause such chaos."

"Yes," Jonah said. "It's quite important."

Zarrani took another sip of his tea.

"Tell me about the end."

"Like I said," Jonah began. "The neurotrophic symptoms manifest themselves from roughly seventy-two hours onward. Although some patients may succumb to incidents and complications arising from these symptoms, they will not be the main cause of mortality. Approximately two-thirds of the way through day four the respiratory elements of the virus come to the fore again, quickly and severely, which will cause unconsciousness in most cases. Internal and external hemorrhaging occurs, followed by convulsions, then death."

Zarrani turned his attention to the TV screen again. He remained silent for a while.

"Play the video."

《《—》》

With the timer in the top corner of the screen reading all zeros they watched Jonah enter the cell and inject first Ronald and then Olivia with Retribution while they slept off the effects of the tranquilizer darts their grandson had shot into them. Jonah then skipped forward twenty-three and a half hours to the first manifestation of symptoms in the pair—a sneeze by Olivia. It was another hour before Ronald let one off. Jonah moved the feed forward to thirty-six hours and the screen showed the Englens in bed, their beds pushed together at this stage. After showing Ronald coughing through a phlegm-filled throat Jonah moved the feed on to forty-eight hours. The couple were again in bed, their labored breathing clearly audible. An untouched food tray lay on the floor by the hatch in the glass. Ronald lay on his side, his body shivering visibly beneath the blankets. Olivia was lying on her back, her face very pale and shiny with sweat. She had one hand on her forehead. The area between her nose and mouth was bright red. She moaned and suddenly launched into a violent fit of coughing.

At sixty-six hours the couple were sitting on the side of Ronald's bed, eating from the food tray. They looked pale and unkempt but their symptoms had clearly alleviated. After drinking some orange juice Ronald coughed and looked out through the glass in the direction of the workbench.

"Well, Jonah," he said. "Is that it? Your little test *done*? You gonna' let us OUT now you...*SON OF A BITCH*!!???" His voice cracked with emotion as he shouted the closing expletive and he picked up an empty glass from the tray. He hurled the glass at the barrier before him and it smashed against it. As Olivia threw her arms up to protect herself from flying debris Jonah moved the footage forward again.

At seventy-six hours it showed Ronald standing near the cell door, his shirt open to the waist, its buttons gone. Ronald's head was at an angle as he gnawed on the left collar-lapel. At one point he paused to sneeze before resuming his chewing. Olivia was in the far corner of the cell, sitting cross-legged on the ground between the beds and the glass. She was staring out through the barrier, a vacant expression on her face.

At eighty hours Ronald was sitting on the toilet, the food tray in his hands. Every now and then he put the tray into his mouth. After a few seconds he would remove it and place a different point of the tray into his mouth. While this was taking place his wife was across the room, the septuagenarian naked from the waist down, one leg astride the railing of one of the beds. She moaned as she slid her groin over and back along the metal bar, her utterances of pleasure occasionally interrupted by fits of coughing.

Four hours later Olivia lay coughing weakly on the ground at the foot of the bed, eyes closed, a small pool of blood on the floor before her open mouth. There were bloodstains and spatters on the bedclothes and bed frame. By the toilet Ronald lay shivering in the fetal position, his ghost-pale face a mask of sweat. The remains of a trouser belt lay by his head, ragged teeth marks at one end. About half a minute into the excerpt of footage Olivia stopped coughing. A minute later Jonah's figure walked into the cell. He passed by his grandfather and went to Olivia. When he arrived at her motionless form he put two fingers to her neck.

"Subject two deceased," Jonah's voice said. "Time elapsed from infection to death…eighty-four hours eighteen minutes."

On his high stool next to Zarrani Jonah moved the footage forward, stopping a little after eighty-eight hours. On the screen Ronald lay on his back, convulsing. There were spatters of blood on the ground around him and lines of blood emanating from the sides of his mouth and nose. Suddenly his convulsions stopped. His left leg twitched a few times and then there was no more movement. Jonah sped the footage forward until his form appeared in the cell. He bent to his haunches at Ronald's side and put his fingers to his grandfather's neck.

"Subject one deceased. Time from infection to death…eighty-eight hours ten minutes."

Jonah rose and left the cell.

The screen went black. Zarrani looked sideways at Jonah who had just stopped the DVD.

"I expect individuals of less advanced age to survive until at least ninety-six hours, maybe a little longer," Jonah said. "The very old and very young will die quicker. Some may not even make it to the neurotrophic phase. Because of the virus's unique origins and makeup it will take the authorities at least four years to develop an antivirus."

Zarrani snorted. "A bit late."

"It'll be too late after four months."

Zarrani drank some of his tea. "The death rate?"

Jonah didn't respond immediately. "Ninety-nine point seven five percent," he said eventually.

Zarrani nodded slowly. He rose and went to the workbench beyond Jonah. He placed his half-finished iced tea on it and turned to Jonah.

"We're going to test it ourselves," Zarrani said, at which Jonah nodded. "If it is successful then we will pay the remainder of your fee. *Thirty* million…not forty. Consider this a…*late* tax."

Zarrani held Jonah's eyes, waiting for a negative reaction to this news. When Jonah merely blinked he said, "Very well. Our business is concluded. I will take the items now."

"Certainly," Jonah said. He put his beer bottle down and pulled out a drawer from beneath his workbench. He took a small briefcase from it which he placed on the workbench and opened. The interior of the briefcase was foam, with three spaces cut out in it. One of the spaces was occupied by a plastic DVD case. He took the case out and opened it facing away from him so Zarrani could see the two DVDs inside.

"Development and genetic sequencing," Jonah said.

Jonah replaced the DVD case and went to the refrigerator from which he removed the virus and antivirus vials. He placed the vials gently in the two remaining briefcase-spaces. Then he went to the DVD player and removed the final human-test DVD from it, which he placed in the plastic case with the other three. He returned to the briefcase and placed the human-test DVD case on top of the one whose contents he had just shown to Zarrani. Jonah closed the case and held it toward his guest.

"When do you plan to use it?" Jonah asked.

"Don't worry, Doctor," Zarrani said, taking the case. "We'll let you know. You'll have plenty time to enjoy your money." He looked around the lab. "Start disassembling all of this equipment immediately. I will arrange for it to be taken away and destroyed within the next few days. Destroy every single record and piece of information you have relating to this project. Is this clear?"

"Yes."

Zarrani nodded. "Then I bid you goodnight, Doctor. I'll see myself out." Not waiting for a response from Jonah Zarrani turned and headed for the door. Jonah took the door's remote-control unit from his pocket and pressed a button. As Zarrani neared the door it began to open, the sham-cellar wall beyond it ascending. Zarrani turned and looked at Jonah.

"By the way, Doctor. I hope you are not keeping any other samples of the virus. If we were to find out that you had sold it to other parties…we would be most unhappy."

Then he was gone.

«««—»»»

Late the following night Zarrani's operative showed up at Jonah's house driving a small dump truck. The two of them began emptying the lab until nothing remained in it except for the stool and chair that Jonah and Zarrani had occupied while watching the test footage. Afterward an exhausted Jonah watched from his front door as the truck set off into the night. When it was gone he went back inside and went to bed.

«««—»»»

A little after three a.m. the wind woke him and he went to the kitchen for a drink of water. Sitting at the table, glass in hand, he pondered the dream he'd been having. In it, Zarrani's operative had dumped the stuff from his lab into the same gulley that Jonah had buried his grandparents in. Jonah stared at the kitchen wall as images of the Englens rising from the ground returned to him, the soil falling from their decomposing faces as they reached eagerly for the debris around and on top of them, their discolored arms packing glass, metal and plastic into their mouths…

He took a drink of water. When he'd been about to embark on human testing of the virus he'd been resigned to having to lure a homeless person or a drug addict to his house some night. But then the idea of using his grandparents had hit him. There would be no need for a trawl through Malibu's trash. And it would mean an end to the Englens pestering him on their annoyingly frequent visits from Pittsburgh. The night he'd invited them to his house for dinner he'd welcomed them at the door and let them in, ushering them past him. After closing the door he'd taken a tranquilizer gun out from beneath his sweater and shot them both in the back. Hey presto, two subjects, minimum of effort. After the testing he'd driven up into the mountains and buried their bodies in a scrub-filled gully.

His eyelids getting heavy, Jonah took one more gulp of water and returned to bed. He was asleep in seconds and this time his rest was dreamless.

‹‹‹—›››

With human testing of the virophage scheduled to begin in less than two months and with Soranor adamant that there would be no time slippage, the heat was really on at Point Mugu. In the weeks after he met with Zarrani Jonah worked seven days a week, rarely getting home before ten any night. Even though he would be utterly exhausted he would always find the energy to go online and spend a few minutes seeing what was going on in Mary's life.

She and Bach (it was hard to think of him as her *husband*—it caused an unpleasant worm to turn in Jonah's gut when he read the word) were doing well, living in the Hollywood Hills now. *He* had recently started work on a big science fiction film and she was busy on an English period drama.

One night as he scrolled his way down through links after Googling her name, Jonah's exhausted eyes flew open, his stomach suddenly a washing machine. He double-clicked on a link and was presented with a photo of Mary and Bach at the Oscars, the couple smiling happily for the cameras. Beneath the photo a headline read:

MARY LEYDON CONFIRMS PREGNANCY RUMORS

Jonah began reading the article beneath the heading, growing sicker with every word.

> Actress Mary Leydon (28) has confirmed recent rumors that she is pregnant with her husband, Oscar-winning director Lowell Bach (33). In a statement issued through her publicist this morning the actress stated that she was one month pregnant and that she was releasing the information to quell mounting paparazzi interest in the matter.

When he was finished reading Jonah gazed at the article for a while, his stomach a vat of nausea. Eventually he rose from the table, his legs feeling like otherworldly stilts as they propelled him toward the bathroom. They weakened a few steps from the toilet and he slumped against the sink, vomiting into it. He sank to his knees, the bitter smell of his ejection filling his nose. After a while he lowered himself to the floor, the cool of the tiles welcome against his body. It was an hour before he rose and went to bed.

《《——》》》

He slept in fits and starts, not drifting off properly until a little before five. When he woke at six-thirty for work he was exhausted but content, happy with the course of action he'd decided upon. After eating breakfast he went into the living room and went to the large grandfather clock standing against the wall. He pushed it to one side, revealing the silver door of a small safe built into the wall. He put his hand up close to the door and clicked his fingers twice, quickly. He paused, then repeated the exercise. A red light on the safe door changed to green and the door opened outward.

In the safe was a rack which held two vials. Jonah reached inside and took the rack out. He gazed at the two vials—one for himself and Mary; the other for *him*, the *creature* he'd planted in Mary's belly, and the rest of the world. Jonah caressed one vial and then the other, staring almost lovingly at the clear liquids inside. After a while he replaced the rack in the safe, closed it and moved the clock back to where it had been. Then he left for Point Mugu.

《《——》》》

When he returned home in the evening he called Wendell Holmes, the paparazzi guy he'd hired to find out the location of Mary's wedding. As he'd hoped, Holmes sounded as hard-up as the last time, being particularly eager to hear Jonah's proposal of fresh business. Jonah told Holmes he'd pay him five thousand dollars to follow Mary around one day and slip something into her coffee when the opportunity presented itself.

"Wohhh," Holmes cut across him. "Now hold up, buddy. I am *not* dosing anybody for you."

"Relax. It's nothing dangerous. You have my word on that."

"Your *word*?" Holmes chuckled. "Man, I hardly *know* you."

Jonah waited a few seconds before speaking. "Ten thousand."

Holmes exhaled loudly. "You're a creepy guy, you know that?"

Jonah didn't respond. No words passed between them for a while.
"Fifteen," Holmes eventually said.
"Twelve."
"Thirteen."
"Ok," Jonah said after a pause. "Come to my place tomorrow night at eleven. I'll give you what you need."

《《——》》

The following night he showed Holmes how to operate the camera recorder on the state-of-the-art spy sunglasses he'd stolen from Point Mugu. Afterward he gave Holmes a small vial of antivirus and sent him on his way.

In the morning Jonah asked Soranor for a day off in the week ahead. Soranor looked at him silently for a few seconds, his face set and even.

"Testing is three weeks away."
"General, I've been working seven days a week for the last month."
"So has everybody else, Jonah. And they're not as well paid as you."
Jonah exhaled loudly. "Just one day, General. Please. To recharge the batteries."
Silence.
"Take Monday," Soranor eventually said.
"Thank you, General." Jonah rose and went to leave the office.
"And Jonah?"
His hand on the door, Jonah looked behind him.
"Don't get up to anything."
Jonah blinked and nodded. "Sir."
He opened the door and left.

《《——》》

The following night Holmes returned to Jonah's house. Jonah connected the sunglasses' camera to his laptop and they watched the recorded footage. It began at the terrace of a coffee shop on Sunset and a knot tightened in Jonah's gut when he saw Mary sitting a few tables ahead of Holmes. Wearing shades, Mary was by herself, reading a book.

"Nothing happens for about ten minutes," Holmes said from beside Jonah.

Gazing at Mary, Jonah gave no indication that he had heard. A little after a minute had passed on the digital clock in the top corner of the screen Holmes let out a long breath.

"There any fast forward on this thing?" he asked.

Jonah ignored him. There was a fast forward but he would not be using it. As the minutes ticked by he stared uninterruptedly at the beautiful woman reading her book, occasionally sipping her coffee or turning a page. Eventually, a little after nine minutes, Mary put her book down and rose from her chair. She went past Holmes in the direction of the shop. Holmes turned and watched her disappear around the shop counter and then he stood up.

"I'm taking out my cell at this point," Holmes announced beside Jonah.

A few seconds later Holmes began talking in the footage as though he were engaging in a phone conversation. On the screen Holmes began moving toward Mary's table, looking around as he did so. There was only one other person on the terrace, a young man who was gazing at his laptop, his fingers pecking rapidly at the keyboard. When Holmes arrived at Mary's table, happily talking away on the phone to no one, he stood with his back to the young man. Holmes gave a sideways glance into the shop and then quickly switched his gaze downward to the half-drunk cup of coffee on the table. The vial of antivirus appeared in his field of vision and its contents were quickly poured into the cup. The vial disappeared from view and Holmes' line of sight lifted to the interior of the coffee shop again.

He turned and began walking back to his table still chatting to himself. As he arrived at the table he ended the "call" and went silent. He sat down. The camera gazed at an empty table.

"How long before she comes back?" Jonah asked, his eyes fixed on the screen.

"Couple a' minutes."

Jonah pressed a key on his keypad and held it down. The footage began fast forwarding.

Holmes groaned. "Man, you had that all *along*?"

Jonah kept the fast-forward going until Mary re-appeared and then he resumed normal playback. She sat down and picked up her book. A few seconds later she lifted the coffee cup to her mouth and drank what remained in it.

"And there she goes," Holmes said.

A gentle relief coursing through him, Jonah hardly heard him.

As Mary went to place the cup back on the table her hand paused in mid-air and her mouth began to work. Her face wrinkled slightly.

"Nope, she's not liking it," Holmes remarked.

Jonah ignored him. Eventually Mary placed the cup on the table. Mary vanished from the screen and there was the sound of shuffling as the camera view moved. The movement stopped abruptly as the sunglasses came to rest on the table in front of Holmes, the camera now focusing on a movie billboard at the side of a hotel. Then the screen went black.

"And that's a wrap," Holmes said. He looked sideways at Jonah. "Happy?"

Still staring at the dark screen, Jonah began nodding. "Yeah."

"Can I have my money?"

Jonah rose and left the living room. Holmes watched him go into the kitchen and open an overhead press. Jonah took out a large, thick envelope and returned to the living room. He held the envelope toward Holmes.

"Count it if you like."

"It was all there the last time," Holmes said as he took it. "I'll give you the benefit of the doubt." He placed the envelope in a small gym bag he'd brought and zipped it closed.

"By the way, if I hear that anything bad has happened to her because of your little potion I'm going to be looking for a *lot* more money."

"Don't worry. She'll be fine."

"Then what the Christ *was* it? It's been buggin' me all day!"

Something you'll be wishing you had yourself in a couple of weeks' time, Jonah thought.

"Sorry. Can't tell you."

Sighing in exasperation, Holmes shook his head. He picked up the gym bag and stood. "Well, I wish I could say it's been a pleasure but it's all been just a bit too weird."

"Goodbye," Jonah said.

"See ya."

Holmes went to the door and left.

Jonah went to the grandfather clock and moved it to one side. He opened the safe and took out the vial of antivirus there. It was half-empty. He went back to his laptop and rewound the footage until he came to the point where Mary was about to drink her cup of coffee containing the antivirus—it would only protect her, not the child growing inside her. With Mary poised to lift the cup to her mouth, Jonah pressed pause. He removed the cork from the vial in his hand. He touched the tip of the vial against Mary's cup on the screen before him.

"Cheers" he said, and played the footage.

At the moment Mary's cup reached her mouth Jonah lifted the vial to his and drank.

‹‹‹——›››

The following Monday Jonah slept in, waking a little after nine feeling completely refreshed. After showering and having some breakfast he rang Nemvicius's people and informed them that he would be enjoying a day off driving around Los Angeles. Then he opened the safe. Before retiring the previous night he'd poured the large vial of Retribution into four smaller vials—one for each major airport, and one for L.A. itself. He took these from the safe and closed it. He put the vials into one of his jacket pockets. He took a baseball cap from a clothes peg by the front door and put it on. He left the house, putting on a pair of sunglasses as he stepped off the porch. It was a beautiful day. He got into his car and headed for the PCH.

«‹‹—›»»

Deciding to work from the bottom up, he headed for Long Beach first. The airport was extremely busy. Being careful not to look upward he entered the first men's room he came across. He went into a stall and locked the door. He took out one of the vials and poured its contents on the ground. Then he left and returned to his car.

An hour later he entered the Tom Bradley terminal at LAX. Feeling a bit peckish after emptying a vial in the men's room he decided to get some food. He went into a quiet restaurant where there were only two tables occupied and sat down. He placed his order and while he was waiting for his food a family came in and sat at the other end of the restaurant. The parents were tough-looking, with hard mouths and tattoos. Their children—a girl and a boy—were similarly defiant in appearance, the girl being grossly overweight and the boy sporting an ugly Mohawk.

The boy was badly behaved, shouting intermittently and going for occasional gallops around the restaurant. As Jonah was leaving money on the table to pay his bill the boy went on one of his runs. Putting away his wallet Jonah saw that the boy had added a new dimension to his dash: the boy was stopping at random tables now and pounding them twice in rapid succession with his fists before taking off again. When the boy came in Jonah's direction the two made eye contact and seconds later the boy's fists BAM-BAM-ed on Jonah's table. Jonah watched the boy continue past him toward the back of the restaurant before facing forward again. Seeing that no one was looking in his direction (the boy's parents seemed oblivious to the racket their son was making, stuffing down huge desserts with their daughter), Jonah took one of the full vials from his pocket and poured a tiny amount from it onto his table.

When the boy went past him on the way back to his family Jonah put his hand on the table, just behind the fluid.

"Hey, kid."

The boy turned and faced him, an obstreperous, what-do-you-want expression on his features.

"Do that again."

"What?" the boy asked crankily.

"Bang on the table again."

The boy walked quickly to Jonah's table and brought his fists down twice on it, a challenging, I-dare-you-to-do-anything look on his face. Jonah flicked the fluid before his hand. It spattered against the boy's face, some of it going into his eyes.

"Ahhhh!" the boy yelped, his hands flying to his eyes. He turned and began walking in the direction of his family. Jonah watched him as he made his way along, bumping against tables occasionally. As he neared his parents Jonah rose and headed for the exit.

"Dad, that guy flicked water into my eye!" Jonah heard the boy whine before he melted into the crowd on the thoroughfare outside.

«« —»»»

He took the 405 north to Burbank, and after emptying the third vial at Bob Hope International, sat in his car and pondered where to open the last one. L.A.'s one. Still undecided after twenty minutes he drove to the Hollywood freeway and joined it heading south. When the sign appeared for Universal City he faintly contemplated taking the exit but then it was behind him so he kept on going until he reached the Vine Street exit which he took. He parked on Hollywood Boulevard and began sauntering casually westward on the thoroughfare. When he came to the intersection with North Cherokee Avenue he turned south onto the smaller street. He walked about twenty meters or so, the only person he encountered being a derelict black man sitting against a wall on his haunches. After walking a little bit beyond the man Jonah stopped and took the last vial from his pocket. He had just removed the cork from the vial when he heard rushed footsteps approaching him from behind. Before he had time to do anything the homeless man appeared beside him.

"That's *mine!*" the man nearly shrieked and snatched the vial from Jonah's hand. A gout of fluid flew from the vial as the man whipped it toward him. "How *dare* you take my property!" The man lifted the half-empty vial to his mouth and downed what remained in it. He pointed the empty vial at Jonah, prodding it at him threateningly. "You *watch* it" the man said. "*Watch* it."

Jonah held the man's mad, weary stare for a few seconds before turning and heading back toward Hollywood Boulevard.

"This is *my* property!" the man shouted behind him.

When Jonah reached the Roosevelt Hotel he went inside and ordered a burger in the bar. Sitting by the window he watched the world go by as he waited for his food. The late-afternoon traffic was thickening. On the sidewalk a woman squatted over a star on the Walk of Fame, smiling up at a man holding a camera. A few seconds later, she stood and went to the man. Jonah studied them as they looked at the camera, their mouths moving soundlessly. There they were, chattering and grinning away, a wretched photo at the center of their universe, both of them oblivious of the man beyond the glass only a few feet away—the man who had spent the day erasing the rest of their lives.

"Here you go, Sir," a waitress said, depositing Jonah's burger before him.

"Thank you."

Jonah lifted the burger to his mouth and began eating it. He'd taken a few bites before a familiar sight appeared on the sidewalk. The homeless man who'd drunk the vial of Retribution about half an hour earlier was standing outside, his hands beneath his neck wrapping his thick coat tightly to him even though the temperature was at least in the low eighties. His lips were pursed and he was looking about defensively as though fearing an attack from somewhere. His eyes fell on a rubbish bin nearby and he went to it. He rummaged about in it for a few seconds and when he left it he was holding a half-eaten chicken drumstick. He brandished it threateningly at passers-by. Even through the thick glass Jonah could hear him shouting:

"This is *my* property! *Mine!*"

The man took a bite out of the drumstick and after shouting, "Watch it!" at a couple passing by him, he began walking quickly away from Jonah. Jonah watched him go. The irony of it was interesting. In a few days' time, when the man would be eating much more questionable items than discarded drumsticks, the public would still pay him little attention, just another crazy homeless guy doing crazy things—the perfect carrier.

«««—»»»

The sun was declining as he pulled onto an overlook on Mulholland Drive. He gazed at the vista before him, his eyes taking in the basin below. From the San Jacintos in the east, he slowly scanned westward. His gaze lingered for a few seconds on the tall buildings of downtown, their spires rising abruptly above the mostly flat expanse, almost like a smattering of mushrooms rising from a cowpat in a field of low grass. He moved on again, tracking the blocks of offices on Wilshire Boulevard. Continuing toward the ocean he shifted his gaze further afield, taking in the smog-obscured cranes of Long Beach, rising against a dull-red evening sky. He moved along the Palos Verdes Hills to LAX and finally to the towers of the power station at El Segundo. As he studied the water beyond, he listened. Engines revved, horns beeped, sirens screamed. The sounds of just another normal evening. What would the basin sound like in a few weeks' time?

He scanned some of the prime residences on the hills below him, his gaze resting on one particularly impressive house, its huge white mass partially obscured by trees. He wondered was it owned by someone in the movie business. A director maybe. Looking for new material perhaps. Well, in a few days' time the greatest reality TV show in the history of civilization would be taking place before their eyes. Yeah, they'd get some incredible footage alright. Before they started eating their cameras. Or trying to have sex with them.

Jonah's eyes moved to the right, in the general direction of where Mary and Bach were living. He knew the address but there was no way he was getting any closer to the house. He was taking a risk even being as close as he was. Were they at home right now? No, he supposed. They were probably filming. In his mind's eye Jonah saw Bach in a studio in his director's chair, immersed in his work, completely oblivious to the horrific end that awaited him. Jonah's heart began to race with the delight of it all. Soon Bach would be gone, as would the stranger he'd planted in Mary, Soranor, and all the other little aches and pains in Jonah's life. Jonah's mother would perish, if she was still alive—an added bonus. The world was being cleansed, or rather, *his* world. He would be left all alone in it with his beautiful Mary, together at last, in peace.

He went to the trunk of his car and opened it. Inside was a cooler which contained a bottle of chilled 1907 Heidsieck champagne, the most expensive in the world. After being lost at sea for eighty years following a shipwreck, two hundred bottles of the vintage champagne had been recovered by divers in nineteen-ninety seven. The bottle Jonah removed from the cooler had cost him two hundred and eighty thousand dollars. With the world about to end, the ridiculous purchase had become justifiable. Soon enough money would have no value.

He uncorked the bottle and took a glass from the cooler. He poured some of the champagne into the glass and put the bottle back in the cooler. He returned to the edge of the overlook and gazed out at the city once more, contemplating, the champagne bubbling in the glass before him.

Retribution. It was a harsh, vicious name for his creation, unacceptably so. Something more sophisticated was warranted, more…graceful. It came to him a few minutes later as a car pulled in behind him.

Unity.

Yes, perfect. His beautiful killer was bringing his beautiful love to him. *Unifying* them. With the sound of footsteps drawing closer Jonah looked sideways to see a man and a woman arrive beside him. He smiled at them and held his glass high in their direction.

"To Unity!" he proclaimed.

He faced the basin again and drank.

PART II

LOVE
EXPRESSED

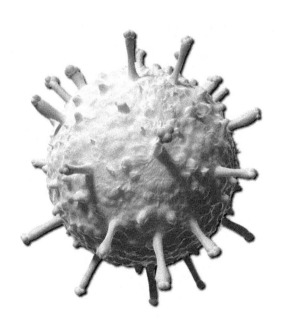

CHAPTER FIVE

lmost a week after Jonah emptied his vials in Los Angeles, accounts of a strange, horrific illness began to appear in small columns of newspapers of major cities throughout the nation. With human testing of his virophage less than two weeks away, Soranor told Jonah and his team not to get distracted by what the media were undoubtedly sensationalizing and to stay focused. The CDC would take care of it, assuming there was anything to take care of. A week later Jonah and his team were summoned to Soranor's office.

"We've been suspended until this 'mouther' thing has been dealt with," Soranor said to the group assembled before his desk. "The CDC can't make head or tail of the goddamn thing. All they've been able to establish is that it's a virus of some sort. All of you have been seconded to Atlanta effective immediately. Your plane leaves from Santa Monica airport at nine tonight. So go home and pack some things." He let out a long breath. "We'll pick up where we left off when this thing is dead." He paused. "That's it. You're all excused."

One by one the scientists left the office, Jonah last. A second after he closed the door behind him he heard a loud "FUCK!" in sync with what sounded like a fist colliding with a filing cabinet. A faint, unpleasant smile lifted the corners of Jonah's mouth and he walked away.

«‹‹—››»

The stretch of the PCH between his house and Point Mugu had grown much quieter during the previous week and on his way back to Malibu Jonah decided to count the number of cars that came toward him. By the time he pulled off of the PCH on to the smaller road leading to his house he'd only counted fifteen. After packing his case he cooked some food. He watched TV as he ate. He flicked through the news channels. At least half of the stations were focusing on the

Mouther virus as his masterpiece had been dubbed. *Philistines*, Jonah thought as he cut the pork on his plate. Whilst still mostly concentrated in the U.S., the virus had turned up in every continent now. After watching a clip of a woman with blood coming from her ears, mouth and nose convulsing in a hospital bed in Sao Paolo, Jonah switched to a station showing some grainy footage of a bearded man, naked from the waist down, attempting to insert his semi-erect penis into a gasoline pump nozzle in Durban. Jonah changed channels again and was presented with a scene from a park in Downtown L.A. in which a teenage girl was running her tongue along the armrest of a park bench.

Jonah turned off the TV and put his knife and fork on his plate. He lifted his half-eaten dinner and glass of water and went down to the basement. He opened the door of what had been his lab and went inside. The only furniture in the room was a little bit ahead of him, a small table and chair. Jonah scanned the room, what greeted his eyes filling him with serenity and bliss.

The walls were Mary's. Every inch of their space was covered with images and photos of her, some taken by Jonah himself over the years, some taken from newspapers and magazines, some downloaded from the internet. Many were blown up to large proportions. Jonah went to the table. It faced the biggest blow-up of all, a giant photo of Mary from her Oscar-nomination night.

"All going according to plan, my love," Jonah said to a beaming Mary. He placed his plate and glass on the table. "We'll be together soon."

He sat down and began eating again.

《《—》》

After finishing his meal Jonah still had some time to kill before his Naval escort came to bring him to the airport so he walked into the center of Malibu. Some shops were open but very few had anyone in them. The sidewalks were practically deserted and the roads were quiet. Jonah went into the only coffee shop he found open and ordered a cappuccino. There was a TV on the wall and it was tuned to a news channel. The screen was split, with the left-hand side showing three people sitting on a couch discussing the dreadful disease that was increasing its presence in practically every half-modern country on the planet. The right-hand side of the screen showed shocking footage of sufferers in the neurotrophic and latter respiratory stages of the illness.

Jonah turned his attention to the woman behind the counter. She was looking worriedly at the screen. She began shaking her head slowly.

"God, it's like something outta' the Bible."

"Sure is," Jonah said.

"They'd better find a cure for it, and fast."

Jonah drank some more of his cappuccino.

«««—»»»

Twenty minutes later he sat down on the beach. He looked left and right. For as far as he could see in either direction there wasn't a single other soul on the golden expanse. He gazed out at the water, savoring the silence which was punctuated only by the rhythmic crash of the waves. This is perfection, he thought. And the only thing that could have made it even more perfect was having Mary beside him. A burst of expectation lit in his gut and he told himself to be patient, it would happen eventually.

He looked to his left and ran his eyes along the L.A. beachfront from north to south. As he moved from Santa Monica to Venice, to Manhattan and Redondo he wondered if there were anyone on them. Had his little killer quietened them too? He figured it probably had. A feeling of power suddenly rising in his veins, he remained gazing at the coastline until movement caught the corner of his eye and he turned his head sharply to the left. Approaching him slowly was a man, an empty expression on his face. As he drew closer Jonah noticed the slight sheen of sweat on the man's face and his red-with-fever cheeks. The man sneezed and a second later caught his foot and tumbled awkwardly to the ground. Jonah watched him slowly get to his hands and knees and then stare motionlessly at what had felled him, a glass bottle. The man gazed at it for a while before eventually picking it up and continuing his study of the vessel. He lifted the bottle to his mouth and began to lick it. A few seconds later, he began biting it. From where he sat Jonah could hear the bright, abrupt sound of the man's teeth coming into contact with the glass:

THEK......THEK............THEK

Eventually the man took the bottle out of his mouth and rose to his feet, sneezing twice as he did so. As the man resumed his progress in Jonah's direction Jonah thought that he looked somehow familiar. He studied the man's face, thinking that he'd definitely seen him before. He was a TV celebrity of some sort—a show presenter. Watching the man sit down a few feet from him it came to Jonah. The guy had interviewed Mary only a few months previously. Except it hadn't been much of an interview from Jonah's recollection, the guy appearing more interested in Mary's chest and legs than on the words coming from her mouth. Jonah remembered that he'd wanted to kill him at the time. As he watched the man pick a clump of seaweed up and begin eating it Jonah felt pleased that this account was being settled.

"Seen Mary Leydon recently?" Jonah asked him.

Chewing contentedly, a strip of seaweed hanging from his mouth, the man looked at him, his eyes simple and cow-like.

"You know, the actress you eye-fucked on your show a couple of months back?" Jonah continued. "*My* Mary?"

The man stopped chewing. He sneezed explosively, shreds of seaweed flying from his mouth. Jonah closed his eyes instinctively as it flew toward him, some of the mess striking his face. Jonah found himself chuckling. "Gee, thanks," he said, wiping his cheek. He looked back at his companion in time to see the man place a fresh helping of seaweed in his mouth. As he observed the man munching his bizarre snack, staring out at the ocean as he did so, a little scene flitted through Jonah's mind: the guy conducting one of his ridiculous, brash interviews, flashing his impeccable dental work (now under pressure) between the interviewee and the audience, and then suddenly stopping mid-ridiculous sentence, his face losing all expression, his figure freezing motionless for a few seconds before coming to life a few seconds later with his hand slowly going underneath his desk and emerging holding a clump of seaweed, then the seaweed going into his mouth and the chewing starting...

The man stopped chewing and swallowed. Still staring out at the ocean he blinked a few times before looking down at the sand by his leg. After a few seconds of observation he dipped his hand beneath the sand's surface and scooped up a healthy dollop of it. He put his hand to his mouth and packed the sand into it, some of it falling onto his polo shirt as he did so. Then he began chewing again.

"Sir, move away from that man!"

Jonah looked behind him to see two men in white protective suits approaching. In the parking lot behind them there was now a white van, a similarly-attired figure behind the wheel. Jonah rose to his feet and did as instructed.

"Sir, did this man sneeze or cough in your direction?" one of the men asked Jonah when they arrived between him and the sand-eater, who was still happily grinding away as he stared out at the water, seemingly oblivious to the two new arrivals.

"No," Jonah lied.

The suited man remained looking at Jonah for a few seconds as though perhaps not fully convinced of the veracity of the response he'd received. Eventually he turned and began helping his companion who was coaxing the sand-eater to his feet. The man did their bidding without objection and they led him in the direction of the van, a hand on each upper-arm. Jonah noticed that the man was carrying the bottle he'd found. Halfway to the van he dropped it on the sand. He bent to pick it up, his handlers stopping to let him do so. When he had retrieved the bottle they continued on their way. As they neared the van the man began biting the bottle again. Jonah could just about hear the faint sound:

THEK............THEK

《《《—》》》

An hour and a half later Jonah was approaching the airport on Pico Boulevard. The thoroughfare was quiet. He looked along the sidewalks. There wasn't much life on them. He wondered what it would be like when he returned.

CHAPTER SIX

I n Atlanta Jonah discovered that pretending to work hard was much harder than actual hard work. Being one of the leading virology authorities on-site, many of his new colleagues looked to and deferred to him in their research on Mouther. (God! That name! Three weeks of exposure to the horrendous sobriquet for his little beauty still hadn't inured him to its awfulness.)

On the eve of his ninth day at the CDC Jonah sat in his room flicking through TV channels. He yawned, tired after another day of bluffing and waffle. The news stations were focusing on little else besides Mouther. One clip showed a man kneeling at the foot of the Eiffel tower, licking its base. Another showed a young boy biting a gate outside a house in England. Yet another showed a two-man-and-one-woman sex-sandwich in Rome, the flushed faces of the trio empty as their bodies pumped and pistoned. A clip from a Moscow hospital showed a sheet-covered body being wheeled from a ward, the camera zooming in on the form's concealed head which had red stains on the area of the sheet covering the mouth, nose, eyes and ears. In some countries the masses were becoming concerned with their leaders' lack of action on this appalling illness that was killing indiscriminately. In New Delhi almost two hundred people had been shot in an attempted storming of the Sansad Bhavan. A close-up on the clip that Jonah was watching showed snatches of blood on the parliament building's walls. In Istanbul the army had had to be drafted in to assist police in quelling a massive riot in Taksim Square which had resulted in over a hundred deaths and the destruction of almost every surrounding building.

All over the world there were increasing incidences of people taking the law into their own hands, the U.S. included. Bands of vigilantes were patrolling streets in smaller, more isolated towns, shooting those infected with the virus (or "Mouthers" as they had been dubbed), sometimes burning the bodies, sometimes leaving them where they had fallen. One brief clip showed a street in Harrison, Arkansas where two pickup trucks were cruising along slowly, the backs of the vehicles carrying men and women armed with guns and shotguns. An aerial clip from Norfolk, Nebraska showed a pickup stopping in the middle of a street by a bus stop. At the side of the bus stop a woman was standing with her pants around her ankles. She appeared to be trying to insert a short pole of some sort into her vagina. The people in the pickup opened fire on her and she flew backward, collapsing to the ground a bloody-rag doll, the shop window behind her accompanying her to the grave. Another station showed a street in Logan, Utah where a furious gun battle was taking place between a group of vigilantes and police.

Jonah continued flicking through the channels, a swell of pride surging through him at the escalating carnage. The world was blundering around, being punched slowly to death by an invisible enemy it knew nothing about. As a child Jonah had enjoyed the Predator movies. What a legend the predator was—this invisible, hostile warrior from God-knew-where who pulped his bewildered, terrified opponents to death's door before finally revealing his horrifying form to deliver the killer blow…*that* was Jonah's baby. His sweet, devastating Unity. His own personal predator. By the time science parted the curtains on Unity's true form (if it succeeded in doing so at all) the world would be almost dead.

Jonah switched off the TV. He stared at the empty screen, his mind picturing the Unity virion on the black surface before him, an austere ball of doom with short protein spikes of death jutting from its surface. It belonged on the roof of the Sistine Chapel! Instead of *The Creation of Adam* should be *The Creation of Unity*. Jonah would take God's place and the virus would take Adam's, Jonah's outstretched finger touching a protein spike, giving life to his offspring.

He wondered if his parents would be proud of him if they were alive. They should be, he thought. After all, what had they done with their lives, a family-abandoning flower-seller and an alcoholic house-painter? Nothing. Bringing him, Jonah, into the world had been their only achievement. And what an achievement it was. They had raised a god. *The* god, actually. The purifier who would cleanse the earth and leave it to the two purest people on its surface—him and Mary. They would be its second Adam and Eve.

He undressed and climbed into bed. He folded his arms behind his head and gazed up at the darkened ceiling. He had yet to acclimate to the perfect silence of his room. As a precaution in the event of things turning bad on the streets of Atlanta, the CDC higher-ups had accommodated the virus researchers four levels underground. Accustomed to being lullabied to sleep by the dull drone of the distant PCH in Malibu, Jonah rarely nodded off in his new surroundings in less than an hour. He found the stillness a bit strange.

He was glad of the security though. In the week since his arrival the authorities had beefed things up considerably. The facility's perimeter was now patrolled twenty-four hours a day by heavily armed marines with Humvees at every gate. Also reassuring was the high-speed underground train (which very few people knew about) that in the event of the facility being compromised would take personnel fifteen miles northwest to Dobbins Air Reserve base where a plane was on twenty-four hour stand-by.

His phone began ringing. Not bothering to turn on the light over his bed he reached out and picked it up from the bedside locker. He looked at the screen and saw that the number was withheld. He rarely answered such calls but on this occasion after staring at the screen for a few more seconds, he tapped the answer icon and put the phone to his ear. Being so far underground the cell reception wasn't great but now there was even more crackle and hiss, as though the call was coming from somewhere remote.

"Hello," Jonah said.

The caller didn't respond immediately.

"I told you not to give it to anyone else, Doctor," Zarrani eventually said.

Jonah felt no fear at the sound of the voice.

"I didn't," he said.

"Liar."

"I'm not lying."

"Treacherous scum. Who did you give it to?"

"I told you," Jonah said calmly. "No one."

"Stop *lying*, you dog!"

"I'm telling you the truth," Jonah said. He paused before adding "I released it myself."

"What?"

"You heard me."

A period of hissing silence ensued, punctuated by the odd crackle.

"Why?" Zarrani eventually asked.

"To be with her," Jonah said softly.

"What?"

"To be with her."

Silence.

"You are a madman, Gates. You test the virus on your grandparents and now you do *this*."

"You could say I'm doing your dirty work for you."

"You should not have done it!" Zarrani barked. "Retribution was *ours* to unleash! At a time of *our* choosing!"

"Its name is Unity."

"What?"

"The virus. My virus. Its name is Unity, not Retribution."

"I will hunt you down, Doctor," Zarrani said quietly. "And when I find you, I will kill you."

The line went dead.

Jonah kept the phone to his ear for a few more seconds before putting it back down on the locker. He closed his eyes. With Zarrani's threat leaving his head as quickly as it had been made Jonah saw himself on the beach at Malibu, Mary by his side. In his silent room Jonah could practically hear the soft crashing of the waves, a blissful sound free to reign now, the din of the world behind him and Mary silenced forever. The last thing Jonah saw in his vision before sleep took him was Mary, free from the shackles of her old life, smiling beautifully at him.

«‹‹—››»

Three days later a fleet of police cars arrived outside the facility. The officer in charge informed the facility's head of security that over a thousand people were marching toward them at that moment from Downtown Atlanta. The police and marines readied themselves and waited.

About an hour and a half later the procession appeared around a bend in the approach road. From the canteen on the fifth floor Jonah watched the human column as it came, and came, and came. By the time it was ordered to stop about fifty feet from the police cars Jonah could see that its entirety was not completely visible, the mass of bodies tailing around the bend in the road. Beside him, Lars Fielsen, Jonah's second assistant from Point Mugu, snorted.

"A thousand people my ass," he said. "Gotta be three thousand out there at least."

The mood of the throng was not one of panic or aggression but rather of upset and worry. A few people had loudspeakers and they took turns airing their concerns. When would the cure be ready? Nobody was surviving this disease. Hospitals, morgues and graveyards were filling up. Looting was becoming a problem. There wasn't a gun to be had in the city, every gun shop was out of stock, some of them having been robbed, their staff murdered. There were rumors of people shooting family members just for sneezing.

Rob Czencke, the head of the research team, defused the situation as best he could. After assuring the assembly that his team were working as fast as they could to come up with a cure, he pleaded with the crowd to return to their homes. The chief speaker, a red-haired man with a beard said ok, they'd go, but they'd be back in three days' time. The throng turned and went back the way it had come.

«‹‹—››»

The following day the team watched the news in silence as they witnessed the destruction wrought by a number of explosions in Downtown Atlanta. The next day they watched as the violence and looting escalated. The authorities were losing control of the city. Some of the police force had given up the cause, others were even joining in the melee. In the evening additional marines arrived at the facility along with some more Humvees.

《《《—》》》

In the morning the police arrived and informed the security team that well over five thousand people were on their way. This was not a peaceful group of concerned citizens like the last time they said, it was a mob, angry as hell.

Looking out of a window on the third floor Jonah heard the multitude before he saw it.

"This doesn't sound good," his assistant Henry Kintaro said beside him.

When the mass became visible Jonah saw that it was moving at a much quicker pace than the previous demonstration. Jonah could see police officers in the huge swarm. There was rage in their strides. Many of them were armed, carrying pistols and shotguns. There were some baseball bats. A lot of hands carried beer cans. The procession stopped at the barricades that the marines had set up and such was the noise that Jonah could not hear what the people with the loudspeakers were saying. Those at the front of the column were particularly animated, pointing their fingers furiously at the police, soldiers and security guards before them.

Five minutes later with no sign of the mob cooling down, the forces facing it put on gas masks. Many in the throng did likewise. The order to disperse came once, twice, three times. Then the tear gas canisters were released. The head of the column fell back a little. As the gas billowed it obscured the front of the procession.

Suddenly a woman wearing a mask emerged from the cloud, a gun pointed at the forces beyond the barricade. She fired. A marine's head snapped backward and he fell to the ground. The guns of the men on either side of him came to life and the woman did a grotesque little puppet-dance before collapsing on the road. A few more gun-wielding individuals appeared from the gas, their weapons firing. Gunfire erupted from the entire security force.

"God," Henry said in a desolate tone as the battle blazed.

"I can't watch this," another observing scientist said, and walked away from the window. A few seconds later Henry turned and went away, another colleague following him. Alone now, Jonah watched the carnage until the gunfire stopped.

«‹‹—›››

As the crowd had withdrawn the red-haired bearded speaker from the previous day announced with emotion in his tone that they'd be back, better-armed and better-equipped. They knew that the cure was in the facility, being stockpiled for the elites. The next time they came they were going inside and nothing would stop them.

«‹‹—›››

The death toll was eighty five civilians killed and ten security personnel. As the bodies were being removed the research team was summoned to the facility conference room. When they were all seated around the table there the President appeared on the screen before them. Jonah had last seen the President on TV a little over a month before, a few days before he'd released the virus in L.A. The President had been in Paris then, at some big conference. The face before Jonah now looked like it had aged twenty years in the interim.

After informing the gathering that he was greatly saddened by the catastrophe that had taken place outside their door, the worried visage informed them that they were the great hope of the nation in the face of this terrible disease that had at this stage manifested itself in every state, except Alaska. They were possibly even the great hope of the world. The Europeans were at a loss as to what they were dealing with and had nothing to offer. Nor did the Chinese or the Russians, at least that they were willing to share. The private sector was stumped. The President asked them to please redouble their efforts. The clock was ticking and time was not on their side. He urged them to be strong in the face of what had happened on the streets outside and to focus only on their work. They were not to worry about their personal safety, they would be protected at all costs. Additional security was en route to them as he was speaking. After wishing them Godspeed, the feed ended. After a few seconds of silence Rob Czencke exhaled loudly at the head of the table. He rose to his feet.

"Ok, everybody," he said. "You heard the man. Let's pick the tempo up."

He turned and left the room, the others filing after him.

That night before going to bed Jonah went for a walk around the facility grounds. Even more marines had arrived, he saw. As he passed the main gate two marines were talking and one of them looked up at the roof of the main building, pointing. Looking up in that direction himself Jonah saw the rotor blades of two attack helicopters.

«««——»»»

"Jesus," Lars Fielsen said as he, Jonah and a few more colleagues gazed out the window. The approach road below them was black with people right up to the barricades before the facility's defenders. About two hundred meters back from the front of the human column in the middle of the crowd was a heavily-armored bus. About a hundred meters back from this was a huge semi, similarly armored and towing a trailer. Hovering over the facility gates were the deadly-looking helicopters that Jonah had first seen on the roof two days previously.

The crowd were ordered to disperse and instead of doing so parted to the sides before the bus. The bus began to move forward. The driver was ordered to stop and when the bus simply gained in speed every gun behind the barricades opened up on it. The high-caliber bullets from the chain-guns of the helicopters proved particularly potent, blasting chunks of the bus's armor clean off. One of the bus's tires blew and it careened to one side, ploughing through a slew of bodies. It overturned, continuing its progress toward the gate on its side. The defenders maintained their torrent of fire upon the approaching vehicle whose roof was disintegrating rapidly under the hail of ordnance. Slowing as it reached the barricades, the bus still maintained enough momentum to burst through and slide onward a few meters before coming to a halt a few feet from an abandoned Humvee.

The crowd parted back to the semi and it began to move forward. Once again the order to stop went out and was ignored. The defenders opened fire. The semi's cab began to come apart but the truck kept coming. Rockets flew from the helicopters and the cab burst into flames. The driver's door opened and Jonah could just about make out the features of the red-haired man who'd addressed them on the loudspeaker on the previous two encounters. His form was burning and bloodied. Jonah turned his attention back to the truck in time to see it smash into the overturned bus which it bulldozed forward through the front gate and fence. It crashed through the security station inside the gate, obliterating it. It kept going until the bus came to a stop a few feet from the main building. The crowd rushed forward toward the newly-created breach in the defenses. The marines and a few Humvees moved quickly into the void and opened fire, the helicopters overhead doing likewise. A female scientist let out a cry of shock as bodies began to fly apart.

The door behind them crashed open and Jonah turned to see four marines with urgent looks on their faces.

"Ok, people, we got to get to the train now," one of them said. "Just as a precaution."

The team followed the marines down the eleven flights of stairs to the platform where the train was waiting, its engine idling. They got on board and waited. In the seat in front of him Jonah could hear Rob Czencke crying softly.

Three-quarters of an hour later they still hadn't moved. Movement caught the corner of Jonah's eye and he looked out the window to see a senior-looking marine approaching the train, two gun-toting soldiers behind him. A few seconds later the senior stood at the top of the carriage, his underlings behind him.

"Ladies and gentlemen, I've been instructed to inform you that you are to return to your workstations immediately—"

"What?" Rob asked in the high-pitched tone of a broken man. "*Return to our workstations*? After what we've just seen?"

"This message is from the President, sir," the senior said calmly.

Rob made no retort.

The senior raised his eyes to the rest of the carriage. "The situation outside is over. The crowd has dispersed and everything is under control. You are to return to your duties as of now. The ground floor of the building and upwards are off-limits until further notice."

"I wonder why?" Jonah heard Rob mumble dully.

The senior's eyes flicked down to Rob then up again.

"Guards will be posted at all lifts and stairwells. Under no circumstances are you to attempt to gain access to the aforementioned levels until restrictions are lifted." He paused. "That's all."

The senior turned and left, his escort following.

Jonah heard Rob begin sobbing again. No one in the carriage spoke or moved for a while. Eventually Henry Kintaro got to his feet and walked toward the door. One by one the others rose and followed, Rob last.

《《—》》

The restrictions on accessing the ground floor and above were lifted late in the evening. At dusk Jonah went for a walk around the grounds. Chinook helicopters had lifted the semi and the bus from where they'd crashed and had placed them lengthways across the breach in the facility wall as a barrier while teams worked quickly at repairing the damage. The bodies had been taken away but the clean-up effort hadn't been meticulous. Here and there Jonah saw blood splashes on the grass and flowers. In a shrub he spotted a finger with a wedding ring at its base. Resting against the edge of a cement path between it and the grass he came across part of a nose.

Jonah went back inside and went up to the canteen. He poured himself a cup of coffee and went to the window. Beyond the semi-and-bus barricade the cleaning of an abattoir was taking place. The walls of buildings along the approach road and their sidewalks were crimson. Some individuals in protective suits were hosing the bloody surfaces while others brushed the red water on the ground toward drains. Sipping his coffee, Jonah watched them work.

《《《—》》》

In the morning Rob failed to show up in the lab. After knocking at his door repeatedly and receiving no answer the marines broke into his room. They found him dead in his bed, an empty sleeping-pill bottle on his bedside locker.

Jonah was made team leader. A little while after the announcement he went to the toilet. Washing his hands afterward he smiled at his reflection in the mirror. It had to be the greatest irony of all time. The man who was destroying the world was now in charge of its rescue.

《《《—》》》

In the evening Henry made the discovery that the virus was distantly related to the Point Mugu virophage. When he articulated his finding to Jonah, his voice quivering with shock and excitement, Jonah had to restrain himself from giving the man a sarcastic round of applause. He'd never had much time for his lead assistant's limited ability but he'd expected Kintaro to have hit this particular nail on the head at least a week earlier.

Together they informed the Pentagon. The decision was made to immediately move the team and its research to Point Mugu. The virophage had been developed there and its equipment would be more suitable for working on its deadly relative than that at Atlanta.

A little over an hour later they were in a plane headed west. As they climbed higher in the sky Jonah looked behind him at Atlanta receding in the distance. Fires burned at random points in the city. A particularly large inferno blazed close to the tall buildings at its center, a thick black plume of smoke rising from the orange ball. Jonah faced forward again and closed his eyes. He fell asleep and didn't wake until they touched down in California.

《《《—》》》

Jonah wasn't happy to receive the news that Soranor was once more his superior. Upon the suspension of the virophage project nearly four weeks earlier Soranor and some other high-ranking Point Mugu personnel had been seconded to the Pentagon. With the announcement of Kintaro's discovery the General had been reassigned to Point Mugu with the task of supervising the newly-transferred research team.

Upon leaving the plane the team were taken to a conference room where Soranor was waiting for them.

"I'll get straight to the point, ladies and gentlemen," Soranor said. "The situation globally is disastrous. The numbers of dead and infected is already in the tens of millions. Each day the number of those becoming infected rises at an exponential rate. Panic, rioting and looting have stricken all of our major cities and cities around the world. As you know, this virus was engineered from a virophage that we'd been developing here up to only a few weeks ago. This virophage was being developed for the betterment of humanity, for the fight against illnesses that have plagued the human race since time immemorial. But unfortunately some as yet unknown entity or entities have gotten hold of our research and have turned it against us. Our fight against this threat is two-pronged, comprised of our intelligence forces and *you*. All over the world, in tandem with local agencies our intel people are turning up the heat on informants and suspects. No stone is being left unturned." Soranor paused. "Which brings me to you, ladies and gentlemen. The Pentagon has run the numbers on this thing. Current estimates are that if Mouther is allowed to progress unchecked, the major urban centers of the world will be de-populated in a matter of months." He paused to let this sink in. Around the table a few eyes blinked in concern. Others dropped theirs from Soranor's. "So the urgency of the situation cannot be over-stated. The lab is next door, it's ready and waiting for you. Your quarters are on the next level down—the rooms are small but they're comfortable. Not that you'll be seeing much of them anyway." Soranor looked around at Jonah, Henry Kintaro and Lars Fielsen. "I know that some of you have residences in the area but I cannot permit you to return to them. The Southern California area has the highest concentration of dead and infected in the nation. Mouthers are roaming up and down the PCH as we speak. Across the highway outside our door they're in the fields eating crops, plastic, earth and anything else they can find. Right now this base is secure and I want to keep it that way. Any questions?"

There were none.

"Ok. Go to your rooms and freshen up. Then get to work."

«««—»»»

The days ticked by. As the situation on the outside deteriorated, the morale of the research team mirrored its downward spiral accordingly. Jonah could see the despair simmering beneath the exhausted visages of people trying desperately to be strong. The infinitesimal progress being made on decoding the virus was coming mainly from Henry with the result that the team began to see him as the de facto leader of the project. Jonah would watch the other scientists coming to Henry, seeking his advice and approval, and at times he would almost burst out laughing at the words that came from Henry's mouth. What a case of the blind leading the blind!

As the days turned into weeks the catastrophe began to hit home in the base as news of deceased loved ones reached them. Every now and then Jonah would see a member of the research team or military personnel sobbing in a corridor or at a table. One afternoon Jonah walked past

Soranor's office and saw the General inside, his elbows on his desk and his head in his hands. A cadet informed Jonah later in the evening that the General's daughter had died from the virus and his wife was now infected.

One evening Jonah left the lab building and went for a walk around the grounds. The cool unprocessed air felt so good in his lungs that for a moment it was hard to believe that the world was dying. But dying it was. Soon enough there would be virtually no one left to enjoy this glorious air. He and Mary would have it all to themselves and they would stroll around together, savoring its sweetness.

He looked in the direction of the PCH, recalling Soranor's words a fortnight earlier. The General had said that infected people were wandering the fields beyond the highway, eating the crops. In his mind's eye Jonah pictured the expanse of the Oxnard plain, the occasional Mouther dumbly wandering its long crop rows, every now and then stopping to bite a sprinkler or to scoop some earth into its mouth.

He turned and began heading back toward the lab. As he walked his thoughts returned to Mary. Things were really bad in L.A. With the authorities having more or less lost control the city was now a sprawling free-for-all of looting, rape, and murder. Jonah supposed that the Hollywood Hills was as good a place as any to be in the midst of the chaos. The area was elevated and not densely populated. Mary had money, her house was gated and she had a security system. Though he was concerned, Jonah felt no fear for her. Mary was tough, a survivor. He knew she would hold out until he came for her.

He had a feeling Bach was dead. And his child. This feeling becoming surer with each step he took, Jonah practically had a spring in his step by the time he arrived at the door of the lab. Upon stepping inside he was presented with the sight of a soldier squatting on his haunches a few meters down the corridor. The soldier had an elbow on one knee, his hand supporting his forehead. As Jonah passed by him the soldier remained in this position, not looking up.

"You guys getting any closer?"

Jonah stopped and looked behind him. The soldier was looking up at him, his eyes shiny. Jonah could see he'd been crying. He was young, but the soldier's breast ribbons informed Jonah that he was clearly of fairly high rank. Looking at the soldier's nameplate he saw Col Matt Gormos engraved there. Before Jonah could reply Gormos spoke again.

"I lost my son today," he said, looking at his hands. "Joshua. He was six. He's got a twin brother, Luke. He and his mother are ok so far, but…"

Gormos looked up at Jonah again.

"Hurry, Doctor. Please."

Jonah nodded at him. Then he turned and continued on his way.

Dolonse Rath Meenah
Rathmines Branch
Fón / Tel: 4973539

«««—»»»

They'd given samples of the virophage to every major health authority and drug company in the world along with detailed files on its connection to the Mouther virus. At first the newly-enlightened authorities had almost collapsed into panic at the sheer scale of work that lay ahead of them in familiarizing themselves with not only something so complex and cutting-edge as the virophage itself, but also its relationship to its deadly offshoot. Jonah had almost felt sorry for them but had had to grudgingly admire them as they'd set about the ridiculous task.

He, Henry and Lars had conference calls with the chief health centers of the world on a daily basis. The whole thing was so hopeless it was almost comical. Not only were the odds stacked so pitifully against the frazzled faces on the conference screen in terms of workload, those frazzled faces were also not very bright at all. They weren't even up to Henry's level. To Jonah it was like snails trying to scale a mountain. A very high mountain. And Henry was the fastest snail. The others couldn't even be called snails actually. They were more like stones.

As time wore on new faces occasionally appeared on the screen to replace old ones as stress and suicide took their toll. One day Jonah and his colleagues called the Indian health center and the hard face of a senior army officer filled the screen. He informed them that unfortunately the center had been compromised by the virus and in accordance with a recent government decree on infection containment all center personnel had been liquidated. India's fight against the virus was no longer a scientific one but a military one. After wishing them the best in their efforts the officer killed the feed.

"I wonder how long before it goes that way here," Lars said.

«««—»»»

One afternoon in the fourth week of their return to Point Mugu, Jonah, Lars and Henry had just returned to the lab after a conference call with some British scientists when Jonah heard raised voices in the hallway outside followed by the sound of automatic gunfire. Everyone in the lab looked to the door, their faces full of shock. There was the sound of rapid footsteps drawing closer and then there was some more gunfire.

The door burst open and Colonel Gormos appeared in the room. He was carrying an M16. Just before the door swung shut behind Gormos, Jonah spotted the horizontal leg of a soldier in the hallway. There was a blood splash on the nearby wall. The door closed and Jonah turned his attention back to the gun-wielding colonel. No one in the lab moved a muscle as a slightly-out-of-breath Gormos slowly looked about the lab.

"A few days ago my son Joshua died with the virus," he said. "Just a few minutes ago there I got a call from my wife. She and our second son Luke woke up sick this morning. She was crying. She told me that she didn't want our little boy to go through what his—" Gormos cleared his throat and when he resumed speaking his voice shook a little, "—what his brother had endured. She didn't want to see Luke become this—" he paused again, "—strange, empty thing like his brother. She didn't want to see him shaking in his deathbed not even knowing he'd ever been alive. So she asked for my permission. To spare him from such a fate. It'd be quick, she said. She had a gun and he was asleep. He wouldn't feel a—" Gormos faltered, his chin trembling. "I said ok," he managed, smiling desolately. "I guess I couldn't bear to imagine my boy trying to eat his own toys." Gormos swallowed, not far from breaking down completely. "She hung up," he said, forcing some strength into his words. "She called back a few minutes later and...and she told me it was done. We talked for a little while longer and then she said she had to go. She wanted to be with the boys. I told her I loved her and ...that was it."

A cold look replaced the sorrow in Gormos' eyes.

"People like you designed this fucking plague. And now you can't stop it. You could say that I'm doing you a favor here. At least this way you won't end up trying to have sex with your own goddamn test tubes."

Gormos opened fire. Henry and Sheila Sonnerland, the nearest people to him, went flying backward. Jonah dropped behind his workbench to a crawling position as the hail of destruction above him continued. The sound of the gunfire in combination with shattering glass and disintegrating electrical equipment was deafening.

And then it stopped. Over the sounds of sobbing and groans of pain, Jonah heard footsteps. "Yeah, he's dead," a voice said a few seconds later.

"Ok people, it's over," a voice said in a louder tone. "It's safe to come out now."

Jonah slowly got to his feet. At the top of the room there now stood two gun-wielding soldiers. At their feet were the bloodied bodies of Henry, Sheila Sonnerland and Matt Gormos.

«««—»»»

Outside of Henry and Sheila who had almost been cut in half by the slew of bullets that had struck them, two more people died in the assault—Max Vorshech and Christian Kramer. Gloria Naiman was in critical condition in sickbay having taken two shots to the chest. Pete Billings was there too but his condition was far less serious, having been shot in the arm and shoulder.

The remainder of the team were summoned to a conference room where they were informed by Soranor that what had happened had indeed been a disaster but they simply could not allow themselves to be beaten down by it. They had to dig deep and slog onward without delay.

Afterward they returned to the lab to find it in pristine condition, every single item of damaged equipment replaced. Not a trace of the carnage remained.

In the evening Jonah and Lars had a conference call with some Australian scientists. When they asked where Henry was Jonah told them what had happened. A look of deflation appeared on the faces before him. It was the same with every research team that Jonah and Lars spoke with in the ensuing days. They were like sheep without a shepherd now.

Chapter Seven

All over the world an exodus began. With the number of dead well past the one billion mark and with no sign of any solution coming from their governments or scientific communities, people began abandoning urban areas and heading for more sparsely-populated territories. In the U.S. the movement began as a small disorderly departure before quickly morphing into a massive, feral scramble. Raised voices and beeping horns became screams and gunshots. Bumper-to-bumper traffic from major cities sometimes stretched for tens of miles, lasting days on end. The last vestiges of authority brave enough to attempt to police these exoduses were either shot or dragged from their motorcycles and beaten to unconsciousness or death by the more amoral elements keen to preserve the lawlessness. Families had their car trunks emptied at gunpoint, their food and supplies for the journey and their hoped-for new lives taken from them. If they were lucky, they were left alive.

Rape was common. At gunpoint male family members looked away as their female counterparts, both young and old, were disgraced on the asphalt or in their vehicles. Sometimes the males were killed and the women would weep as they were violated on the ground beside the dead bodies of their loved ones. Those in the cars ahead and behind would close their eyes or look away, trembling and praying that they would not be next.

The armed forces were drafted in to restore some semblance of order and the situation ameliorated somewhat, but not by much. Many of the soldiers were disillusioned, seeing their task as pointless. Believing the world to be in its death-throes they figured they might as well enjoy the end-times and joined in the free-for-all.

During the emptying out of L.A. Jonah would gaze at the far-off PCH on his evening walks around the base. He could just about make out the line of cars on it, bumper to bumper for as far as he could see of the highway in either direction. He would hear screams, shouts, gunshots, music, religious nuts preaching through loudspeakers, the odd explosion. Sometimes he came out to look at it at night if he was unable to sleep. There would be fires burning at irregular intervals along the line as people strove to stay warm. On his fifth day of observing the depressing sight Jonah heard on the news that the tailback in the distance was one of the worst in the nation, stretching at times from the outskirts of Oxnard all the way back to Santa Monica, a distance of almost fifty miles.

Not everybody in the exoduses was well. People in the early respiratory stage of the virus joined in the flights from the cities, hoping against hope that the tickle in their throat was just the flu. They would sit in the epic traffic jams, holding back the coughs and sneezes, their fear rising as their symptoms worsened until they were discovered by those around them. They would be shot in their vehicles or fleeing from them.

Jonah had seen an aerial news clip showing a young couple in a traffic jam leaving Chicago. The banner beneath the footage had read:

MOUTHER EXECUTIONS
ON RISE IN CITY EXODUSES

The couple were looking frantically behind and ahead of them as shotgun-wielding men approached their car from the front and rear. The woman was particularly distraught, crying with terror. The men approaching from the rear reached the car first and pointed their weapons at the occupants. The mouth of the young man in the driver's seat moved quickly as he attempted to negotiate with the owner of the gun facing him, his eyes pleading. And then his head disappeared behind a red mess on the windshield. A second later the face of his passenger vanished behind a similar veil of crimson.

Another memorable news clip had shown a traffic jam on a mountain road outside Phoenix. Three armed men were walking along the road in the direction of a heavy-set mustachioed man who was hastily emerging from a car some way ahead of them. The man ran as fast as he could from them, his flushed, sick face full of panic. The men fired at him, one of them staggering drunkenly as he did so. As he was going around a bend in the road the moustache's hand flew to the side of his neck. Seeing an armed man and woman approaching him from the opposite direction he ran toward the guardrail, beyond which lay a steep, craggy slope ending in a gulley. He then scrambled over the guardrail and held onto it as his feet made their way down along the treacherous slope. A second after he removed his left hand from the guardrail his right hand flew apart after being struck by a bullet and the man pitched backward sickeningly, crashing down the slope and out of view, his resting place obscured by some trees. His executioners collected at where he had gone over the guardrail and began shooting into the gulley.

Some of those targeted for elimination went down fighting. Armed themselves, sometimes heavily, they struck back against their would-be executioners, wounding and killing some of them before eventually being corralled and dispatched by superior numbers. In a gripping news clip Jonah had watched a father and son team put up a hell of a battle outside New York. With a death-squad of five approaching them from the rear the duo burst from their car in perfect synchronicity and began firing. Two members of the squad dropped to the ground. Another, a policewoman, stumbled behind a pickup truck clutching her stomach. The two remaining unscathed members of the group scrambled for cover behind a station wagon. A furious gun battle ensued during which most of the windows of the vehicles between the two opposing forces were shot out, covering the occupants cowering inside them with glass. Some of these occupants, unable or unwilling to endure the storm taking place over their heads, slid out onto the road and crawled away. The father and son killed one of the duo facing them leaving only one member of the squad to fight on. He wasn't on his own for long before three reinforcements arrived on the scene. Very quickly after their arrival the son fell to the ground. The father fired a few more shots before running around the front of his car where the unmoving form of his son lay. He knelt beside his son and put his gun down. The camera remained focused on them before eventually changing angle a little to show the four executioners arriving on the scene. The executioners watched the father and son, guns at the ready. Eventually the father looked around at them. In the grainy footage Jonah could just about make out the grief in the man's face. The father turned back to his son again. The death-squad let him mourn his son for a little while longer before eventually opening fire on him.

Jonah thought about Mary. He had no doubt that she was sensible enough not to be in one of the mad lemming-rushes from L.A. (there were catastrophic, violent traffic jams on every major exit from the city, not just on the PCH). He wondered how she was taking the fact that she had been spared while all around her were probably dead by now. She was undoubtedly curious. And he couldn't wait to sate that curiosity. He couldn't wait to tell her that he had cleansed the world for her and that now she could walk its purified soil like a queen, her king by her side.

Jonah looked at his watch. It was almost seven and he had a conference call with a French research team on the hour. He turned and headed back toward the lab building. He was sick to death of these pointless check-ins with his colleagues around the world. Although he knew the charade would be coming to an end soon. With every day that passed he could see the light of hope growing dimmer in their dull-witted, terrified eyes. Even tough old buzzard Soranor was crumbling. The loss of his family to the virus coupled with the scientific community's haplessness against it were grinding the good General's resolve away. These days when Jonah passed Soranor's office and the General was inside, Soranor was invariably sitting at his desk, staring at the wall ahead of him, tumbler of whiskey in hand. Jonah figured his departure from the base wasn't far off. It was only a matter of time before the soldiers under Soranor's command stopped taking his orders or that the General simply dissolved his authority and let everyone do what they liked. Being the proud old dog that he was, Jonah reckoned that Soranor would embark upon the latter course of action before the first occurred. Either way Jonah knew he would be taking his trip to the Hollywood Hills pretty soon.

He reached the lab and went inside. On his way to the conference room he passed Soranor's office and glanced inside just in time to see the General with his whiskey tumbler at his lips. An image flashed in Jonah's mind's eye in which Soranor, his face red and eyes thread-veined with the virus, was biting the glass, all interest in the fluid it contained gone completely. The General's office receding behind him, Jonah hoped that fate might perhaps conspire to let him see such a sight in reality.

CHAPTER EIGHT

After the great exoduses came relocation, a process that proved even more dreadful than its predecessor. In rural areas all over the nation, millions of people pitched their tents (literally) and parked their caravans and RVs by streams, rivers, lakes, bays and the open ocean. As numbers rose and personal space diminished, fear of Mouther grew quickly, culminating in a whirlwind of violence and slaughter. The rivers of the country ran red with blood from the bodies in them.

In many areas, locals not willing to allow relocation forced the refugees onward at gunpoint. Frequently, armed groups of refugees refused to comply and held their ground. Gun battles ensued. In one such battle in northwest Kansas which Jonah watched footage of on TV, over a hundred people died.

Of course the virus tagged along in the exoduses. The death-squads had not eliminated all of the infected. Mouther tore through the settlements like wildfire before catching in local populaces. Three months after its release in Los Angeles the virus was now killing in every crack and corner of the nation. In the abandoned metropolises of the country mouthers wandered the empty streets, the sounds of their teeth clamping on fire hydrants and railings echoing faintly while in the rural areas the infected shambled along in fields and on riverbanks, occasionally pausing to eat stones and twigs.

《《《——》》》

With the first reported outbreak of the virus having come from Los Angeles, the U.S. was seen as the mothership of the disease. Millions of her citizens felt the need to evacuate the country. Hundreds of thousands of people living close to Canada and Mexico decided to cross the border into these neighbors. Anywhere was better than the Armageddon of their homeland. With enormous Mouther problems of their own, Canada and Mexico were keen not to let their situations degenerate further. They moved fast to quell the migrations onto their soil issuing warnings to the panicked floods approaching them. When these went unheeded they resorted to drastic action and the border areas became graveyards. Such was the volume of people seeking to cross into Mexico from California that the Mexican army had to draft in their country's more questionable elements to beef up their boundary forces. Drug cartel killers stood side by side with army soldiers as they opened fire on the occasional attempted storming of border checkpoints. Drug and immigrant tunnels, now filled with traffic going in the opposite direction, were dynamited, often with people making their way through them.

With Alaska continuing to report that it had yet to encounter the virus on its territory, the state began to be seen as a promised land. From docks, harbors, ports and airstrips all along the west coast of the U.S. vessels and aircraft of all shapes and sizes embarked upon the desperate quest north. The first ship to enter Alaskan waters was the *Nereus*, a cruise liner that had come all the way from San Diego. Over ten thousand souls had packed themselves on board in California. Two thousand had died on the way, having been executed upon showing symptoms of Mouther. Their bodies had been flung into the sea. A slew of officers had fallen victim to the virus including the captain and his second in command. Their place had been taken by a passenger, retired Navy Admiral Myles Hocke. As the *Nereus* made its way toward the Alaskan mainland Hocke was contacted by General Eugene Ives at Joint Base Elmendorf-Richardson in Anchorage. Ives informed Hocke that the First Republic of Alaska was closed to foreigners as were its airspace and waters. Hocke was to leave Alaskan waters immediately. Hocke told Ives that no one on board was symptomatic, that the ship was Mouther-free. Ives told Hocke that he understood, but Alaskan territories were off-limits. He repeated his demand that Hocke exit the country's waters. Hocke killed the communication with Elmendorf and maintained his progress. A few minutes later two Raptor fighter jets appeared and strafed the water on either side of the *Nereus* with cannon fire. Hocke ploughed on. On their second pass the Raptors' cannons demolished the *Nereus*'s glass viewing area and top deck. Still Hocke maintained radio silence and kept his course. On their third pass the Raptors unleashed their missiles, two of which struck the liner below the waterline. Hocke sent out a mayday signal which was ignored. Hundreds of people lined the piers and docks of Anchorage, watching the sinking of the *Nereus* through binoculars in silence. It was gone in a little over an hour and then the really grim work began. Only a few die-hards remained watching from the piers as half a dozen Raptors set about the grisly task of eliminating every single survivor. All over Anchorage people covered their ears in an effort to block out the sound of cannon-fire and missiles exploding as they struck lifeboats. When the Raptors were done, a few marine-laden coastguard boats headed out to the scene of the slaughter. Any signs of life they encountered were quickly eradicated by the marines' automatic rifles.

The fate of the *Nereus* caused many in the north-bound flight to hoped-for sanctuary to change course. Some went to try their luck in the Hawaiian Islands, others decided to chance British Columbia. A hardy few ploughed onward, convinced that the Alaskans would not have the heart for another *Nereus* and would soften. But it was not to be. The First Republic of Alaska remained steadfast in its position. All newcomers were instructed to alter their course and head elsewhere. A few ultra-rich refuge-seekers, their planes and vessels laden with gold and jewels, of-fered their entire cargoes in exchange for sanctuary but were denied. Most of the rejected turned and left for alternative destinations but a few, brave with desperation, maintained their course for Alaskan soil. There was no point in going to Hawaii or British Columbia, the virus was al-ready in both places. Not to the same extent that it was in others, but it was only a matter of time before both areas were engulfed like every-where else. Seeing themselves as having no other choice, these frantic souls drove their vessels onward in the hope that the Alaskans would blink first. General Ives didn't, and the *Nereus* was repeated over and over again. But the First Republic's defenses were not completely im-pregnable. Smaller vessels, even some planes, made it through the security net, particularly ones that steered well clear of Anchorage. Russians, Japanese and Chinese landed undetected on Alaska's remote west coast. When Anchorage found out about the budding colonies in its outer regions it took immediate action. The death squads carried out their grim task and brought the virus back to the capital with them. And so at the end of its fourth month of freedom in the lab of the world, Mouther set about conquering the city that had held out against it for so long.

«««—»»»

In Europe, Iceland was clever enough not to continuously proclaim its virus-free status as Alaska had done. In the second month of Mouther with the global crisis beginning to accelerate, the Icelandic government began discreetly purchasing as much weaponry as it could on the black market. With fear and paranoia having firmly taken root in the human psyche all over the world at this stage, Iceland ended up paying multipliers of normal pricing. Normal social services were completely suspended with all monies being directed toward national defense. With no standing army of its own outside of ten Italian jet fighters and their pilots, Iceland had to buy in mercenaries, paying them fortunes to keep their mouths shut as to why they were going to the north Atlantic island.

The mercenaries stayed quiet but the story of Iceland's good fortune inevitably leaked out as the government had expected. By then the island's defenses were in half-decent shape at least. Most of the able-bodied men and women had received basic weapons training from the mercenaries and manned posts alongside their highly-paid protectors. First to chance their arm were the Italian government. Their country boiling with Mouther, Italian politicians desperately attempted to use their pilots and planes on the island as leverage, asking the Icelanders to grant them and some of their (wealthier) citizenry sanctuary. The Italian pilots told the Icelanders to put the phone down—as far as they were concerned they were Icelandic now and the jets were the property of the Icelandic government.

And then came the exodus. From all over northern Europe and Scandinavia planes and boats headed for Iceland. Though the Icelanders had thought the Alaskans silly with their repeated utterances on being Mouther-clean, they thought their American counterparts completely correct in their reaction to those insisting on being given sanctuary in their territory. Like the citizens of the (now Mouther-infested) First Republic of Alaska, the Icelanders looked at the planes and boats approaching from the east and south and saw death coming. The refuge-seekers were told to desist and turn away, which most of them did. Some didn't, however, and the guns of the hitherto most peaceful nation on earth opened up on them. A few travelers attempted landings in the more remote parts of the island but with there being heavily-armed garrisons scattered throughout the landmass they were quickly stopped in their tracks.

As law and order began to dissolve all over Europe so too did the military forces of its countries. More interested in staying alive than in following orders, rogue units from every country in northern Europe abandoned the extermination of their infected citizenry and headed north in aircraft carriers, warships, submarines, jets and bombers. Along the way they fought with each other and weaker forces were consigned to the bottom of the ocean. A large Norwegian contingent was first to arrive in Icelandic waters and gave the nation a chance to surrender. The defenders said they would rather die fighting than succumb to Mouther, and opened fire on the invaders. The battle was a stalemate until the arrival of a British force who allied with the Norwegians and quickly subdued the defenses of Iceland's southern coast.

The small towns in the north, west and east of the island were outraged at the taking of Reykjavik by the outsiders and told the city's new overlords that if they did not leave Iceland immediately the rest of the country would unite, march south and fling them into the sea. The British and Norwegians decided to keep things diplomatic. After apologizing for the damage done to Reykjavik and for the loss of life involved in its capture, they invited the impassioned leaders of the island's outer regions to look at things clinically. Why upset the current situation, they asked. The conquerors were a strong force to have in Reykjavik. They would be a huge boost to Iceland's southern defenses. None of them had Mouther and they were willing to be examined to the last man by local doctors to prove this.

The leaders of the outer regions grudgingly consented to this line of reasoning. Three days after the agreement they received an urgent message from Reykjavik. Come quickly they were told, a huge French and German contingent was less than two days away. The southern force would not be able to handle this one on its own. The regional towns and villages emptied out and raced south across the ashy wastes of the Sprengisandur. They didn't make it in time. Fifty miles from Reykjavik they could hear the bombardment of the city. By the time they approached its outskirts the guns had mostly gone silent. The intended rescuers gazed disheartened at the wreckage of their capital, practically in ruins after its second sacking. They launched their assault nonetheless, fighting gallantly but unsuccessfully.

The new invaders, now the undisputed masters of the territory, sent out a message to the world. Iceland was open for business. For the right price you could buy sanctuary in a Mouther-free modern, western country.

Laden with gold, jewels, drugs, whores, catamites and other vices, the mega yachts and private jets started their engines. Sheiks, oligarchs, business moguls, gangsters, dictators and despots headed north in their droves. Unfortunately they also brought Mouther along with their wealth and temptations. Soon Reykjavik was full of the grunting of sex in its freezing ruins and the clacking of teeth biting down on its scorched rubble.

⟪⟪—⟫⟫

And so it went all around the world. The first urge of those with the will and the means to re- locate was always to go somewhere where there were at least *some* other human beings. And the same thing that had happened in Alaska and Iceland happened in these places too. In

South America, the high altitude Andean town of La Rinconada became the place to go. When word began to leak around Peru and its neighboring countries that the mining shantytown of over thirty thousand people was completely Mouther-free they flocked to its location on a permanently frozen glacier which was only accessible by treacherous, winding mountain roads. In a matter of weeks the population ballooned six-fold before the inevitable arrival of Mouther resulted in its total decimation.

The same bubble and burst pattern predictably occurred in numerous other isolated habitations: in the Cape York peninsula in Australia, in Matuo County in China, and even in Tristan da Cunha, seventeen hundred miles from the southern coast of South Africa.

In desperation people eventually began fleeing to completely uninhabited places, mostly islands. They packed their boats and yachts with as much provisions as their vessels would safely bear and they set sail. Many crafts were wrecked on perilous coasts, their passengers lucky if they made it ashore. Here they lingered, helpless without their supplies. Most of them died in a matter of days. The ones that made it to dry land with their provisions set themselves up as best they could, and began waiting.

CHAPTER NINE

Soranor gazed absently at the last remaining bit of whiskey in his glass. He tilted the glass slowly this way and that, watching the amber liquid quiver as he did so. He snorted softly as some of the youthful scrapes he'd gotten himself into as a result of his fondness for the stuff flashed through his head. Bar fights, shouting matches with his parents, tiffs with teachers, cops and girlfriends…this bewitching fluid before him had fueled it all.

He'd practically given the stuff up during his early years in the Air Force but his old enthusiasm for it had returned somewhat after meeting Corine. A flash of desolation lit in his stomach. That tall, blonde girl had been as willful as she'd been beautiful and he'd opened up the whiskey tap a little to help him cope with her ways. The tap had opened up more and more over the years culminating in him hitting her one night after an Officer's ball. She'd told him there and then that if he didn't quit drinking she'd leave him. So he'd quit, completely this time. It had been hard, having no anesthetic to help him endure her fiery ways. He'd never been a man for drugs but had been contemplating hash when Corine had fallen pregnant. Being pregnant had mercifully had a mildly calming effect on his wife. During Natalie's birth there had been some complications and afterward Corine had been told that she couldn't have any more children. Corine had been crushed for a while and Soranor had been sure that the old, passionate Corine would return. Thankfully she hadn't. Gradually her mood had lifted and the pleasant pregnancy-Corine had re-emerged.

Natalie had grown up to be a wonderful child and an even more remarkable young woman. She'd been popular in school, great at sports and had excelled academically (and very importantly had never developed her father's fondness for hard liquor). She'd only been in her first job with an accountancy firm in Newport Beach for a few months when Mouther had broken out. When she'd called her mother to tell her she'd become infected Corine had immediately gone to her despite Soranor's pleas to the contrary. He didn't want to lose the two of them. The old, headstrong Corine had returned and she'd shouted down the phone at him (he was on base at the time, unable to leave) that there was no way she was going to let their baby die alone. Natalie had died three days later. A day after contracting the virus Corine had called Soranor to say goodbye. She was standing on a bridge, ready to jump. After they'd bid each other farewell she'd hung up. Soranor had cried then, the first time he'd done so since his teenage years.

Soranor knocked back the last of his whiskey. He placed his glass down and gazed at the photo of Natalie's graduation on the wall opposite him. In it a beaming Natalie stood between her proud father and mother. Soranor blinked as an awful image flashed in his brain—Natalie running her tongue slowly along the open lid of her jewelry box, her eyes, once full of life, promise, and education now dull and cow-like, emptied by Mouther. A wave of anger rose within him. He picked up the glass and flung it at the wall where it shattered below the photo.

"FUCK!" he roared.

The blood pounded in his ears. He sat back in his chair. He exhaled loudly. The rage he was feeling dissipated and was replaced by resignation. So this was it. The end. The end of civilization as they knew it. Seven billion dead and rising. Science had nothing. At least nothing that would be of any use for a couple of years. There were immunes of course, as anticipated. People whose systems simply killed the virus when it entered their systems. Some of them had given themselves to research teams around the world to be analyzed. Soranor's own team had taken blood and tissue samples from a few that had come out from Los Angeles (one of them had been Eddie Nemvicius, the detective who'd been in charge of Jonah's stalking case with Mary Leydon—what were the odds!) but again the issue was time. However their bodies had dispatched the virus would one day be decoded, but again that day would be years down the line. And they only had months, if even that.

And they still hadn't the first clue as to who had released the fucking thing! Not to mind who'd cooked it up for them. The FBI and

NSA had come down ferociously hard on informants and suspects, all to no avail. The CIA and the Brits had water-boarded half of Pakistan and nothing had come out of it.

Yep, it was all falling apart. The President was sending his "be strong" messages from Cheyenne Mountain now, the emergency operations center beneath the White House having been compromised by Mouther-infected anarchists two weeks previous. But what the Christ was there to be strong *for*? Ninety percent of the population were either dead or dying, the remainder would be heading that way soon. Hell, it wasn't even a *country* anymore. Its once great cities were empty, ransacked skeletons, some of them burning, populated only by scavengers, corpses, and those who didn't know whether they were dead or alive. Its rural areas were nationwide wild wests where nothing was sacred. Law, order, morality…all gone. It was every man for himself now.

Show's over, Alec. Time to give up.

He felt lazily disappointed at his defeatism. He'd never given up on anything in his life. He'd always been tenacious, had always been ambitious. A knot tightened in his stomach. Ah, *ambition*. That was why he was sitting here now wasn't it, his family and most of the world dead? Indeed it was. He'd seen an opportunity with the virophage to put a rocket under his career and he'd grabbed it with both hands. He'd seen the virophage's killing power firsthand and had gone ahead with its modification anyway. But his intentions had been *noble*, too! He'd have gotten the top seat at the Pentagon but the world would have gotten a cure for the flu virus! Fuck, but that sounded like a fair bargain to him.

But that dream had been whipped away and replaced with a novelesque tragedy. An intended boon for humanity had become its grim reaper. A potential cure for an illness that had plagued civilization for eons had been twisted into a monstrosity that made you want to eat your own clothes and have sex with your toaster before killing you horribly. Soranor opened one of the drawers at the side of his desk and took out the bottle of whiskey he'd replaced there only a few minutes earlier. He placed the bottle on his desk, and still holding it, studied it. It occurred to him that he should never have stopped drinking. If he hadn't he probably wouldn't have gotten into the Air Force. He wouldn't have met Corine. The virophage project might never have been embarked upon. The fucking thing might just have been left doing its thing on the launch-pads at Vandenbergh. Seven billion people wouldn't be dead. Beautiful Natalie Soranor would never have been born. She wouldn't have had to-

Soranor uncorked the bottle and put it to his mouth. He took a deep swig of the whiskey and put the bottle back down on the desk where it landed with a bang. He gazed at it blankly. Movement caught the corner of his eye and he looked up. He watched two scientists walk past his window and disappear in the direction of the labs. He supposed it was time to give the research team the option of leaving. Let them go to their loved ones, if they were still alive in the anarchy beyond the base gates. They had no way of even knowing if they were still alive, of course. The internet and cell phone networks were no longer functioning. The only channel left on TV was the emergency government channel which was only used to transmit the President's occasional addresses.

The military personnel under his command still did his bidding but Soranor could see the apathetic glaze in the eyes of his subordinates becoming more pronounced with each passing day. They were good people, all of them—professional, dedicated—but they knew the game was in its final innings.

The phone on his desk rang and he picked it up.

"Yes."

"Sir, I have base gate on line one."

Soranor pressed the number on his phone.

"Yes?"

"Sir, I've got Detective Nemvicius here at the gate. He says he's got something extremely important to show you."

"Send him in."

"He says you've got to come out to him, Sir. And follow him."

‹‹‹—›››

Late that afternoon Jonah was about to take a break and go for a walk around the base when Lieutenant Napier, one of Soranor's chief assistants, entered the lab.

"Ladies and gentlemen," Napier said. "I have a message from General Soranor-."

"Ah, where *is* General Soranor by the way?" Elizabeth Frei, one of the scientists, asked. "I've been wanting to speak with him all day."

"I'm not at liberty to say," Napier answered. "The message is as follows—as of this moment you are free to leave the base should you choose to do so. For those who wish to remain, there are enough provisions on site to cater for the facility at full occupancy for approximately six months. Military personnel have also been permitted to leave and I've been informed that most intend to do so." He paused. "That's all. Good luck, everybody."

Napier turned and left the lab. Nobody said anything for a while. Lars Fielsen broke the silence with a loud exhalation.

"So that's it, then," he said.

Jonah's heart was pounding in his chest.

Finally.

《《—》》

After packing his things Jonah hitched a ride to Malibu with three soldiers who were heading into L.A. to check on their families. The twenty-mile journey to Malibu took nearly two hours. There were a lot of abandoned cars on the route and they had to weave their way around them. A few times they had to get out and move cars out of their way. Not all of the cars were empty. Some held bodies in various stages of decomposition. There were bodies on the road too which they took turns in moving if they were blocking their progress.

They ran into the occasional mouther. One of them, an elderly woman, was licking the top of an open car door as they approached. She lifted her head to watch them as they passed by, her eyes tracking them absently. Eventually she lost interest in them and returned to her licking. They came across a male Mouther having sex with a dead girl against the side of a car, the girl's upper body splayed haphazardly on the car's trunk, her head turned sideways facing them. Her eyes were open and gazed unseeing at the approaching jeep and its occupants. Her blue face and arms jerked lightly as her rider thrusted at her from behind. As the jeep passed by the man looked up from his labors to see a gun pointing at him. A glob of snot hung from one of his nostrils. The dull eyes in the red, sweaty face betrayed no fear as their owner pumped away at the dead flesh beneath him. A shot rang out and one of the Mouther's eyes disappeared, flying out of the back of his head with more of his skull's contents. The Mouther collapsed backward. As they drove slowly onward Jonah watched the Mouther's still form on the asphalt for a few seconds. Movement caught the corner of his eye and he watched the dead girl slide off of the car trunk onto the road. He faced forward again.

«««—»»»

As he walked up the short driveway to his house Jonah looked to his right. About a hundred yards or so down the road was the house of his neighbors, the Bomris. Standing by her little red sports car was Martha Bomri. She was running her mouth along something long and black that she was holding in her hand. From where he was, Jonah thought it might have been a windshield wiper. He dropped his eyes to the windshield of her sports car and saw that one of the wipers was indeed missing.

As he neared his house Jonah saw that the front door had been forced open. He went inside tentatively and saw that the cellar door ahead of him was open. He went to the kitchen as quietly as he could and opened an overhead press. He took the tranquilizer gun that he'd shot his grandparents with out from behind some soup cans and crept down into the cellar. The door to what had been his lab was open and a figure in a protective suit was sitting at the table where Jonah had eaten his meals in the three months between giving the virus to Zarrani and being seconded to Atlanta. Jonah stepped into the secret room, the tranquilizer gun pointed at the man a few feet ahead of him. He saw that there was a bottle of whiskey on the table.

"Nice décor," Soranor said, not turning around.

Jonah stopped moving. Keeping his gun trained on Soranor's back he was unable to resist a glance upward at the huge blow-up photo of Mary at the Oscars on the wall facing him.

"You should have buried them deeper, Jonah."

Jonah looked back down at Soranor just in time to see the General's thumb press the screen on the tracker device which was keyed to the bio chip in Jonah's leg. Jonah shrieked, dropping the tranquilizer gun as the unforgettable pain he'd experienced almost a year earlier in Soranor's office returned to his thigh. His hands flew to the area of his leg experiencing the horrific electrical buzz and he fell to the ground. When the agonizing crackling inside him stopped abruptly he could have cried with relief.

"I've just spent the afternoon with Detective Nemvicius," Jonah heard Soranor say. He looked up to see the General still sitting in his chair, but facing him now, the tracker in his hand. Jonah could see the drink in Soranor's eyes. "Turns out he and a few other immunes have formed a body disposal team in L.A." Soranor went on. "Yesterday they were up in the mountains looking for some fresh dumping locations and give a guess what they found?"

Panting after his ordeal, Jonah remained silent.

"Hmm?" Soranor asked. "Any idea what it could have been?"

Jonah said nothing.

"Well, it was something very interesting. Two bodies, a man and a woman, partially dug up by coyotes. Not much damage done by the coyotes interestingly enough. Guess there was something about the corpses they didn't like." Soranor paused, holding Jonah's eye in silence. "Anyway, there's not much left of the bodies but the killer's amateur enough to have left the man's driver's license on him. Ronald Englen is the man's name. The woman has no ID on her but Nemvicius presumes it's his wife. The surname sounds familiar. And then it comes to him. Crazy Jonah Gates' grandparents. Now, one of the guys on Nemvicius' body disposal team happens to be a doctor. Nemvicius is curious and asks the doctor to carry out an autopsy on the bodies, as a favor. So they take the bodies away and spend a few hours examining them. And here's where it gets *really* interesting. In their stomachs, well…where their stomachs *used* to be, the doctor finds some peculiar objects. In Ronald's stomach he finds pieces of a credit card, a few keys, and bits of a trouser belt. In the woman's case—" Soranor raised his eyebrows in a mock-questioning manner. "Olivia, isn't it?" he asked, and went on without waiting for a response. "Well, in her stomach he finds half the heel of a shoe and some jewelry. The doctor finds that the teeth of each individual are damaged, probably from biting and chewing all this stuff."

Soranor leaned forward in his chair. His eyes became dark and when he spoke again the false levity was gone from his tone.

"He makes out that the bodies have been dead for at least six months. Which means they died of Mouther *before* the outbreak." He paused. "You tested your little killer on your own grandparents, you sick *fuck*."

"AAAAAHHHHHH!!!" Jonah screamed as the unearthly pain leaped into life in his thigh again. It went on and on and on. Just when Jonah thought that his leg would burst the agony vanished. His heart pounding, Jonah whimpered shakily with relief. He was dimly aware of a musky smell in his nostrils. He saw that Soranor was standing over him. The General kicked the tranquilizer gun away.

"Huh," Soranor snorted. "So, you've pissed yourself. Good. At least now I know I have your full attention, you mass-murdering *fuck*."

An excruciating bolt of pain flashed in Jonah's gut as Soranor's boot collided squarely and at speed with his exposed abdomen. Moaning, he curled up instinctively, hardly able to breathe.

"*Who* did you give it to?" Soranor barked down at him. "Who did you sell out to, you treacherous piece of shit!"

Jonah groaned.

"Tell me, Jonah! Tell me, or we go for round three!"

"It doesn't matter," Jonah mumbled.

"What?"

"It doesn't matter," Jonah said, a little louder. He felt like throwing up.

"What? What do you mean it doesn't matter, you *prick*?"

"It doesn't matter because it wasn't them who released it. It was me."

Silence.

"You?" Soranor asked incredulously. "Why the Christ did *you* release it? They pay you *extra* for that?"

Jonah let out a long breath. "No."

Then why, for the love of God?"

"I did it for *her*."

Soranor didn't respond immediately. "Who?"

"Mary."

"For *Mary*?"

"Yeah. To set her free. So we could be together."

Again Soranor went silent for a while. "To set her free," he eventually repeated in a low voice. "From a life she was enjoying. So she could be with a SICK PUPPY who she rejected and who harassed her for years. This…selfish, pathetic delusion is the reason that my wife and daughter and seven billion other people are dead." He paused. "You crazy FUCK!!!" he bellowed and kicked Jonah savagely between the legs. Jonah's entire body jerked as a white hot ball of agony exploded in his groin. Incapable of making even the faintest noise of pain he coiled into an even tighter ball than after the previous kick and vomited weakly.

"So that hurt," Soranor remarked. "Good. I didn't think you *had* anything down there."

Jonah heard the sound of clothes creasing and when he heard Soranor's voice again it was inches from his ear, the smell of whiskey strong.

"I'm going to kill you now, Jonah. Slowly, and painfully. It'll be an undignified death, like the one you inflicted upon my daughter. And I'm going to enjoy it. I'm going to kick you, beat you and cook you until there's nothing left but a…pulverized barbecue." Soranor paused. "But first I'm going to have a drink."

Jonah listened to Soranor walk toward the table. Hearing him pour some whiskey into a glass Jonah wondered if this might be the end. The destroyer of the world was about to be ignobly dispatched from it, forced to endure the rank smells of his own bodily emissions before his departure. And all on the day of his intended visit to Mary! The poetic tragedy of it was excruciating. He looked at Soranor who was drinking his whiskey and then shifted his eyes to where his tranquilizer gun lay. In his current state he hadn't a hope of getting to it in time. Soranor would press his accursed little torture-zapper and that would be the end of that little burst of heroism.

And then he remembered. Jonah's eyes flew down to the breast pocket of his shirt. He hardly ever clipped a pen there but he'd done so this morning. Mercifully the pen was still there now. And it was one with a sharp nib. This was not a fluke of course. It was his destiny to meet Mary on this day. Fate had made him clip the pen to his shirt earlier. Actually no, not fate.

Her.

Taking the pen quickly from his shirt he looked at the photo of Mary on the wall facing him. *Thank you*, he mentally said to the smiling face there. He held the pen between his legs behind his clasped hands. To Soranor it would look like he was still nursing his injured genitals.

"Ahhh!" Soranor said in satisfaction and placed his glass down on the table. "Ok!" he said and began walking toward Jonah. Jonah clicked the nib of the pen out. With one eye shut he gazed at the approaching legs, timing their stride. When they drew close he whipped the pen out and drove it as hard as he could into the side of Soranor's calf.

Soranor roared in pain and keeled sideways, the tracker device falling from his hand. The second it hit the ground Jonah kicked it away, sending it skittering off toward the far end of the room. He looked at Soranor on the ground clasping his leg, his face a rictus of pain. Jonah grinned cruelly. He'd gotten the bastard good alright. Feeling that he might be able to stand, Jonah attempted to do so and succeeded. He limped toward where the tranquilizer gun lay, his recently-shocked leg uncertain beneath him.

"You FUCK!!!" Soranor barked behind him. "You fucking… FUCK!!!"

Jonah bent and picked up the gun. He turned and took a few steps toward the fallen General who was groaning in agony, his hand clamped around the bloody wound in his calf. Soranor looked up at Jonah who responded by lifting his gun and pointing it downward.

"Go on," Soranor said, a look of sullen resignation in his half-drunk eyes. "Put me out of my misery."

"Not yet," Jonah said, and fired.

Soranor looked down at the dart protruding from his chest and then looked up at Jonah, a look of surprise in his eyes as though he'd expected to see a bullet hole in his suit and not a tranquilizer. His eyelids fluttered briefly before closing and he fell unconscious.

《《—》》

The Bomris had moved into their house a little over a year previously. A few weeks after doing so they'd invited Jonah over for dinner. He'd accepted the invitation. After that evening the only contact that both parties had engaged in had been hand salutes from a distance or as they passed each other on the road. That suited Jonah just fine. The evening he'd spent with them had been tough. They'd been too effusive, too full-on.

As Jonah neared their property he watched Martha who he'd seen earlier with a windshield wiper in her mouth. The wiper now lay discarded on the ground beside her and she was licking the prancing-cat hood ornament of her Jaguar like it was a lollipop. She lifted her eyes to watch Jonah walk up the driveway toward her. Her licking of the hood ornament slowed a little but didn't stop. She let off a sudden sneeze and the ornament fell from her grasp to the cement. She stared dully down at it for a few seconds before bending slowly and picking it up. Jonah went past her toward the house. As he neared the open front door he heard the dull clink of Martha's teeth on the ornament.

Jonah entered the house and walked slowly along the hallway toward the kitchen. The main reason he was here was because Joe, Martha's husband, had a motorbike. With the PCH being the way it

UNITY

was, Jonah figured a motorbike would be much more practical for his trip to the Hollywood Hills than a car. With Martha being infected Jonah presumed that Joe was either infected or dead himself and wouldn't be needing it. The second reason Jonah was skulking around his neighbors' was because he'd thought of a little parting gift for the good General back in his basement.

"Joe?" Jonah called.

He received no response.

When he arrived at the half-open living room door he sniffed. There was a faint odor of something unpleasant in the air. He pushed in the living room door. By the wall to his left was a fold-away bed and on it lay Joe, the bed clothes only half-covering his discolored body. Joe's dead, cloudy eyes were open, staring at something on the ceiling. Dried blood trails emanated from his nostrils and from the sides of his mouth.

Jonah turned from the scene and continued on to the kitchen. Upon arriving there he went to a key-holder by a bank of overhead presses and took the key of Joe's Honda Shadow from it. He also took keys labelled "Surgery" and "Garage." He went out the back door and walked toward the building at the rear of the house. Nearly the size of a small bungalow, the building he was approaching was divided into Joe's veterinary surgery and a garage. He went into the surgery first and after a few minutes of searching found what he was looking for, a hypodermic needle. Then he went into the garage and climbed onto Joe's Shadow.

He cruised slowly down the driveway, stopping by Martha who now had her dress pulled up, her underwear at her knees. She was rubbing the head of the Jaguar's hood ornament against her vulva. Leaving the bike running Jonah dismounted and went to her. He inserted the hypodermic needle in her upper arm. Martha did not flinch at the sudden invasion of her person. Not desisting from her bizarre self-pleasuring she looked down at the needle as it slowly began to fill with blood. Over the idling motorbike engine Jonah could just about hear an occasional grunt of arousal from her.

The *change* of it all was incredible. It was hard to believe that the… person before him was the owner of two art galleries, one in Santa Monica and another in Beverly Hills. The confident, articulate woman that Jonah had encountered on the evening he'd been invited to dinner was gone for good now, replaced with this shameless, wordless simpleton.

Jonah withdrew the needle, put its cover back on and put it into the Shadow's satchel. He climbed back on and left Martha to her gratification. When he arrived back at his house he took the needle from the satchel and went inside. He realized he was still wearing his soiled boxers and jeans. In all the excitement he'd forgotten to change them. Doubting if Mary would be impressed with a smell of urine from her savior he headed upstairs and put on fresh clothes. Then he went down to the secret room where Soranor lay in oblivion. He squatted by the General's form and inserted the needle into Soranor's buttock.

"Here you go, General," Jonah said and injected its contents into Soranor.

When the needle was fully depressed Jonah withdrew it. He rose and went across the room to where the tracker device lay. He opened it and removed its battery. He went back to Soranor and tossed the tracker on the inert form.

"Some food for later."

He left the room and pressed a button on the remote control for the door. He gazed at the picture of Mary on the back wall of the room, growing smaller as the door began to close.

I'm coming my love.

CHAPTER TEN

HUM

Sitting on the couch, Mary remained motionless. She hadn't moved at the sound of the first explosion a few hours earlier either. To will yourself into movement meant you had to care about something. And that was the problem. She didn't care about anything. She had nothing to care *for* anymore. She looked around the room. It was losing its light, she saw. When she'd sat down and placed the glass of water on the table before her (it was still full) it had been early afternoon. It was twilight now. In the past month she'd begun engaging more and more in this empty sitting, letting the day roll by, not moving until the basic needs of hunger, thirst, or bodily evacuation stirred her into action.

She yawned. She was constantly tired these last few weeks. In the early days of the chaos she'd spent her days in a state of hyper-vigilance which had left her exhausted at the end of every day and she'd slept like a log at night. Now, with the city's coffin all but nailed shut, the raids on the house had all but stopped. Her days were long and pointless with the result that her sleep was lukewarm at best. She lifted the glass of water from the table and drank some of it. She looked sideways at the shotgun and the pistol on the sofa beside her. She'd killed the last raider over three weeks ago but she still kept a weapon close to her at all times, just in case. The guns beside her had killed fifteen people over the previous few months. She'd buried the bodies in the scrubland beyond the house.

Most of the raiders had come for money or jewelry but a few had come for her, too. One time she'd been shoveling the last few loads of dirt onto a grave (that of the tenth raider she'd shot, a knife-wielding teenage girl) when she'd looked up to see two men approaching her. Both of them had been sick, their faces shiny and bright with Mouther.

She knew what they'd wanted by the look in their eyes. One last fuck before their brains left them and they ended up doing it with God knew who or what. One of them just had time to cough up a mouthful of phlegm before she whipped the pistol from the waistband of her jeans and put two in him. She turned the gun on his companion, and showing no mercy to the terror in his eyes she fired twice more. She buried them beside the girl she'd killed earlier that morning.

Indeed she'd become quite the gunslinger over the past few months. Before Mouther she'd only ever handled a gun, a blank-fire pistol, on the movie set of *The Lower Ones*. In the movie she'd shot and killed another character, her husband. It had been well-choreographed, the actor's blood bags bursting neatly before he'd tumbled to the ground. She'd found the experience a little unsettling.

After she'd shot her first house raider the finality of what she had done combined with the smell of copper from the raider's blood had caused her to vomit and pass out for a while. She'd gotten her pistol, a Sig Sauer P238 on an afternoon in Burbank about a month and a half after the outbreak of Mouther. With crime rising and looting beginning to raise its head in parts of the city she'd decided she needed something more potent than Lowell's baseball bat to defend herself with. The first two gun stores she'd called to had been closed for days, sold out of stock and unable to come by any more. As she walked into the third store a tough-looking bearded man came toward her carrying a box full of weapons and ammunition. He looked at her as they neared each other and he gave her a little nod before walking on by.

"We're all sold out," the man behind the counter told her just as she noticed the complete bareness of the store. As she was walking back to her car feeling a little worried a pickup pulled up at the curb beside her.

"Hey."

She looked into the pickup and saw the bearded guy from the shop, his box of guns and ammo on the seat beside him. He fished a small gun from the box.

"Catch."

He tossed the gun out the passenger window to her which she caught.

"Some magazines."

He tossed a small cardboard box to her.

She studied the two items for a second or two before looking back at her unexpected benefactor.

"Thank you," she said. "How much do you want for them?"

He shook his head. "Forget it." He smiled softly, a little shyness in the expression. It had a warmth that Mary would not have anticipated seeing in such a tough visage. "You were great in *The War Beneath*," the man added.

Mary smiled. "Thanks."

The man nodded slightly and looked out his windshield.

"Guess you won't be making any more movies any time soon, huh?"

"I guess not."

Neither of them said anything for a few seconds. The man turned to her again.

"Well, you take care of yourself."

"You, too. And thanks again."

The man nodded and drove off.

After she'd learned how to use the gun she'd gone over to Franklin Canyon Park and fired a few practice shots at some cans.

The shotgun she had, a state of the art Benelli, had belonged to Tony Ricardi, her next-door neighbor. She'd gotten it the day after the dreadful raid on the Ricardis' house. She'd been in her bedroom when the gunfire had started, about to get undressed for bed. The battle had finished after about half a minute and then Madison, Tony Ricardi's wife, had begun screaming. Mary had put her fingers to her ears to block out the terrible sound and had curled up in a ball on her bed. She knew if she went over there to try to help she wouldn't last seconds. From the amount of gun action she had heard she knew there were a few raiders at least. She fell asleep like that and woke a little while later to the sound of two more gunshots. Her heart pounding, she stared at the ceiling, wondering if they'd come for her next. She reached out and lifted her pistol from the bedside bureau. As she drew it toward her she looked sideways at her hand holding the gun and watched it trembling in the moonlight for a few seconds. She laid the gun beside her on the bed and stared up at the ceiling again. An hour passed before she drifted off to sleep, her finger on the pistol's trigger. She woke a little after dawn but it was nearly midday before she could summon the courage to venture over to the Ricardis. As she climbed over their wall she knew that what she was doing was dangerous, there was a possibility the raiders might still be in the house. But she hated the thought of Tony and Madison having being left bound and gagged, waiting helplessly for someone to come to their rescue. Her heart sank as she tried to rustle up some optimism that this second scenario was what lay in wait for her. The recollection of Madison's screams and the two late gunshots filled her with desolation. Her worst fears were confirmed. In the living room of the ransacked house she found the couple, dead. Tony had been shot several times, his shotgun on the ground beside him. He'd gone down fighting she saw. A raider's body lay amidst the glass of a shattered coffee table.

The sight of poor Madison was almost too much for Mary to bear. She could only face it for a second or two before having to close her eyes and draw a deep breath. When she opened her eyes again she gazed at the lifeless form of her neighbor. She felt utterly deflated, her stomach a rolling washing machine. Madison was naked except for a few torn remnants of her clothing. There were two bullet holes in her chest. Mary felt a lump in her throat at the thought of what she'd gone through. After they'd slaughtered her husband they'd had their fun with her, and after that they'd executed her. Mary felt a dull anger swelling inside her at the outrageousness of it all. The woman before her had been a surgeon who'd worked crazy hours in Cedar Sinai. In the little bit of free time she'd had she'd worked in a free clinic in East Hollywood and in a Downtown homeless shelter. You didn't *kill* people like Madison Ricardi. And yet here she was, lying raped and murdered and left to rot on her own living room floor. It was a while before Mary could force herself into action. She laid Tony and Madison to rest side by side in their lawn and buried the raider with the others in the scrubland. Afterward she took Tony's shotgun from the living room and combed the house in search of some additional ammunition for it. After finding a few boxes of shells in a utility room she went home. She ate some food and then even though it was only early evening, went to bed. Utterly exhausted by the trauma of what she had seen next door and all the grave digging, the haunting images of the Ricardis living room that crept into her brain only kept her awake for a few minutes before sleep stamped them out. She slept until late the following morning. After breakfast she learned how to use the Benelli with the aid of a YouTube video. A few days later she used it for the first time on two semi-feral homeless raiders.

She'd had a few close calls. On one occasion she was pouring herself a glass of water at the kitchen sink when she heard a gunshot and a hole appeared in the window before her. She looked out to see a man in the yard by Lowell's car, his gun pointed at her. She dropped to the ground just before a second shot smashed through the glass. She crawled out into the hallway where she'd left the shotgun leaning against the wall. She filled it to the brim with shells while her intended killer shouted that he'd give her ten minutes to leave the house. Then he was coming in, and if she was still there he'd kill her. She could hear nerves in his voice. This coupled with the fact that he was a terrible shot at close range gave her confidence. She went into the living room, picked up a cushion from one of the sofas and hid behind it. Twenty minutes elapsed before she heard the man attempt to break the front door down. With no hope of the rock-solid Spanish-style door giving way he quickly abandoned his efforts. After a period of silence she heard the kitchen window shattering. Listening very carefully she could just about hear the faint squeak of the man's shoes as he went from room to room. She heard his footsteps draw closer and closer before going suddenly silent. At that point she knew he was on the living room carpet. She tossed the cushion into the air and heard his gun discharging three times. She sprang to her feet and saw the man standing wide-eyed, his gun pointing in the direction of a shower of cushion feathers. He just had time to snap his head in her direction before she blasted him in the chest. He flew backward, his insides hitting the fireplace before the rest of him.

On another occasion she'd fallen asleep at the kitchen table after eating some cereal, unknowingly having left the front door unlocked. She woke at the sound of a cornflake crunching on the ground and looked up to see a huge, longhaired baseball bat-wielding man towering over her. Murder in his eyes, the man lifted the bat over his head. Realizing she was about to be bludgeoned to death, Mary reached behind her and snatched up the pistol from the countertop. She shot the man in the throat just before the bat began its deadly descent. The man dropped the bat and his hands flew to his ruined windpipe. His mouth making gagging sounds, he gazed wide-eyed at her, a *what did you do that for?* look in his eyes. With the man showing no signs of going down she shot him twice in the chest, still sitting at the table. Still he did not fall. She raised her gun and put a bullet in his forehead. Finally he collapsed to the floor.

But the realization of how lucky she'd been on these occasions was nothing compared to the luck she'd felt at being spared from Mouther. She was an immune, she supposed. There were others like her in the city and across the nation. Not that she cared anymore.

She blinked, drew a deep breath and exhaled loudly. She realized she'd been staring at the shotgun and pistol beside her on the couch all the time she'd been reminiscing. Reminiscing about murder. She waited to feel any emotion at this grim realization but none came.

I'm dead.

Yes, except for the fact that she was still warm and breathing, she supposed she was. Over the past few weeks she'd been *feeling* less and less. She'd seen a TV movie once about a planet in a far-away galaxy whose core was cooling, leaving the remainder to become a barren, icy waste. That was *her* now. Her humanity was ebbing, leaving behind this empty, apathetic shell that didn't bat an eyelid at having to blow someone's brains out and bury them.

The irony was rich. Mouther hadn't touched her but had taken everything else in her life bar her pulse. It had snatched away all she'd ever cared about, leaving her soulless and alone. The poets would love it. The screenwriters too, if any were still alive. There would be no more movies. She would never again stand under the lights and before the cameras. Never again perform the magic that was transforming mere lines on a page into a living, breathing human being for the world to behold. Never again watch the man she'd loved smoothly run a set and turn a batch of A4 pages into a spectacle that could captivate and mesmerize…

She picked up the pistol from beside her and stood. She left the living room and went to the kitchen, her legs a little stiff after sitting for so long. She went out the patio door and onto the lawn. At the end of the lawn, just before where the grass ended and the garden began, were two graves, handmade crucifixes at the head of each. Lowell was in one grave and their child, little Esther, lay in the other.

Lowell had begun sneezing and coughing one afternoon a little over a month after the outbreak. After he'd instructed her to keep her distance from him he'd attempted to lighten the situation. You'd never know he said, it might just be the flu. She'd watched in desolation from the kitchen door as he'd taken some food from the presses, gloves on his hands, and put it into a bag. When he was finished he told her to step back from the door and move down the hallway. She started sobbing at that point and did as he requested without a word. When he appeared in the hallway he offered her his best effort at a smile and then turned and went upstairs. She heard him shut a bedroom door and lock it. Mary went upstairs, took a chair from one of the other rooms and sat outside the bedroom he'd gone into. She kept a vigil there, talking to him, only moving when she had to relieve herself or get some sustenance from the kitchen. She would eat, drink and sleep on the chair. When his condition deteriorated and he took to his bed she remained by his side, passing the time by reading (when she could concentrate) and listening to music. She walked up and down the hallway every half hour or so to stretch her legs. When Lowell's condition improved and he began talking again Mary couldn't help but be hopeful. His illness was in keeping with the phases of Mouther but as the hours ticked by and he seemed to be getting even better she allowed herself to believe that yes it was a quick, bad dose of flu that he'd had and now he was on the mend. When a flat tone began to creep into his conversation and he began to make some grammatical errors she was devastated. As she fought to keep her voice from cracking a wave of nausea began to swell in her gut. She told him she'd be back in a minute and went to the bathroom. She walked first so as not to alarm him but ended up having to run. She barely made the toilet bowl in time for it to receive the dinner she'd eaten an hour earlier. As she rinsed out her mouth afterward she could feel a dull ache in her abdomen but thinking this to be nothing more than tenderness in her gut after vomiting, she brushed it aside and went back to her chair outside Lowell's door.

As the hours went by the pain in her abdomen grew slowly worse and she eventually began to get cramps there. She realized she was having a miscarriage. She began to feel almost ethereal. This hell couldn't be real. Her sexy, intelligent husband being slowly reduced to an inarticulate simpleton behind this locked door with their child dead inside her. No, this type of nightmare only happened in the movies, it didn't happen in reality. That was it! She was acting. At work, earning the crust. This *had* to be a movie. She was just getting too deep into a role. Any second now someone would shout CUT! and the set and its environs would come to life with the bustle of bodies and *reality*. But the scene went on and on and on. Lowell continued to mumble his flat, by now almost unintelligible sentences and her abdominal pains and cramps felt abysmally real. As did the feeling of dampness between her legs when it came. She went to the bathroom and when she saw the blood on her underwear the wave of despondency that swept through her made her lightheaded. She reached out and held onto the bath handle until the sensation left her. She remained sitting on the toilet until she passed a large blood clot and after cleaning herself up she went back to her chair. She was horrified by what Mouther had wreaked upon the man she loved but she was emptily glad that it had rendered him oblivious to the many treks she took to the bathroom in the ensuing hours. She passed five more clots until the fetus finally came. She didn't know what its sex was but she had a feeling it would have been a girl. She'd had a deal with Lowell—if they had a girl it would be called Esther, after Mary's mother, and if it was a boy they'd call it Nicholas after Lowell's grandfather. Crying, Mary put little Esther into a plastic zip lock bag which she placed in the fridge. She returned to Lowell's side and after a while fell asleep. She woke to the sound of the bedroom door handle before her clicking back up into position. Exhausted, she kept her eyes on the handle until it began to move slowly downward. It kept descending for a few more seconds before suddenly flying back upward again. A horrible, ominous feeling dawned in her gut as she watched the now still handle. It remained motionless for a few more seconds before embarking upon its slow descent again. Mary's heart pounded as she watched the handle go down, her face flushing with terror. She blinked when it snapped back upward. A dreadful scene began to play in her mind's eye— Lowell on his knees in the bedroom, one hand pressed against the door, the other against the wall, his once confident and intelligent eyes now vapid as he ran his tongue slowly along the door-handle, pressing it downward as he moved along it…

She fled to the kitchen. She collapsed into a chair at the table, put her head in her hands and began crying. She felt she could cry all night such was her desolation but exhaustion prevented her from doing so. She fell asleep and when she woke she saw it was dawning outside. Another day being born over a dying city. After having some breakfast she turned on the radio. There was nothing on it but Mouther, Mouther, Mouther. Her desolation turned to rage and she wanted to pick up the radio and hurl it against the wall. In the end she simply turned it off and sat gazing into space. Her need to be near her husband grew with each passing minute. Even though he was lost to her now, a deficient zombie waiting to die, she still wanted to be by Lowell's side. But she'd made a promise. Not long after he'd locked himself in the bedroom Lowell had made her promise that as soon as he began to exhibit the more…unpleasant symptoms of the disease she'd walk away and not return until he was dead.

She held out until mid-morning. With the thought of Lowell being up there alone proving unbearable she went upstairs. As she made her way toward the bedroom door she kept her eye on its handle. It remained stationary. When she arrived at the door she stood facing it. She could hear no sound outside of the blood pumping in her ears. Knowing it would be a futile exercise she called out Lowell's name (he'd stopped answering to it the previous evening). No sound came from the room. Her stomach rolling unpleasantly she walked to the door and pressed her ear up against it. Her eyes snapped shut in response to what she heard. It was barely audible but there was no mistaking the sound. She listened, her heart breaking, to the sound of her husband's moaning as he released into or against God knew what in the bedroom. She recalled the blissful occasions she'd heard that sound before, those sweet nights he'd thrusted inside her, his body and breath hot against her. The sound he'd made when he'd given her little Esther.

She bolted from the door and nearly fell as she dashed down the stairs. She did not return upstairs for the rest of the day and slept that night on the living room couch. When she woke in the morning she knew he was dead. She had some breakfast and walked up the road to the DeWieckes' house. Claire and Clarence DeWiecke had left the city with their children the previous week. The reason she was here was because she needed an axe, and Clarence, an amateur carpenter in his spare time, had one in his workshop. She climbed in over the front gate and made her way up the long driveway toward the house.

When the house came into view she saw that one of the living room windows had been smashed and the front door was open. She went to a small building at the side of the residence which housed Clarence's carpentry workshop and tried the door on the off-chance it might be unlocked. It wasn't. She returned to the front of the house and went inside. She noticed that Clarence's ornamental clock was gone from its place on the wall inside the door. The rather simple-looking painting of a lighthouse (which Clarence had told Mary and Lowell had cost him sixty grand) that had hung alongside it was gone too. On her way to the kitchen Mary glanced into the living room and saw that the place had been ransacked, the expensive ornaments and figurines gone from over the fireplace.

On a key holder in the kitchen she found the key for the workshop. She went back out to the workshop and went inside. She spotted the axe almost immediately, resting against the wall beneath a tool shelf. She picked it up and held it in both hands, thankful that she'd been a gym bunny. It was very heavy but she figured she'd be strong enough to use it alright.

Her eyes fell upon the half-completed bed headboard on the workbench before her. Having graduated from small tables to chairs and then to bedside bureaus, Clarence had told Mary the last time they'd met jogging that he was ready for a serious carpentry challenge now—a four-poster bed complete with ornamental finials. Mary moved her eyes around the headboard, recalling the previous occasion she'd been in this workshop. Lowell had been with her. It had only been a few days after they'd moved into the neighborhood. Clarence had invited them to call over some evening and they'd taken him up on the offer. Toward the end of their visit he'd taken them out to the workshop and had been in the middle of showing them a table he was working on when his seven year-old daughter Ursula had shown up at the door. She'd said that she couldn't sleep and had asked her father if he'd read her a bedtime story.

Mary's eyes went to the spot by the door that Ursula had stood in that night and she could see the little girl as clearly as though she were standing before her at that moment—a beautiful child with long blonde hair holding a little teddy bear in her hands, a slightly put-out look on her face at not being able to sleep. Feeling a lump rising in her throat, Mary swallowed it away and left the workshop. She walked quickly down the driveway but she could not keep the image of little Ursula from her mind. The lump returned to her throat and this time there was no resisting it. As she neared the gate her face crumpled and her eyes began to fill. When she reached the end of the driveway she put the axe down, folded her arms against the gate and cried into them.

When she finished she tossed the axe over the gate and climbed over after it. She returned to the house and went upstairs. Lowell had told her that if he died she should just leave his body and leave the house. If she buried him she could contract the virus. As she looked at the bedroom door before her she braced herself, gripping the axe tightly in her hands, about to go against her husband's words once more. There was no way she was leaving him to rot in there. She lifted the axe over her shoulder and swung it as hard as she could against the door. She repeated the exercise until the timber eventually gave. She aimed her blows around the newly-created breach until she had a fairly sizeable hole made. She put her hand in through the hole and felt around until her fingers alighted on the key of the door. She turned it and withdrew her hand.

She put her hand on the handle and closed her eyes. She listened to the blood pounding in her ears for a few seconds and then she opened her eyes. She looked down at her hand holding the handle which she saw was trembling a little. She pushed the handle down and opened the door slowly inward. She steeled herself against the awful things that she saw scattered about—his tooth-marked wallet, the ragged remnants of business cards, half a toothbrush beside part of a shoelace—and she went to where Lowell lay between the bed and the door of the bathroom.

She knelt by his form, naked except for his boxers, and kissed him gently on the forehead. She put her cheek against the side of his head and held it there for a while. It felt so alien and depressing to feel him so cold. Eventually she straightened herself and took a deep breath.

The work began. She cleaned Lowell and dressed him in his best suit and shoes. Then she put her hands under his armpits, lifted his upper body from the ground and began dragging him toward the stairs. She was relieved he'd lost some weight over the previous few months. If she'd been dealing with his original thirteen and a half stone she'd have been in trouble. By the time she got to the bottom of the stairs she could feel the sweat rolling down her back beneath her t-shirt and she still had a long way to go. She drank a few glasses of water and got going again.

When she got to the end of the lawn she laid his upper body down gently on the grass and collapsed beside him. She remained there for nearly half an hour and then she went inside for some sustenance. Afterward she went back out and dug Lowell's grave. She laid him inside, gave him one final kiss and covered him with earth. When she was finished she dug a small grave beside his. She went into the kitchen and took their child from the fridge. She placed Esther in the grave and filled it.

Spent, she dropped to her knees before the graves. She sat back on her haunches and placed her hands on her thighs. She studied her exhausted, quivering fingers, brown with dirt. She looked up at the late-afternoon sun shining unhindered in a cloudless blue sky. Another beautiful L.A. day. And here she was, just finished burying her family. She wondered if anybody else in the city had just done the same thing. She looked back down at the graves, listening to the faint sound of sirens from somewhere in the basin below. Suddenly it hit her.

My family. Gone.

She felt completely devoid of substance, hollowed. It was as though a giant hypodermic needle had been inserted in her chest and had sucked every bit of vitality from her body. She tumbled bonelessly to the grass. It was a while before any feeling returned to her form and when it did it came in the form of a horrible, all-consuming want. An image of Lowell smiling appeared in her mind's eye and she groaned with longing for him. She curled into a ball and pulled at the grass like a heroin addict in the grip of a brutal craving. She saw Clarence DeWiecke lifting little Ursula into his arms that night in the workshop and she ached for her own child. Completely exhausted after her labors, she fell asleep. When she woke up it was almost dark. She went inside and went to bed. She slept through until the following morning and such were her pains and aches after the previous day's exertions that she could barely walk down the stairs. After having some breakfast she did some light limbering-up exercises and when she felt a little suppler she went back upstairs. After cleaning out the room Lowell had been in (a task that had some very trying moments) she went to Clarence

DeWiecke's workshop where she cobbled two wooden crosses together. She brought them back to the house and placed one at the head of each grave.

She cried at the foot of the graves every day after that. Then the raids began and as the bodies began to pile up in the scrub beyond the wall she began to cry a little less on each occasion. Eventually she stopped crying altogether.

Now, nearly five months on from the day she'd laid Lowell and Esther to rest she stood over their graves, wishing she could mourn them. She knew the grief was still there, still warm and alive, but buried beneath a deep layer of cold. Would she ever be able to feel it again? She didn't know.

"Hello?"

In a semi-trance, she ignored the voice.

"Hello? Mary?"

She turned her head slowly toward the house, the direction she'd heard the voice coming from.

"Mary, are you in there?"

Mary blinked. Slowly surfacing from her torpor she felt glad at hearing the sound of a human voice but she was also a little unsettled. She couldn't quite place the voice from this distance but it was familiar to her. And not in a good way.

"It's Jonah, Mary."

Mary blinked in astonishment. It couldn't be. Jonah Gates, the creep who'd stalked her on and off for years had somehow survived the Mouther plague and was standing nearby somewhere? Christ, what were the odds? She was on the point of telling herself that she was hearing things, her mind was finally cracking, when he spoke again.

"Listen…I know you're probably not glad that I'm standing outside your gate but…I just wanted to know if you and your husband are ok."

Staring in the direction of his voice Mary blinked repeatedly. This was *unbelievable*.

"Mary?"

Still Mary remained silent. Her disbelief beginning to melt, she snorted inwardly. This had to be the most ironic moment in human history. The first human voice she'd heard in nearly two months and it had to be *this* harassing weirdo. But she needed to talk to someone. To see someone. Living, that was. Even if it was an ex-stalker.

"I'm here, Jonah," she called out. "I'm ok."

"Aw, that's great to hear," came the reply. "Just to let you know, I don't have the virus."

"Ok. Neither do I. I'm coming to the gate now."

"Great."

She went back inside the house and out the front toward the gate. As she neared the gate she was glad of the pistol in her hand. Any weird stuff on his part and she'd point him back out with it. When she stopped before the gate she tucked the pistol into the waistband of her jeans. Then she opened the gate a little.

He was standing by a motorbike. His face was the same, serious, no different from the one she'd taken the ridiculous hairpiece and moustache from after he'd gate-crashed her wedding a year before. The situation felt surreal. She hadn't spoken a civil word to him in years and now…here they were. She wondered if he'd really had that GPS chip that Soranor had mentioned implanted in his leg. She'd only turned on the tracking device the General had given her for it a couple of times and had often wondered if that arrow on the screen had really been pointing at Jonah. When the arrow hadn't come near her location in the first few weeks she'd put the tracker away. She couldn't recall where.

"Hello," she said.

"Hello."

Her eyes went to the gun tucked in his waistband.

"You have to use that much?" she asked.

"Couple of times. It's just a tranquilizer." He looked at her own weapon. "You?"

"A good bit."

A silence fell between them. Mary found herself remembering the many silences on their two dates all those years ago. At least those ones had had the noise of the world to fill the void. With the world dead around them now this silence was much worse than those had been.

"Do you want to come inside?" she asked.

"Yeah. That'd be nice."

«««—»»»

They talked at the kitchen table. Or rather she talked. She told him how lucky she was that Lowell, at the beginning of the outbreak, had stocked the cellar with a huge supply of non-perishable food in the event that the reports of the dreadful new virus were for real. She told him about Lowell's sickness and death, the loss of their child, the raiders, the Ricardis.

When she finished speaking he rose from the table. She watched him go to the sink and gaze out at the darkening world beyond the window. Same old silent Jonah. Even the end of the world didn't change some people. He hadn't even offered his condolences on the passing of Lowell and Esther.

She went to his side by the window. She looked at the two fireballs burning at the distant oil refineries in Carson. She blinked as a third fireball was born.

WHUMP

She watched the new conflagration, larger than its siblings, as it set about pushing a thick, black plume of smoke into the air above it. She wondered idly what had caused the infernos. Lack of monitoring of the facilities? Bored immunes? Mouthers straying into the complexes and dining on vital technical equipment? Not that it mattered. She looked across at Jonah. He wasn't looking at the fires she saw. His gaze was trained on something closer. The crucifixes in the lawn. There was a strange look in his eyes that she wasn't sure she liked.

"The one on the left is Lowell," she said. "The other one is our baby. Esther."

"Can I go out to them?"

She nodded. "Ok."

She led him outside and across the grass to the graves. They stood side by side looking down at them. She heard Jonah sniff and she looked across at him. She wasn't sure with the dusk but she thought his eyes looked shiny. He sniffed again and wiped first one eye and then the other. He released a shuddery breath. Christ! He *was* crying. She couldn't believe it. She'd never have thought him capable of showing such an emotion. And he was crying for her loss. Touched, she looked back down at the graves.

"You're free now."

Mary blinked. What had he said? She looked sideways at him, puzzled. There was a smile on Jonah's tear-streaked face now, another expression she'd not seen him produce before.

"You're free," he repeated. "Free from the old world. From your old life." He paused before adding, "We can *be* together now."

She gazed at him in amazement. "What the hell are you talking about?"

"I did it for *you*, Mary. It was mine. I made it, and I let it out. For *you*. And I kept you safe against it."

It took a few seconds for realization to dawn in her. When it did, it caused a horrible heat to swirl in her stomach. Jesus, it couldn't be true. He wasn't *that* crazy. Was this some LSD hallucination perhaps? Had she taken something earlier to get her through the emptiness of the day? She decided to humor this fantasy and opened her mouth.

"*You* created Mouther?" she asked weakly, her tongue feeling heavy.

"Yes."

"*You*…caused the outbreak. For me?"

"Yes," he said in a shuddery voice, and sniffed.

He was on the verge of crying again she saw. Tears of happiness at having killed her husband and child and seven billion other people. This…monster had cleared the world for him and her. Her stalker. Now the greatest serial killer in the earth's history.

She took her gun from her jeans and pointed it between his eyes. He whipped his arm up just in time to bat hers to the side as she fired.

She became aware that the heels of her palms were burning. She'd grazed them in her fall. She picked herself up and went back inside. She washed her hands under the tap. When she was finished she turned her palms upward. As she looked at the cuts and grazes on them it began to rise inside her. The enormity of it all. Her hands shook and her heart began to pound. Feeling weak, she gripped the sink tightly. Her vision blurred as her eyes filled with tears. The strength left her legs and she slid to the floor, crying.

It was all her fault. All of it. Lowell, Esther, the world. He'd done it all for her. And she'd let it happen. She'd had three chances over the years to press charges against him and she'd let him off on each occasion. Lowell had been angry with her after she'd let him go for the third time. He'd been very upset after Jonah had ruined their wedding day and had thought that any man capable of turning up at the wedding of a woman he was obsessed with was dangerous and needed locking up. He'd been right of course, so right. She saw Lowell before her in her mind's eye and her grieving intensified.

"I'm sorry!" she lamented. "I'm *so* sorry!"

She curled into a fetal position and rubbed her stomach, aching for the life that had once resided there. She cried until sleep took her.

«««—»»»

At the same time Mary was mourning the loss of her husband and child, Jonah was also grieving. As he shambled along Laurel Canyon Boulevard, his legs twitching with exhaustion after his flight from the house, he wept for only the second time in his life (the first had been back at Mary's, tears of joy that now seemed like they'd happened an age ago, or on another planet). He sobbed as he made his way along the silent road, the moon his only light.

She tried to kill him! He couldn't believe it. Had she gone mad? After all he'd done for her! All he'd endured for her. Granted he knew there would be some pain in bursting the boil of her previous life but to turn on the man who loved her more than anyone she'd ever met…

he couldn't understand it. *Bach* hadn't loved her. It frustrated Jonah to think that she thought he had. Bach had just been using her to push himself further up his degenerate Hollywood ladder. She'd just been a status symbol to him and Jonah had given the filth what he had deserved. And the child Bach had given her? If she'd been expecting it to grow up to be any different from its father then she'd been naive in the extreme. It would have turned out just the same as its old man—ambitious, grasping and using.

Jonah's ear was killing him, the pain there ferocious. He'd broken into a house a few minutes earlier and had poured some whiskey he'd found there onto the wound. He'd nearly passed out with the bolt of agony that had followed. At least the bleeding was lessening somewhat. He could feel the blood beginning to dry on his neck and under his shirt. That was what you got for sacrifice and devotion to someone. An attempt on your life and a piece of you shot off.

As well as the shock and bitter disappointment of the whole horrendous experience he'd just been through, Jonah was also worried. Had she really meant it when she'd said that she'd come after him and finish the job? She'd sounded pretty resolute about it alright. She had that goddamn tracker. She could be upon him in no time, that brute of a shotgun she had and her pistol both loaded up to the max…

Panic rising inside him Jonah looked behind him. Nothing moved in the road amidst the occasional abandoned car. Forcing himself to maintain his composure he drew a deep breath. Would she calm down? Yes, he figured she would. But not for a while. And he didn't think that hanging around waiting for it to happen would be a good idea. Right now he figured the best course of action would be to put some distance between them.

«««—»»»

About half an hour later he came across what he needed. At the side of the road was a motorbike, its half-decomposed owner lying alongside it with two bullet wounds in his chest. The bike's key was still in the ignition and when Jonah turned it the engine coughed and spluttered uncertainly for a few seconds before eventually catching and roaring into life. Jonah's spirits lifted a little when he saw that he had a half-tank of gas. And he had saddlebags too. He wondered which way he should go. Should he continue south, the way he'd been going, or should he try one of the other three points on the compass?

He kicked the bike into gear and headed for the Hollywood freeway. When he got to it he was heartened to find that it wasn't too littered with vehicles. He headed north. It broke his heart to be leaving his love but she needed time. Time to purge herself completely of her old life and to realize what she now had—a man who loved her more than anything in the world and who would do anything for her. Then she would come to him and they would be together forever.

PART III

LOVE PURSUED

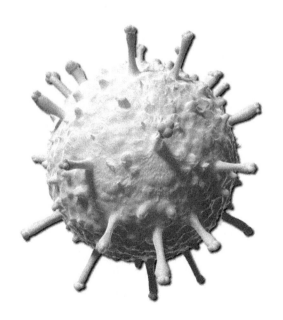

CHAPTER ELEVEN

ary woke a little after dawn. After having some breakfast she went looking for the tracker that Soranor had given her. She began in her bedroom, searching the drawers beneath her mirror first. Not finding it in the bedroom she moved on to the next bedroom up.

By late morning she still hadn't found it, having searched the entire house and the garage. Tired and sweating, she returned to her bedroom and sat on the edge of the bed. Even though she'd searched it from top to bottom something told her that the tracker was *in this room*.

She gazed at the drawers under her mirror. Eventually she rose and went to them. She searched them again, this time taking each drawer out as she went through it. She found the tracker on the ground behind one of the bottom drawers, resting on a bank statement that she'd been looking for before the outbreak.

She turned on the tracker and blew the dust from it while she waited for it to load up. When the map appeared on the screen it had an arrow pointing at Buttonwillow, just off the Interstate 5, west of Bakersfield. At the bottom of the screen was the distance between him and her—one hundred and twenty two miles. My my, he hadn't hung around, had he? She'd obviously scared him rightly. A bitter pleasure rolled in her stomach. *Good.* She imagined how he must be feeling. How blind, how exposed. She could see him but he couldn't see her. The vicious satisfaction she was feeling intensified. She hoped every second of helplessness he was feeling was eating the bastard up.

As she rose from the bed her eyes fell on the bank statement which she had left on the dresser. She doubted it would be of any use to her for a very long time, if ever again. She recalled the bank runs that had taken place in the second month of Mouther, the news footage showing mile-long queues outside bank branches. The banks had run out of cash within days and then things had turned bad, particularly so in L.A.

Some of those who had left it too late to withdraw their money had in desperation turned to violence, returning to branches bearing arms and threatening slaughter if they were not given their money. A few of these desperate individuals had followed through on their warnings and had gunned down counter staff and security personnel before going down themselves in a hail of police and SWAT fire. Mary could recall one particularly dreadful occasion in which a man had detonated a powerful explosive device in a bank on Wilshire Boulevard, killing himself, some police officers, fellow customers that he'd taken hostage, and every single member of the bank's staff.

Mary looked at the tracker in her hand again. This *arrow* before her was responsible for all of that. All the panic, confusion, violence and death. All of which he'd done in her name. How *dare* he! He wasn't a *man*! He was an abomination, a monster. Boiling with fury she had to fight against a powerful urge to hurl the tracker against the wall. It felt like she was holding pure evil in her hand.

She put the tracker in her pocket before she did anything silly. She went downstairs and upon entering the kitchen saw that her transport requirements were no longer an issue. On the table beside the bottle of beer he'd half-drunk Jonah had left the key of his motorbike. She felt her skin crawl a little as she picked up the key—she was loath to touch anything that he'd laid his hands on (she left the beer bottle where it was, there was no way in *hell* she was going to touch anything that his *lips* had been in contact with).

She went outside and got on the bike. She'd ridden bikes before but not since she'd left Wyoming, a long time ago. And none of those had been as big as this one. She fired it up and went out onto the road. To get a feel for the handling she drove down Laurel Canyon Boulevard as far as the intersection with Hollywood Boulevard and then she returned to the house. The bike was heavy and would not be easy going but it was powerful and comfortable and she had a feeling she had a lot of driving ahead of her.

She filled one of the bike's saddlebags with as much food and essential supplies as she could pack in and put the shotgun, (half of it—

the barrels poked out under the side-flaps at the sky) its shells, and ammo for the pistol into the other. Ready to leave, she went out to the graves. Kneeling between the two of them she placed a kiss first on Lowell's and then on Esther's. She would have vengeance for them. For the city. For the world. For the survivors who had had everything they'd held dear taken away from them.

She rose to her feet and went to the bike. She started it up and drove toward the gate. As she drew closer to it something on the ground caught her eye. She stopped by the curious item and bent over it for a closer look. There was a ragged line of what looked like blood on one side of it. Eventually she realized she was looking at part of an ear. So the bastard hadn't escaped unscathed. Good. She continued toward the gate.

«‹‹—››»

Jonah swung his feet to the floor and sat on the edge of the bed, his head lowered, yawning. He was exhausted. He'd woken in agony in the middle of the night after rolling over on his wounded ear and had only slept in fits and starts afterward.

He rose and went into the bathroom. His ear had bled a little during the night. There was dried blood around his earlobe and on his neck. There was no discoloration around the wound which was good. He'd gotten to it in time with the alcohol. He moved his head a little closer to the mirror and examined the injury. The line the bullet had sheared was fairly straight. He ran his finger along the scab that had formed, flinching at its raw, vulnerable feel. He moved his head back from the mirror and studied what looked back at him. A mutilated, bloodied man, his face pale around haunted, heavily-bagged eyes. Part of his body rotting in a yard in Hollywood under the hot Californian sun. It shocked and depressed him to think that his love had done this to him. A knot of worry tightened in his stomach as an image of Mary barreling up the I5 toward him, a homicidal look in her eyes, formed in his mind. Was this *actually* what was taking place right at that moment? He figured it was a distinct possibility. Christ, this not knowing was hell. It was like being the blind man in a game of blind man's bluff in which there was only one other player but she was heavily-armed and furious—with the blind man.

His heart sank at the thought of getting on the bike again, especially in his current exhausted state. He briefly wondered if maybe it would be worth the risk to just stay where he was and wait. Maybe she was still in Los Angeles. Maybe she was on her way, but calm, ready to begin her new life with him. This second thought sent a momentary feeling of bliss coursing through him before it quickly dissipated, allowing bleak reality to return once more. *No,* a voice in his head advised. *Best to go.* One day would not be enough for her to clear her head. She would need a couple at least.

He went back into the bedroom and tipped out two antibiotic pills from a bottle on the dresser. He'd found the pills in an almost-bare pharmacy down the road. He swallowed them and went downstairs. On his way to the kitchen he couldn't resist a glance into the living room where the dried-out husk of a corpse lay by a coffee table. A brilliant beam of early morning sunlight was streaming in the window, shining directly down on the shriveled remains. The idea of spending a night in a house with a decayed body was morbid to him but the two houses he'd tried before this one had both had two carcasses in them. By the time he'd arrived where he was now he'd been so exhausted that he'd accepted his lot and had fallen into bed after eating some beans he'd found in the kitchen.

In the kitchen Jonah opened the press he'd found the beans in and looked at his options. There were four cans before him, containing peaches, tuna, chicken and sausages. He took out the peaches and tuna. An odd mix, but it would silence his stomach.

His hunger sated he took the two remaining cans and went to the dining room, where the motorbike was. He'd brought it inside the previous night, not wanting to risk it being stolen. He'd been lucky enough to come across it in the first place. He put the cans into one of the bike's saddlebags and wheeled the bike out into the hallway. Remembering the antibiotics he went back upstairs for the bottle. He stowed it with the food cans and wheeled the bike out the front door of the house. When he reached the driveway he started it up and drove down to the sidewalk. He looked up and down the street.

He turned right onto the road, heading west. Buttonwillow, small-town California. The warehouses, machinery yards and one story houses faded quickly behind him and were replaced with crop fields. The only reason he'd come across Buttonwillow at all was because the I5 the previous night approaching Bakersfield had begun to get quite clogged with cars, many of them inhabited with corpses. The moon had illuminated them in all their decayed glory for Jonah to see as he'd made his way around and between vehicles. Carcasses of all shapes and sizes had greeted Jonah's reluctant eyes: the small forms of children, the larger ones of teenagers and the fully-grown remains of adults. Every now and then he'd looked behind him, just to make sure none of them had risen from their graves and were following him. His discomfort had grown as he'd progressed through the cemetery so much so that by the time he reached the off-ramp for the 58 highway his heart was pounding in his chest. Half the way down the off-ramp he'd looked behind him half-expecting to see a battalion of the dead shuffling down the asphalt toward him. Unable to dislodge images of the sepulcher on the Interstate from his mind he'd been re-lieved to come across a living human being, a male teenage Mouther, on the outskirts of Buttonwillow. Rake thin, his clothes hanging from his malnourished frame, the kid had been standing next to a WEL-COME TO BUTTONWILLOW sign, an abandoned station wagon nearby. The kid had been licking a fully-opened roadmap. He'd paid no attention to Jonah as he'd pulled up in front of the pickup. Jonah had spotted a tire iron on the ground by the station wagon and had picked it up. He'd held it before the kid who'd stopped licking the map and had stared at the tire iron for a few seconds before dropping the map and taking the tire iron from Jonah. He'd begun alternately licking and biting it while Jonah had taken the map from the ground before continuing on his way.

Jonah pressed the accelerator down a little further and the bike sped up a little. The tiny little town of McKittrick was next on his route. After that there was nothing before he hit Paso Robles, where he would join the 101 highway. Suddenly the sprinklers in the fields on either side of him burst into life. Jonah was surprised that they were still working. Eventually the fields were behind him, the sprinklers continuing to water food for a world that was gone.

«‹‹—››»

A few miles north of Castaic Mary pulled onto the shoulder of the road. She took the tracker from her pocket. He was north of Soda Lake now she saw, still headed west. She was still wondering why he'd left the Interstate. Not that it mattered of course.

She was starving. She put the tracker back in her pocket and took two cans from one of the bike's saddlebags, one of cooked chili and the other of fruit cocktail. Dinner and dessert. She caught the pull-cover on the can of chili and went to open it. She had it opened a fraction when the tab broke off. She was immediately relieved she'd thought to bring along a can opener. She took one from a saddlebag and opened the can the remainder of the way. It was interesting to see how the end of the world could change the value of something as everyday as the humble can opener. It had probably only cost her a couple of dollars but she figured it was worth many multiples of that now.

She looked about her as she ate. She was surrounded by the gentle slopes of the San Emigdio mountains, green against a clear blue sky. A beautiful, peaceful scene. Completely artificial of course. The road she was on had been one of the busiest in the state, alive with engine noise twenty-four hours a day. And Jonah had put a stop to all that. She realized he'd made the world like himself, empty and quiet. A planet made to reflect a personality. She wondered how he was coping with the handiwork she'd done on his ear. Hopefully it had hurt (and was still hurting) like hell.

After she finished eating she zipped up the saddlebag. As she did so she found herself recalling a scene from Hoffa, the classic film with Jack Nicholson and Danny DeVito. In the scene she was thinking of a guy had opened a package he'd received and found a jar inside containing a man's penis and testicles preserved in vinegar. Mary thought that maybe she should have picked up the part of Jonah's ear from the ground back in Hollywood and similarly preserved it. She could have taken it along with her and let Jonah have a look at it when she found him. Before she killed him.

But that was the type of stuff psychos did. The type of stuff Jonah did. She climbed back on the bike and got moving again. Gaining speed, she wondered again why he'd come off the Interstate.

《《—》》

The reason was revealed to her in the afternoon. At first the corpse-bearing vehicles appeared in dribs and drabs but the trickle of death quickly grew to a sclerosis. She could feel sweat tickling her back as she made her laborious progress through the charnel house in the afternoon heat. Leaving L.A. had been bad in a few places, especially around San Fernando, but it had been nothing compared to this. She kept her eyes from the vehicles as much as possible, focusing on her tortuous path around and between them but there was no shortage of carcasses on the ground either. Some of them had died violent deaths, many having gunshot wounds in their skulls. One corpse she came across had no head. A few had no remnants of clothing on them. She blinked as she made her way past these tragic forms, desperately trying to expel scenes of rape from her mind.

On a few occasions she had to dismount from the bike to move bodies out of her way. This she found particularly trying. She scrunched her face at the dreadful scuffing noise the husks made against the ground as she dragged them to their new resting places. The lack of weight in the dried-out forms was also close to unbearable. As she moved each one she prayed that the carcass wouldn't come apart—if it did she figured it would be something she would not recover from.

By the time she came to the highway 58 off-ramp she was physically and mentally drained. When she reached Buttonwillow she stopped in the middle of the street, not far from where Jonah had spent the night. She looked at the tracker. He was on a minor road to the left of the 101, between Templeton and Paso Robles. She had a feeling he'd run into more *congestion* on the route and was turning around to join the 46 highway which was a few miles south of him. She put the tracker away. She was so tired she contemplated finding lodgings there and then for the night but figured she had a few more miles left in her so she drove on.

When she came to McKittrick which was even smaller than Buttonwillow, she pulled up in front of the first half-decent house she saw and went to the front door. When she found it locked she broke a small hole in the glass over the handle with her pistol and put her hand in through it. She found that the key was in the lock beneath the inside handle and twisted it. She turned the handle and pushed the door inward. The pistol by her side, she checked the living room and dining room and found no signs of life. There was nothing in the kitchen either. Just before leaving the kitchen she glanced out the back window. In the lawn, in the shadow of a tree, were two graves, crucifixes at the head of each. One of the graves looked a lot fresher than the other. She left the kitchen and went upstairs. When she found nothing there she went back outside and began wheeling the bike toward the door.

She was tired, hungry and sunburnt. She couldn't wait to get some food inside her and hit the hay. She was just about to push the bike into the hallway when she heard a voice.

"Hey, there!"

A worm of defensiveness tightened in her stomach and she looked in the direction that the voice had come from, her hand ready to go to the pistol in her waistband if she didn't like what she saw.

Across the street a little way down the road a tall old man was standing on the front porch of a house. In one hand he was holding a bottle. Behind him a shotgun rested against the wall of the house by a chair. When the man saw that he had her attention he nodded.

"Hey," he repeated, in a lower voice this time.

Mary didn't respond immediately. The man didn't look dangerous. He sounded normal enough too.

"Hey," she eventually replied.

"You thirsty?"

Again Mary took her time in answering.

"Yeah."

The man raised his bottle a little.

"Wanna' beer?"

Mary could feel herself softening. She hadn't talked to a regular person in months.

"Sure," she said.

‹‹‹—›››

The beer was warm but welcome. They drank at the kitchen table while he cooked some food on a gas cooker. When he asked her where she was headed she said Santa Margarita. When she didn't elaborate any further he dropped the issue.

His name was Gerald Verlayne and he was eighty-two years old. He'd lived in McKittrick all his life, working on the oilfields surrounding the town. He was the only person left in the town, everybody else was either dead or had left. Up until a fortnight ago Gerald had had the company of Alberto Roa, the owner of the house she'd broken into. Neither Gerald nor Alberto had caught Mouther. They'd had a routine of drinking beer on Gerald's porch every evening. One evening Alberto hadn't turned up so Gerald had gone over to his house to see if everything was ok. He'd found Alberto dead in his lawn at the foot of his wife Manuela's grave. With Alberto having been on the portly side Gerald had guessed it had probably been a heart attack that had taken him. Gerald had buried him next to Manuela.

"Sorry about going into his house," Mary said.

Gerald lifted his hand in an "it's-nothing" gesture. "Might as well be used for *something*." He paused before speaking again. "It's funny. Alberto and me'd been living across the road from each other for years and we'd hardly spoken beyond saluting each other. We weren't on bad terms or anything like that. We just moved in different circles." He paused again. "Then along comes the end of the world and we're drinking buddies."

He drank some more beer and then he rose and went to the cooker. He began transferring the food to plates.

"You need some help with that?" Mary asked.

"Nah, it's ok."

A few seconds later he placed her plate before her. "Thank you," she said.

The meal was modest, consisting of pasta, potatoes and onion, but it was cooked and fresh. Not having had any electricity in her house for months Mary's diet since then had consisted mainly of cold package-sealed and canned food. The hot pasta in her mouth now tasted glorious. Gerald had picked the vegetables only a few hours before in the fields outside Buttonwillow. She found it difficult to resist the urge to eat at speed. Dessert consisted of some canned creamed rice.

Afterward they went out on the porch where they continued drinking. Mary's chair was comfortable and this combined with her full belly added to her exhaustion. She figured she'd be saying goodbye to Gerald before long and heading to her bed across the road before she fell asleep where she was. Her eyes heavy, she looked up and down the silent street which was rendered ghostly in the twilight. For the past five months she'd watched night fall over the Los Angeles basin from her location in the Hollywood Hills, the lights of the night growing fewer and fainter as time had gone by and the sprawl of life below her had succumbed to Mouther. Eventually there had been nothing but a black blanket. It was no harm to be away from that sight. Still though, the contrast with her present situation felt a little surreal. Here she was, drinking beer with an octogenarian in a tiny little town in the San Joaquin Valley.

She took the tracker from her pocket and looked at it. The arrow was pointing at Cambria, on the coast. She put the tracker away and took a gulp of her beer. She was half-expecting a question from Gerald about the device but none came. Eventually he spoke.

"You lose anybody?"

She looked sideways at him. His features were half-shrouded in the gathering darkness.

"Yeah. My husband and child."

He expelled a breath.

"Christ, I'm sorry," he said. After a brief pause he began speaking again. "I lost my wife, Norma. She died a few weeks after the outbreak. One of the first to catch it in the town. Spread like wildfire after that. The graveyard was full in a month. After that people started burying their folk in their back gardens, or fields." He paused again. "I'm glad Norma is in the graveyard. I don't think I could bear looking out the back window and seeing a cross in the lawn. I don't visit her grave at all. I think about her too much, you see. It starts out good and then it goes bad. In my mind I might see her coming in the door...or gardening...or cooking...and then I see her—" he stopped and she heard him swallow, "—licking or biting things..." He went silent again. "Thank God we didn't have any children. I can't even begin to imagine what it must be like to lose a child to that...*thing.*"

Thing. Mary pondered the word. Yes, that was a good word for Mouther. Better than *virus.* It was a terrible, terrible *thing.* Like a beast. And created by a beast.

"I was six weeks pregnant when the outbreak happened," she said. "My husband caught it about a month later. I lost the baby while he was dying."

Mary's heart pounded in her chest. She felt a lump rising in her throat and swallowed it away. The words had been painful to get out but she realized she'd needed to say them to someone for months.

"God, Mary," Gerald said softly. "I...I don't know what to say. That must have been..." He trailed off.

"I buried them side by side behind our house."

Gerald made no comment on this. Mary took a drink of beer.

"What was it like being in L.A.?" he asked. "Was it really bad?"

In her mind Mary suddenly saw herself shooting raiders and burying their bodies.

"Yeah," she said. "It got pretty bad around the time of the Chevron fire. It stayed bad for a couple of weeks and then things began to quieten down."

A series of explosions had rocked the Chevron refinery at El Segundo while the exodus from the city had been taking place. First one storage tank had gone up and then a series of others had followed suit. Mary had seen footage of the explosions on TV. The roads around the refinery had been lined with every manner of vehicle at the time. The force of the blasts had lifted cars, SUVs and pickup trucks from Sepulveda Boulevard as though they were toys. Vehicles had been hurled from Vista del Mar into the sea, a distance of half a kilometer. At that stage, in the third month of the virus, most of the city's firemen and police had abandoned their posts. Those dedicated souls that had remained rushed to quell the ensuing inferno. What little decorum that had existed in the metropolis at that stage completely collapsed and the less morally inclined saw everything as fair game. It had been during that period that Mary had done most of her raider-killing.

"Christ, that fire was really something alright," Gerald said. "Saw it on the TV. It looked like something outta' the *apocalypse*." He snorted humorlessly. "Guess it *was* part a' the apocalypse. They sure were lucky they got that rain. Otherwise it looked like the whole city could have burned down."

It had looked that way to Mary at the time. The fire had quickly spread beyond the refinery, destroying the community between it and LAX to the north of it and threatening Hawthorne to the east before heavy rain had come to the rescue of the authorities and ended the blaze. The inferno had raged for over a fortnight.

"Another one started yesterday," she said. "In Carson."

"Yeah?"

Mary took another drink of beer.

"Jesus," Gerald said.

A silence ensued. Mary knew what he was thinking. There were a lot of big refineries close by each other in that area and if they all went up the resulting conflagration, with no one left to stop it, could very well destroy the entire city.

"That why you got out?" Gerald asked.

"Yeah," she lied, her voice little more than a mumble she was so tired.

A scene flashed into her mind and she felt a knot tighten in her stomach as she saw herself sitting inert on the sofa back in Hollywood as she'd been only the previous day, staring blankly out the window at the red, burning world, the heat from the blazing trees and scrub outside almost stifling...the flowers wilting in the garden...cracks beginning to make their way along the glass...the paint beginning to bubble on the walls...and still she remained where she was, unmoving...

Taking a deep breath, Mary purged the movie from her mind.

"You're actually the second living person I've seen today, you know," Gerald said in a lighter tone.

She looked sideways at him.

"On the way to Buttonwillow earlier I came across a guy picking food cans off of the road and putting them into a motorcycle bag. I was slowing down to stop and help him when he turned and looked at me." Gerald paused briefly. "Now I hadn't seen another living soul in months before this guy and I wanted to help him and have a chat but... there was something in his eyes I didn't like. Just kinda' freaked me out I guess. So I kept on going. I don't know Mary, maybe I'm being kinda' paranoid but...keep an eye out for this guy on your travels. He's tall, fair-haired and well-built. There was something funny with one of his ears. I think he was *missing* part of it."

Mary looked back across the road again, her eyes slowly closing with exhaustion. So Gerald had almost come to the aid of the man who had killed his wife and wiped out the town Gerald had lived in all his life. Her eyes shut and Mary saw Jonah's face before her in the darkness. She focused on the eyes that had unsettled Gerald. The attractive blue eyes that had been part of the reason she'd accepted Jonah's offer of a date that night in Malibu. (How long ago had that been? Five years? Six? God, it seemed like it had happened a *millennium* ago. An *age* ago. On a different planet.) She'd been stupid, vain, impressed with his looks. Unwilling to look deeper into those pretty eyes at the ...*nothingness* behind them. The nothingness that Gerald had spotted and avoided straight off. Mary focused on this nothingness now, boring deeper and deeper into it, determined to come to its rotten heart. She moved forward...forward...forward. It felt like she was in a tunnel. Eventually a dull sliver of light appeared ahead in the gloom. As she made her way toward it she became aware of something else. Sound. A horrible, seething, swarming sound that grew in tandem with the sliver of light. She was approaching the mouth of the tunnel she saw. When she reached its end she gazed about her. She was standing over a flat, moonlit plain that stretched as far as the eye could see in every direction. Every inch of the expanse was covered in a thick, boiling blanket: maggots, worms, lice, centipedes, millipedes and every other manner of verminous creature imaginable. All feasting on the millions of bodies beneath them.

Sleep took her.

«««—»»»

She looked behind her. Lowell smiled at her from his director's chair, film script in hand. She smiled back at him and turned her attention to the beautiful little girl sitting quietly beside him. Little Esther was the image of her father, with thoughtful eyes and dark hair. Mary waved at her and Esther waved back, a soft smile appearing on her face.

Mary faced forward again. A few seconds later someone shouted "action!" and she rose from her desk. She walked to the witness box from which a man eyed her nervously. She arrived before him and unleashed a barrage of questions and facts which she interspersed with presentations of evidence from her desk. She was a district attorney and she was loving the role. Her lines flew from her mouth with confidence and conviction.

At one point she turned toward the jury box and what she saw there made her stop mid-sentence. Every member of the jury was staring straight ahead of them, their bodies motionless, their eyes blank and sweating faces affectless. A male member of the jury lifted the end of his tie toward his mouth and began dully chewing it. Movement catching the corner of her eye, Mary shifted her gaze to the back row of the jury where she saw a woman running her tongue along the sleeve of her blouse. Mary heard a clacking noise coming from beside her and she looked up to see the judge biting the handle of his gavel. Panicking, Mary looked behind her. Clad only in his boxers now Lowell was still in his chair, licking one of the armrests. Terror rising inside her, Mary's eyes fell on Esther. The little girl was bent over, picking her father's film script from the ground. Her movement was slow and cumbersome. When she sat back into her chair and her face became wholly visible a bomb went off in Mary's stomach.

Her daughter's eyes which had been full of intelligence only a few minutes earlier were now completely barren. Esther's face gleamed with sweat and there were cherry blossoms of fever on her cheeks. She slowly tore a page from the film script in her lap and balled it up, the movement of her hand in the latter action being methodical and labored. She put the balled-up paper into her mouth and began chewing. Mary screamed for all she was worth.

«««—»»»

Mary! Mary!

Somebody was calling her but she couldn't see who in the darkness. Then her sleep-dazed mind realized she still had her eyes closed. She opened them and found herself in a moonlit room. She looked around, having no idea where she was.

"Mary! Mary!"

She looked at the old man beside her. Crouched by her bedside he was clad only in a vest and boxer shorts. He had his hands on her shoulders.

"Mary!" he said. "You're *awake* now! It's ok!"

And then she remembered who he was. The guy from the porch the night before. She became aware that she was screaming. She stopped, her breath coming in quick deep gasps.

"It was just a dream, Mary," Gerald said softly. "You're awake now. It's alright."

Mary could feel herself shaking in his gentle grasp. Her heart was racing in her chest. Reality began to return to her. Lowell and Esther didn't have Mouther. They were dead. She wasn't playing a D.A. in a courtroom drama because the movie business was also dead. Like everyone else in the world. Images from the previous few days rushed into her mind—Jonah, the bike, the bodies, the heat.

She began to cry. Gerald stroked the side of her face comfortingly as she lamented what she had lost and what lay ahead of her.

"Let it out," he said soothingly. "Let it out."

«« — »»»

After she'd fallen asleep on the porch the previous night Gerald had tried to wake her but she'd been so out for the count that he'd quickly abandoned his efforts and had simply lifted her upstairs and put her in the room next to his.

When she woke in the morning the first thing she did was look at the tracker. The needle was still pointing at Cambria. She got out of bed, determined to get moving quickly. On her way downstairs she saw her bike in the hallway. How thoughtful it had been of Gerald to bring it over.

On the kitchen table she found a plate containing a chopped up kiwi, some melon slices and a bunch of grapes. She ate a few of the kiwi slices standing. She took two more from the plate and went to the back window. Popping one of the slices into her mouth she looked up at the sky. There were only a few wisps of white against a sea of blue. She went back to the table and finished off the remainder of the kiwi. The melon tasted so good she couldn't help sighing on occasion as she ate it (she'd always loved melon but hadn't had any in almost six months). She tore a small clutch of grapes free from the bunch and went out into the hallway. She saw no sign of Gerald in either the living room or dining room, not that she had expected to.

Seeing that the front door was off the latch she went outside. Gerald was sitting in his chair asleep, a glass of water on the deck beside him. Mary walked to the front of the porch and looked up and down the empty street. There was a little dust in the air, being blown by a light breeze. She heard Gerald yawn behind her. She turned to see him open his eyes.

"Morning," he said, a croak of tiredness in his tone.

"Morning. I ruin your sleep last night?"

"Nah. I never get much sleep these days anyway. I get bad dreams too."

Mary remained silent for a while.

"Thanks for breakfast," she said eventually, raising the clutch of grapes in the air. "And for bringing my bike over."

"You're welcome." After a pause Gerald spoke again. "So. You hitting the road soon?"

"Yeah. As soon as I finish these." She popped another grape into her mouth.

"You, ah…in a hurry to get where you're going? I mean, you can stay as long as you like."

Mary looked at Gerald and felt a wave of pity. Here was this nice old man, not an ounce of malice in him, all alone in a ghost town in the middle of nowhere. After she left when would he have company again? She quickly brushed her pity to one side and smiled gently at him.

"Thanks for the offer, Gerald," she said. "But I gotta' get going." She lifted her eyes to the road beyond him. "I've got someone to meet. And it's important."

<<<—>>>

"Well," she said. "Goodbye, Gerald."

They were standing on the driveway beside her bike. He smiled but the smile didn't reach his eyes. They were sad at the prospect of returning to solitude.

"Goodbye, Mary."

In her mind's eye Mary saw Gerald in his porch chair, gazing down the street, eyes squinting against the dust. An ember of anger reddened to life inside her. She decided to give him something that might prove a bulwark against the emptiness.

"The guy you saw yesterday, Gerald," she said softly. "He's responsible for the plague."

He stared dully at her, as though his brain were incapable of processing what she had just said. "What?" he eventually asked.

"The man you saw on the road. He's a scientist. He created Mouther, and he let it out."

Gerald's face was a mixture of shock and confusion.

"He...let it *out*?"

Mary could feel her heart beating a little faster.

"Yes," she said. "He told me himself. He's a very sick man, Gerald. He's running from me now. I told you I was going to meet somebody. It's him. And when I find him, I'm going to kill him."

Gerald exhaled loudly. Looking like he'd been punched in the stomach, he dropped his head.

"Christ," he said in a deflated tone. "The fucker say *why* he did it?"

Mary felt her face flush. "No."

"I had the shotgun in the car with me yesterday. I've had a gun all my life, since I was old enough to have one. Never fired at anything more than a beer bottle." He paused. "If I'd have known yesterday what I know now...I'd have blown that guy's head off without a thought."

Mary remained silent.

"Seven billion people," Gerald mumbled. He shook his head. "Jesus. And I was within a few yards of him." He looked at Mary. "So how're you going to find him?"

She fished the tracker from her pocket, giving a quick look at the screen before turning it toward Gerald. Jonah had left Cambria and was headed north.

"The arrow is him," she said.

Gerald took the tracker.

"Then you'd best get going," he said, studying the screen. "Cambria's over a hundred miles away. You've got a big gap to close."

He handed the tracker back to her and she put it away.

"If it was twenty years ago I'd be going with you," he said.

"I don't doubt it."

They held each other's eyes for a few seconds. Mary leaned forward and kissed him on the cheek.

"Take care of yourself, Gerald."

"You too," came the reply. A cold look appeared in Gerald's eyes. "And when you come across that guy…you put one in him for me. Ok?"

Mary nodded. She turned and got on the bike. As she approached the end of the driveway she looked in her rear view mirror. Gerald was standing in the same place, watching her. She turned onto the road.

CHAPTER TWELVE

onah looked to his left. It was a beautiful scene—waves forming and crashing against rocks not far from the shore, scrub shimmering in a soft breeze above the beach. He saw a rest area up ahead and imagined himself and Mary sitting on its grassy verge with their arms around each other, gazing out at the lovely vista. As he passed on he felt a dart of anguish. Here he was, fleeing from his love instead of being with her! His sense of frustration was almost enough to make him want to stop the bike and tear his hair out.

He looked in his rear view mirror. Since leaving Cambria he'd been casting anxious glances in the mirror every so often. He'd had a horrible dream the previous night. In it he'd been driving along the highway and Mary had appeared around a bend behind him. Her eyes invisible behind sunglasses, she'd narrowed the gap between them with terrifying speed and drawn her gun when she was only a few meters behind him. She'd fired, and when Jonah had put his hand to the ear she'd mutilated back in Hollywood he'd found that it was completely gone, his hand re-appearing before his eyes covered in blood. For a brief moment he'd threatened to lose control of the bike but had managed to keep it on the road. He'd looked sideways to see that Mary was now level with him. She'd smiled, a terrible dark grin that had made him glad he could not see her eyes. She'd pointed the gun at him again, this time point blank at his face. The muzzled had flashed.

He'd woken up then, his heart hammering in his chest. After that his sleep had been broken and when he'd gotten up he'd been even more exhausted than he'd been on the previous day. On his way out of Cambria he'd stopped at a shop (the third he'd tried) and had found three cans of energy drink scattered about on its dusty floor. He'd downed them all before leaving. He needed to remain as sharp and focused as possible. Tiredness had cost him his remaining tranquilizer darts the previous evening between Paso Robles and Cambria. It had almost cost him the motorbike (and everything on it) too. On a wooded stretch of the road he'd stopped to take a piss. As he'd done so he'd looked at a charming little brook babbling nearby. After zipping himself up he'd sat on a log and had watched the brook, his exhausted eyes growing heavier as he'd done so. The sound of the bike revving to life had snapped him from his doze and he'd looked up to see a man and a woman on the bike's saddle, the man in the driving position. As the bike had moved onto the road Jonah had leaped to his feet and given chase. He'd fired at the thieves but it had taken him three shots before he'd struck the woman with a dart. After she'd fallen from the bike, Jonah, knowing that he was down to his last dart, had taken careful aim at the man (who hadn't even cast a glance behind him at the loss of his companion) and fired. To Jonah's relief the man had fallen from the bike. Jonah had been even more relieved to find that the bike hadn't been damaged after its tumble to the ground. But that was where his luck had run out. A quick frisk of the thieves' forms had revealed them to be unarmed.

Jonah tightened his grip on the bike's handlebars. His hands were tingling unpleasantly and his heart was thumping in his chest, presumably as a result of the energy drink but he felt wide awake and alert which was the main thing.

With no darts for the tranquilizer gun he felt vulnerable. In Cambria he'd searched houses, stores and cars for a replacement weapon but had come across nothing besides bodies. Every second he remained unarmed he knew he was pushing his luck. He would have to check every vehicle and building he came across until he found something.

Seeing a station wagon parked haphazardly up ahead at the roadside he pulled in behind it. There were two mostly skeletal forms inside, one in the driver's seat and one in the passenger's. Jonah checked under their seats before popping the trunk. There were two suitcases there which he opened and emptied out on the ground. He found no weapon amidst the contents. He drove on. He had no luck in the next two vehicles he tried but when he pulled in by a still-upright police motorbike he struck gold. On the ground beside the bike was a carcass with a hole in its skull. At its side was a gun. He picked it up and took out its magazine. He saw that it was nearly full and slotted it back into the gun. He gingerly removed the holster from the belt of its previous owner and strapped it to his own. He put the gun into it and drove on.

Feeling safer, his anxiousness abated a little. He cast a glance at the entrance road to Hearst Castle as he passed by it. He'd been there once as a boy with his parents and brothers. They'd been on a driving holiday to San Francisco and they'd stopped there for a few hours. Someone had taken a photo of them by the Castle's spectacular Neptune Pool. It had been one of their nicer family photos (not that Jonah could remember many)—their mother and father standing on either side of the by then quite tall Mark and Kelsey, with little Jonah in the middle. A few months after that photo had been taken their mother had left with the hippies.

Bitch.

What had it been like for her, he wondered, his little beast. Had she enjoyed the taste of her wretched hemp jewelry and chain maille earrings before she'd gone? Putting her out of his mind Jonah imagined himself back at the incredible Neptune Pool at Hearst Castle. There was a breathtaking view of the Santa Lucias, the coastline, and the ocean from there. When Mary's anger faded and she warmed to her new future with him, she and Jonah would stop at the Castle on their return to Malibu and enjoy that view. Yes, that would be nice.

«««—»»»

With the roads around Monterrey and Santa Cruz not being too congested he made it to Pacifica late that afternoon. With the air being much cooler than it had been when he'd left Cambria he went into the first clothes shop he saw and got himself a light top. He'd just put it on when a noise behind him caused him to whirl around. A young female mouther, emaciated to the point that she was little more than a skeleton was standing by a clothes rail, alternately biting and licking a timber clothes hanger. Her long blonde hair was woefully unkempt and clumped weed-like in places and her face was deathly pale. She was missing teeth. Jonah watched the pitiful ghoul as she went about her bizarre oral examination of the clothes hanger.

She reminded him of the young man he'd encountered licking the roadmap outside Buttonwillow. He supposed they were "Zombers," a nickname that was a combination of zombie and Mouther. It was the sobriquet given to those who for some unexplained reason hadn't progressed from the neurotrophic phase of the virus to the final and fatal respiratory phase. These unfortunate souls were destined to live out the remainder of their lives in the neurotrophic stage of the disease, their brain damage irreversible. Most of their diet would consist of non-nutritious substances, the normal instinct for nutritious foodstuffs only being listened to when the body's vital systems were in danger of failure due to starvation. It had been a fascinating development in the course of the virus's existence in the lab of the world that Jonah hadn't anticipated at all—those it had manifested itself in being consigned to the neurotrophic phase indefinitely, the normal dietary instinct occasionally kicking in to perpetuate the state. The liberation of death being denied.

As Jonah made his way past the girl she paid him no heed, being completely engaged with her hanger. After having some food he drove to a beachside parking lot and parked next to a large pickup truck. There was a surfer out on the water. Jonah watched the figure weaving in and about the waves. He supposed he should maybe get a move on. He'd made good time getting this far. He still had a few hours of daylight and wasn't too tired.

The surfer was leaving the water. He raised an arm in salute. Jonah raised his own in return. As he drew closer Jonah was glad that he had his gun. The guy was tall and big and had a slightly wild look in his eyes. A tattoo snaked its way out of the neck of his wetsuit up as far as his ear.

"Hey," the man called.

"Hey."

"How are ya'?"

"I'm good."

"You're the first person I've seen alive in nearly a month," the man said. His eyes dropped briefly to the gun at Jonah's side before re-ascending. Jonah watched the man walk past him and place his surfboard in the back of the pickup.

"So where're you from?" the man asked.

"Malibu. You?"

"Santa Cruz, born and raised," the man said and opened the front door of the pickup. He reached across to the far side of the seat and pulled a gym bag toward him. Jonah's eyes lingered for a second on the assault rifle resting on the floor of the cab against the seat before moving to the powerful-looking handgun lying haphazardly next to it. The man took a towel from his bag and began wiping his face and hair vigorously.

"So, Malibu," he said. "Some good breaks down there. You surf?"

"Not since I was a kid."

The man tossed his towel back in the bag and looked out at the water.

"You know this time last year you could hardly catch a proper ride out there it was so crowded." He snorted. "Guess I was never much of a people person. Part of me was actually *glad* when the plague hit. I could catch all the waves I wanted. No more fucking outta' towners and tourists. Now I kinda' miss all those assholes."

He turned toward Jonah.

"So how does it feel?"

"How does what feel?"

"Being immune." The man smiled. "One of the *chosen* ones. You feel lucky?"

Jonah blinked. He was growing tired of the conversation.

"I don't know," he said. "I never really thought about it. Listen, I've got to get going." He nodded at the man. "It was nice meeting you."

"Oh yeah," the man said. "Sure. Likewise. So where're ya headed?"

"North," Jonah said, straddling the bike-saddle.

"Anywhere in particular?"

"I'm not sure yet."

"Well if you're not in a hurry to get there we could head over to my place. I got a serious selection a' stuff, man. Coke…crystal…

1...when the dealers croaked I took *all* a' their shit-."

ĸs, but I've really got to get moving."

Jonan started the bike.

"You sure, man? I've got *juice* at my place. I got two generators out the back. We could turn the music up loud and get *really* wasted."

"I appreciate it, but I've got a lot of ground to cover before dark."

"Oh. Alright. That's cool."

"Take care of yourself."

The man nodded. "You too, man."

Jonah began turning the bike around.

"Hey, man."

Jonah looked at the surfer.

"I don't know how far north you're thinkin' a' goin' but...two guys passed through here a month ago, on the way down from Seattle. Nice guys, kinda' quiet. Like you. I took 'em over to my place and we drank and had some stuff. One of 'em became real talkative then. He said that when they set out from Seattle there was *six* of them. Four men and two women. By the time they hit redwood country there was still six of 'em." He paused. "When they got out of Prairie Creek State Park there was only him and the other guy."

"What happened to the others?"

The surfer didn't respond immediately.

"He said some cult killed 'em."

Jonah remained silent.

"A cult?" he asked eventually.

"Yeah. Some crowd of crazy tree-worshippers he said. They captured the guy and his friends and slaughtered them one by one in some fucked up ceremony. Offered them up to the trees or some weird shit like that. The guy and his other friend managed to escape before it was their turn. Crazy, huh?"

"Thanks for telling me."

"Listen, I know it sounds fucked up but...I just thought I should let you know."

"I appreciate it."

"No problem. Safe travelling."
"Thanks. Goodbye."
Jonah drove off.

«««—»»»

With Daly City approaching in the distance Jonah pondered the man's tale. Back during the plague when it had become apparent to the common man on the street that the world was losing the fight against the virus, stories of bizarre religious cults had begun to appear in the more sensationalist appendages of the media. The tales had emanated from the more undeveloped parts of the world at first but as the vice of Mouther had tightened the accounts soon began to emerge from the backward armpits of the U.S. Animal sacrifices at first, then human.

Not having really believed the incredible tales to begin with, Jonah found the idea that some group of murderous, superstitious freaks were hiding in the woods of Northern California to be an even farther stretch. And then there was the fact that the escapee from the alleged slaughter had been on a drug binge with the drug-loving surfer when he had delivered his story. Fuck's sake, the two supposed visitors to Santa Cruz mightn't have existed at all. For all Jonah knew they were products of the surfer's acid-enhanced imagination.

Adding all of these doubts and rationalizations together helped to dampen the little bit of unease he felt in his stomach. He looked at the sun slipping lower on the horizon and drove a little faster. He wanted to get across the Golden Gate before dusk.

«««—»»»

He decided to chance approaching the bridge directly through San Francisco but Nineteenth Avenue was clogged with vehicles and the dead so he headed out to the seafront and drove along the relatively clear Great Highway. As he made his way along the neck of the peninsula on El Camino del Mar he stopped to have a look at the bridge. He was relieved to see that it was intact. He'd seen the severing of the Bay Bridge during the great city exoduses. With desperation escalating all over the country, some of the more hardline elements on the eastern side of the Bay decided to stem the flow of potential disease carriers from the San Francisco peninsula into Oakland and Berkeley by detonating an enormous amount of C4 on the stretch of the bridge between Yerba Buena Island and Oakland.

Jonah had seen the explosion on TV. All manner of vehicles had been blasted into the bay. A few minutes later a sizeable chunk of the bridge on the Yerba Buena side immediately behind the newly-formed gap in the structure had pitched suddenly downward into the water, plunging a further slew of unfortunates into the brine.

When he arrived at the Golden Gate he switched off his engine. The wind whistling in the bridge's support cables overhead, Jonah regarded the tightly-packed graveyard of unmoving steel and decayed flesh that stretched before him for as far as he could see. A crow cawed at him from a rear-view mirror. He drew a deep breath and moved forward.

The going was slower and tougher than anything he'd experienced up to that point in his journey, even worse than Bakersfield. There was very little wriggle room between vehicles. Not many of the vehicles were occupied but he occasionally glanced at the shriveled forms inside those that were. He supposed it must have been terrible for them, spending their final moments in their metal cages surrounded by thousands of others, like sardines in a can. Dying on a bridge, neither here nor there, water rushing obliviously beneath them, the breeze continuing to blow when their hearts stopped as it had done while they had still been beating. Fleeing an illness that had ultimately got them, or that they'd probably already had. Tragic, but not as terrible as Jonah's own plight. Here he was, fleeing like they'd had, but he was trying to escape the clutches of the person he loved more than anything in the world. Who he wanted to *be* with more than anything in the world. Who he'd protected, and set free…

With a cry of frustration he dealt a savage kick to a body that lay in his path. The light, desiccated remains spun sideways to allow him passage. A few minutes later his stomach rumbled loudly. Having only had a snack in Pacifica he was hungry. He looked up ahead of him and saw he probably had about three quarters of a mile to go. At his current rate of progress he figured he'd be back on land in little over half an hour so he decided to plough onward and hold off on eating until then. But as the minutes went by his stomach grew more insistent so he decided to oblige it. He stopped between a station wagon and a pickup and opened one of the saddlebags. He took out a can of sausages and a packet of wheat crackers. He placed two sausages between two crackers and began eating. He looked at the cars and pickup trucks around him. Only one of them, a Buick, contained a corpse. Jonah looked at the car ahead of him. It was a Bugatti Veyron, one of the most expensive in the world he knew. He found its shape vulgar and loud and its awful yellow-and-green color even more so. It was unoccupied, its driver door open. Jonah could imagine its owner (a stockbroker, or movie-star…maybe even a director like that asshole Bach), arrogant even in the face of death, stepping brashly from the car and striding through the sea of vehicles toward the end of the bridge, not even bothering to close the door behind him. Determined not to be held back even if it meant proceeding on foot. Jonah wished he'd been there to witness the peacock's undoubted swaggering strut. Would the peacock have been frightened? Jonah figured that he would have been. The peacock would have done his utmost to hide it, putting on his best mask of bravado, but the terror would have been lurking beneath the surface alright. It would have been discernible deep in his eyes. Jonah would have called out to the peacock and told him that he, Jonah Gates, was the reason he was fleeing for his life, all his worldly possessions now worthless behind him.

Jonah looked ahead to the end of the bridge and then behind him the way he'd come. He wondered if much praying had been done on the nearly two-mile stretch of road and imagined there had been. Multitudes of impassioned entreaties flowing from trembling mouths and minds that hadn't uttered or thought anything remotely spiritual in years, now suddenly inflamed with religious vigor. The long-ignored help of Jesus and Allah now being sought with ferocious zeal. Please, God, keep it away from me, please, please. The tears coming as the first sneezes were vented. Please, Lord, let it be just a cold, please. The prayers becoming more desperate as the symptoms worsened, supernatural figures being abandoned as the death-squad appeared in the rear view mirror, the begging for mercy now being directed at the gun-carrying, hard-faced mortals drawing closer with each step...

Jonah finished eating and got back on the bike. He'd only gone about ten yards when his path was blocked by the small skeleton of a child. Not bothering to move it out of his way Jonah simply drove over its lower legs. As the thin, brittle bones broke Jonah wondered if anyone had prayed for the child before it had died and a flame of anger lit within him. How...insane the concept of prayer was! How deluded people had been to think that some all-powerful being might perhaps deliver them from his sublime creation!

There was a god alright. But he had chosen to destroy the world, not save it.

«««—»»»

Jonah scanned the length of the crevasse, his heart pounding with frustration. Only a quarter of a mile from land and...*this*. He was standing at the edge of a roughly bowl-shaped recess in the bridge. At the center of the recess was a gaping maw through which he could just make out the distant water of the bay hundreds of feet below, its dark surface rippling in the gathering dusk. Lengths of twisted steel hung slackly below the maw, creaking in the wind.

There had been an explosion of some sort. The cars behind him were scattered about haphazardly, charred and blackened, their windows gone. A few were upside down. At the other side of the mini-ravine the scene was more or less the same. Laterally, the crater extended all the way to the steel railing on Jonah's right. To his left it stretched to within two feet of the railing. Jonah drove over to this thin strip of road surface left to him.

A wave of anxious dismay coursed through his stomach when he saw the thin cracks running across the strip from the crater to the railing. If the surface gave way beneath the bike he could end up tumbling down the slope of the crater and that would be it, out through the maw he would go. The other option was to head back to San Francisco, spend the night there and teach himself how to drive a powerboat in the morning. He looked behind him. The sight of the mile and a half long darkening graveyard of man and metal was almost debilitating. The prospect of making his way back through it…

No. He turned around and faced his precarious road-sliver. He lined up the bike as straight as he could with it and took two deep breaths.

He went for it.

He had the front wheel on the safety of the far side when the road gave beneath the rear wheel. Terror erupted in Jonah's gut as the wheel slid onto the slope of the crater and the bike dipped downward. He could think of nothing to do but floor the accelerator. His sickening fear lasted for one more second (which felt like an eternity) and then the tire caught and he was up and out of the hole.

When he was well clear of it he paused to collect himself, the bike's engine idling beneath him. When the trembling in his hands stopped he put the bike into gear and moved forward.

«««—»»»

By the time the bridge was finally behind him it was fully dark. He turned off of the highway onto Alexander Avenue. Utterly exhausted, he drove slowly and cautiously on the descent into Sausalito for fear he might veer off the road in the event of falling asleep.

He forced his way into the first decent looking house he came across and couldn't even face climbing the stairs. He went into the living room and collapsed onto the couch. He wondered where Mary was. He didn't even have time to opine before sleep took him.

«««—»»»

He woke in the middle of the night, cold and hungry. He went upstairs and in one of the bedrooms found a Stanford University sweater. He pulled it on and went back downstairs. In the kitchen he had some food. As he ate he thought about Mary. How was she finding the road? How was she coping with the traffic and the bodies? He wondered what she was doing at that moment. Sleeping, he supposed. He stopped chewing a mouthful of beans as he pictured her lying in a bed somewhere, her hair tousled about her beautiful face.

The air left his chest like he'd been winded and the spoon he'd been holding fell from his grasp as an ache of longing tore through him that was so strong it was almost disabling. His spoon clanged lightly to rest in his plate, splattering his sweater with flecks of bean sauce.

He needed to see her again. It had only been two nights since he'd been at her house but already it seemed like an eternity. Focusing on her sleeping face in his mind's eye he wondered if she were dreaming.

She is, a voice said in his head. *About killing you.*

He swept the thought from his head as quickly as it had sprouted there. No, he told himself. She's calm now. She's had time to reflect. Sense and realization had come to the fore and pushed her emotion to the side.

He picked up his spoon and began eating again. When he was finished he went upstairs and went into the bedroom he'd found the sweater in. He got into the bed there and closed his eyes. Feeling sleep approaching quickly he welcomed the veil of serenity that preceded it.

Yes. Mary was no longer coming *for* him. She was coming *to* him. His love was ready for them to be together.

《《——》》

He woke in the morning feeling refreshed. After some breakfast he poured himself a glass of water and went out the door at the rear of the kitchen onto a lovely deck. It was a beautiful, crisp morning, the sky cloudless. Beyond him was a sloping wood. He drank some water, relishing the smell of the fresh, forested air on its way to his lungs. He listened to the birds twittering in the trees for a few seconds and then he walked down the steps at the front of the deck. He walked a little way into the wood before turning and facing down the slope.

He could see two more houses amidst the trees below him before the slope flattened out into the town of Sausalito. Beyond it lay the expanse of the bay almost totally obscured beneath a blanket of fog. In the distance Downtown San Francisco looked like a heavenly city rising from clouds. A magical city, now full of nothing but silence and the dead. He drank some more water and shifted his gaze to the waterfront of Sausalito. It looked pretty. He'd head down there in a few minutes and take a leisurely stroll along it. He might even do some fishing. Get a rod in a shop, get a few bottles of beer and sit on the dock. Lovely.

He was in good spirits. The prospect of a relaxing day off of the bike was an uplifting one. He'd decided that he'd remain where he was until Mary showed up. Having had a good night's sleep he was in a more even-minded state than when he'd arrived at the house. In the clear light of day he was still confident that Mary was ready now to have him as her man, but he wasn't going to meet her with his hands hanging at his sides either. He'd have to take some precautionary measures. He looked about him at the trees. Yes, out here would be a good place for them to meet.

CHAPTER THIRTEEN

At the same time that Jonah was scanning the trees around him Mary was looking at the tracker. The arrow was pointing at Sausalito as it had been the previous night. She put the tracker away and fired the bike into life. She put it into gear and got moving.

《《—》》

She didn't check the tracker again until she stopped to eat in Monterrey. She was a little surprised to see that the arrow hadn't moved. When she stopped again in Pacifica she was even more surprised to see that it was still in the same place. She began to speculate. Was he sick? Dead? A dart of disappointment flashed in her gut at the second prospect. *She* wanted to be the reason for his passing to the next life.

She pondered the first scenario. In her mind's eye she saw herself walking into a room to find Jonah before her, lying in a bed, incapacitated. She saw herself raising her gun and pointing it at him. Would she be able to pull the trigger in such a situation? Yes, she thought she would. What if he begged? She reckoned that would make the job easier still.

She wondered what other reasons there might be for Jonah's lack of movement all day.

A trap.

Was that it? Had he grown tired of the road and running from her and was now waiting for her, ready to face her down and resolve the issue one way or another? Did he have the guts? She didn't think he did. He'd killed nearly seven billion people alright but he hadn't had to look them in the eyes as he'd done it. No, Jonah Gates was too weak for that.

He misses you.

Yes. The more she dwelled on the preposterous notion the more she found herself accepting it. He was waiting for her. His deranged mind had pushed logic to the side and had managed to convince itself that there was perhaps hope for them as…

She shivered. It was cold, but that was not her reason for doing so. She could see Jonah standing at a window, gazing out through it, his yearning for her barely visible in his barren, pale eyes. She was looking forward to putting the light out of those pretty, sick-puppy eyes forever.

The shadows were lengthening. She finished eating and drove on.

«‹‹—››»

When she got to San Francisco she followed the route Jonah had taken the previous evening but drove past the Golden Gate and continued on toward the Marina. She'd seen how long Jonah had spent on the bridge and had no intention of being on it herself when darkness fell.

At the Marina it took a while for her to find what she was looking for but she eventually did—a large powerboat with a loading ramp. The first hurdle cleared, she climbed on board. She blinked at the sight of a carcass that lay on the ground not far from the controls. Her heart did a little jump when she saw the keys of the boat in the ignition. She went to the controls and turned the key. The engine started. She saw that she had about a quarter tank of fuel. She switched off the engine and climbed onto the loading ramp. She jumped up and down at its center. It seemed rock solid. But she wasn't even a hundred and twenty pounds. She figured the bike was well over four hundred. She stopped jumping and looked down at the ramp. Would it hold five hundred pounds? A knot of tension tightened in her gut. It would have to. She looked at the shifting water on either side of the ramp. It was deep. She took a deep breath and walked back onto the dock.

She climbed onto the bike and fired it up. She gazed at the ramp before her for a few seconds and went for it. She arrived safely onto the boat deck, her heart racing. After securing the bike against the side of the boat for the crossing she retracted the loading ramp. She started the boat's engine and scanned its control panel. Not long before the outbreak Lowell had bought a powerboat and had shown her how to pilot it. The boat she was on now was much bigger, with much more instrumentation but she figured she could handle it.

When she felt confident of her bearings she undid the boat's mooring and moved it tentatively forward. She slowly navigated her way out of the Marina. When she reached the open bay she applied more throttle. She saw that there were teeth marks on the throttle lever. And on the steering wheel. She looked down at the remains beside her. The driver, she supposed. She could imagine him shuffling along the dock of the Marina, the city lost to the virus behind him, him struggling in vain against the rot of Mouther that was stealing his brain, just about managing to climb onto the boat, his last sensible act being the placing of the key in the ignition.

She faced forward again. The docks of Sausalito were coming into view.

«‹‹—››»

Jonah was sipping some warm beer on the deck at the rear of the house when he heard the faint buzzing sound.

He'd had a relaxing day. After going for a stroll around the town he'd spent a while fishing at the dock. The arrival of a large, bloated corpse in the water had distracted the fish for a while as they'd become more interested in it than in Jonah's bait. When he'd grown tired of fishing he'd walked back to the house and had gone for a walk in the woods.

The buzzing growing louder, Jonah turned his head in the direction of the bay.

A boat was approaching in the distance. A knot tightened in his stomach, a mixture of mostly excitement and a little apprehension. It was her, he knew. He kept his eye on the boat as it drew closer. When it disappeared behind the barrier of trees below him he went back inside the house.

«‹‹—››»

She looked at the tracker, the bike idling beneath her. She lifted her eyes to the tree-covered slope rising behind the picturesque town. She looked at the occasional house in the wood. Jonah was up there somewhere. She left the dock and drove onto the road.

《《—》》

From his hiding place behind a tree Jonah listened to the sound of the bike engine growing louder. In his hands was a shotgun that he'd found in the basement of the house. He had no intention whatsoever of firing it (he'd die rather than do that), no matter how bad things got. If he had to use it at all it would be the stock end he'd be calling on and he thought the odds of that happening quite low. She was coming to be with him, drawing closer, closer-

The bike's engine went dead. Movement caught the corner of Jonah's eye and he looked up to see a squirrel observing him from the branch of a nearby tree. The squirrel kept its gaze on Jonah for a few seconds before it lost interest and began eating a nut it held in its paws.

He heard the front door of the house opening. In the silence that followed Jonah visualized Mary moving slowly along the hallway, her beautiful eyes going from room to room. His heart sped up a little.

The back door opened. He heard her footsteps on the deck. He looked up and saw that the squirrel had stopped eating and was staring motionlessly in the direction of the house. At the sound of boots on the steps at the front of the deck the squirrel bolted along its branch and disappeared into a hole in the trunk of the tree.

A silence fell. When Mary spoke her voice sounded as though she were only a few yards away.

"Jonah. It's ok. Come on out. I'd like to talk."

Jonah closed his eyes for a second, his grip tightening on the shotgun lest he should drop it to the ground and present himself to her, arms outstretched in welcome and relief.

"What happened in L.A…I'm sorry. I've had time to think, and… I'd like us to make a fresh start."

Jonah was just about to lift his leg to step out from behind his tree when the most depressing sound he'd ever heard shattered his feeling of complete and utter joy.

Click.

The sound of a gun's safety catch being thumbed off. The shotgun began to quiver in his clasp.

She appeared ahead of him on his right, a gun in one hand and something else in the other.

"Mary."

She froze.

They remained like that for a few seconds, she with her back to him, he with his eyes trained on her unmoving form. She flashed into movement. Halfway through her turnaround to face him Jonah cracked the stock of the shotgun against her temple and she crumpled to the ground unconscious.

«‹‹—›»›

She came to in the middle of the night, her head aching terribly. She could feel that she was in a bed of some sort. Her hands were tied behind her back. She slowly opened her eyes and found herself facing a moonlit wall. She moved her eyes along the wall until she came to the darkened figure of Jonah sitting in a chair. He was asleep, a shotgun cradled in his arms.

She lifted her head from the pillow a little and the pain in her head worsened, making her feel nauseous. She let her head drop back down and the pain abated to its previous level. She was absolutely exhausted, the travels and labors of the previous today having taken their toll.

She looked at Jonah sleeping in the corner. The minutes rolled by with her maintaining her gaze upon him. Eventually sleep came to end her stare.

«‹‹—›»›

When she woke in the morning she told him that she needed to go to the toilet. He said that he wasn't going to untie her.

"Then you'll have to help me," she said.

"Ok."

In the bathroom she watched his cheeks redden as he undid the button of her jeans. After pulling it and her underwear down he left the bathroom. When she was finished he dressed her and they went downstairs. In the kitchen he fed her and gave her some water to drink.

"We need to talk," he said.

"About what?"

"About *us*."

"I came here to kill you, Jonah."

He blinked, his face becoming unsettled. "Don't say that. You don't mean it."

"I do."

"No, you don't. You just haven't had enough *time*..."

"All the time in the world wouldn't change how I feel about you."

A silence fell.

"I could keep you here. Like this. Until you stopped living in denial."

"I'd rather you killed me."

"Stop talking like that!"

"Talking like what?"

"Talking about *killing*."

"That's rich coming from you."

A look of frustration appeared on Jonah's face. "I didn't set out to...*kill*. I just wanted to be...left alone with you."

Mary lowered her head and shook it. "You're just so fucked up."

"Don't *talk* to me like that!"

"Fuck you!" she shouted. "You cried tears of joy at the graves of my husband and child! You were *glad* you'd killed them! You took everything I had and left me alone in this...*desert*! So I'll talk to you any way I goddamn like, you sick, murdering bastard!"

He stared at her, remaining silent.

"And you're a virgin too, aren't you?"

"What?"

"You're a virgin."

Jonah blinked disconcertedly, his face flushing.

"In the bathroom earlier," she said. "That was the first time you'd ever undressed a woman, wasn't it?"

Jonah stayed mute.

"I get the feeling you've been out with girls before me alright," she continued. "Pretty ones, even. But they probably all went like it did with me. A few dates, and…gone."

"Stop it."

"You probably stalked a couple of them, too."

"I said *stop* it."

"Couldn't take the flick so you skulked around after them like a lowlife."

"Be QUIET!!!"

She smiled bitterly.

"Poor old Jonah Gates. The virgin virologist."

"SHUT UP!!!" he roared, flying to his feet. He hit her full force in the face. Her head snapped backward and then fell forward. It hung over her chest, unmoving. The blood pounding in his ears and his hands trembling, Jonah gazed at the unconscious form before him. Christ! What had he done???!!!

You lost it, you weakling a voice in his head informed him.

He'd never struck anyone before in his life and now he'd just punched the person he loved more than anything in the world into a coma. Breathing hard, he placed his palms on the table and closed his eyes. Jesus, she hadn't *meant* it! Her goading had been terrible but she'd just been…*releasing*! He should have been man enough to take it, let her have her rant.

He'd made a mistake meeting her so early after Hollywood. Yes, that was it. She clearly wasn't ready and needed more time. Feeling calmer he looked back at his handiwork. He flinched inwardly. There was a thin line of blood on her face, beneath a small cut. Jonah went to the drawers by the sink and took a cloth from one of them. He wetted it with some water from a bottle. He pushed the hair back from her face and wiped the blood gently from her cheek, his heart breaking as he did so. When he was finished he studied the gash on her skin. The flesh around it was going red already. He imagined it would swell terribly, such had been the force of the blow.

He felt depressed and angry. This disaster had happened because of his childish impatience. He went to the sink and poured more water on the cloth. He squeezed it, watching the reddish drops of water that fell from it.

He turned to the inert form again. He tilted the downturned head gently backwards and gazed down at the lovely, damaged face. He bent and kissed her gently on the forehead. He straightened and resumed his stare at her.

Time.

Yes. That was all she needed. She'd lanced the boil, ejected the poison. *Now* the healing could begin. And when she was whole…

He felt his spirits lift. He took the tracker from his pocket and placed it on the table before her. He gathered his things together and loaded them onto the bike. He cut the rope tying Mary's hands and left.

«‹‹—››»

Mary opened her eyes and found herself looking at the tracker. Her brain didn't register the information displayed on the screen however, it was more concerned with her state of well-being, or lack thereof. The entire right side of her head seemed to be pounding in pain. Her right eye wanted to close with the horrible swelling she could feel beneath it. An image flashed in her head of Jonah standing over her and launching his fist at her.

Her left temple was still aching where he'd clobbered her with the shotgun the previous evening. She lifted her head and found that her neck was sore too, presumably after the punch.

The bastard.

She felt like crying. A lump began to rise in her throat and she swallowed it away. She wasn't going to give in to the fucker. She brought her hands before her and gently massaged the chafe marks left by the rope. At least he'd untied her. She looked at the tracker again. The location arrow was pointing a little bit beyond Santa Rosa.

She got to her feet slowly. The effort caused the pain in the right side of her head to strengthen a little. She saw he'd left a half-empty bottle of water by the sink and she drank what remained in it. She walked tentatively to the bathroom. By the time she got there she was in agony, the pain in her head had amplified so much.

The sight in the mirror of the damage he'd done allied with the dreadful pain she was in caused her resolve to crack and a sob escaped her. After allowing a tear or two to fall she swallowed. She steeled herself and took a deep shuddering breath. She needed some painkillers. There was no way she could travel in her state of agony. She saw that the mirror before her was the door of a cabinet and she opened it. Inside was bare except for a nearly empty bottle of mouthwash and some cosmetic items.

She searched a few drawers and presses in the kitchen to no avail. She went upstairs, the effort involved wreaking havoc in her skull. She cursed herself for not having thought to pack any medicine before she'd left Hollywood. After a fruitless search of the upstairs bathroom she went into the room she'd spent the night in and found nothing there either. Dizzy and nauseous with pain she collapsed onto the bed.

She closed her eyes. Eventually the pain abated a little and she drifted off to sleep.

«««—»»»

She woke in the middle of the afternoon. She rose slowly from the bed and went downstairs. She was relieved when the exertion involved only slightly exacerbated her pain situation. The swelling in her face had worsened during her rest, however. She could only open her right eye a little way.

In the kitchen she looked at the tracker. The arrow was pointing at Ukiah, about a hundred miles north of her. She went out to her motorbike and opened one of the saddlebags. Jonah had returned her gun she saw. It lay before her amidst the food cans and packages. She put it in the waistband of her jeans and took some food from the saddlebag. She went back inside and ate. When she was finished her pain was on the ascendency again so she drove down the hill into Sausalito. In the third pharmacy she searched (the first two had been picked clean of everything bar male and female scents) she found some Excedrin. After swallowing three tablets she returned to the house.

A half an hour later, the pills having gone to work, she went out onto the deck. She looked across the bay at the spires of San Francisco. She felt reasonably good, rejuvenated by her sleep earlier, the pain in her head reduced to a bare throb. She didn't want to chance the motorbike on the open road though, not with her eye as bad as it was. And besides, she knew it didn't matter how much ground he put between them. His words echoed in her mind.

You just haven't had enough time.

He was keeping the game going. He'd left her alive with the tracker, and the gun to protect herself as she followed him. Eventually he'd stop and let her catch up again, thinking she'd changed her mind. She'd be smarter next time. She wouldn't meet him with the gun in her hand. She'd smile and charm, put him completely at ease.

She'd put on the performance of her life.

Chapter Fourteen

She rose early the following morning and looked at the tracker. The arrow was pointing at Garberville, where it had stopped moving the previous evening. A distance of nearly two hundred miles. She went to the bathroom and a knot tightened in her stomach at the transformation that had taken place on her face overnight. The huge bruise there had changed from red to a hideous purple. The swelling had receded a little though and she was able to open her right eye a bit more.

She went downstairs and had some food. Afterward she climbed onto the bike and got on her way.

«« — »»

With the trees of Prairie Creek State Park growing thicker on either side of him, Jonah felt a worm of unease coil in his gut as he gripped the bike's handlebars a little tighter. He was thinking of what the drug-head surfer back in Santa Cruz had told him about the group of six that had come down from Seattle through redwood country. According to the surfer only two of them had made it out of this very park, the other four having been "offered to the trees" by some bunch of lunatics.

Well, whether the fantastical tale was true or not Jonah would give any potential aggressors a fight. He had ten rounds in his handgun and he had six shells in the shotgun he'd taken from the house.

The sun disappearing behind the soaring trees, Jonah pressed a little harder on the accelerator.

«« — »»

Darkness was falling as Mary pushed the bike in the front door of a house on the outskirts of Scotia. After having some sustenance she looked at the tracker. He was in Oregon now, in a city called Gold Beach.

«««—»»»

Jonah gazed out the window at the darkening ocean. That stupid fucking surfer. He scolded himself for having been fearful enough to have let the idiot's hallucinations spook him. Outside of a few birds and a fox Jonah hadn't seen a single other living thing in Prairie Creek State Park.

Movement caught the corner of his eye and he saw a seal flopping its way from the water below him onto the sand. When it stopped moving Jonah figured it was going to sleep. He recalled being on the beach one time back in Malibu with his brothers as a boy. They'd spotted two large seals sleeping on the sand and Mark had dared Kelsey to go right up to one of them and pet it. After petting one of them lightly Kelsey had gotten brave and had touched the seal again, letting his hand linger on its body the second time. The other seal had begun barking loudly causing its companion to come similarly to life. The seal Kelsey petted began thrashing its tail, knocking Kelsey to the ground. Luckily Kelsey had rolled out of danger's way before a follow-up sweep of the seal's tail arrived at where his face had been only half a second earlier.

Gazing at the inert form below him on the beach Jonah felt his eyes begin to grow heavy. He thought about Mary and wondered where she was right then. Or more importantly, how she was. He still felt absolutely terrible for what he had done. He'd knocked the love of his life unconscious twice in the space of twenty four hours! In his mind's eye he saw himself striking her face and he cringed inwardly. Christ, but he'd hit her hard. He hoped he hadn't broken her cheekbone. How could he have done something so vicious to something so perfect?

It hadn't even been two days and already he was aching to see her again. How long would he have to wait? A week? Two? He ground his teeth in frustration. The reunion would come, though, and it would be worth every second they had been apart. He would kiss the cheek he'd struck, the temple he'd butted with the shotgun, and apologize profusely, apologize for everything. She'd smile and say it was all ok they were together now, the past was water under the bridge.

He turned from the window and went upstairs. He went into one of the bedrooms and stopped inside the doorway. The curtains were partly open allowing moonlight to spill onto the bed. In the corner of the room furthest from him was a chair. In his mind's eye Jonah saw himself sitting on the chair as he'd done two nights earlier in Sausalito, gazing at Mary in the bed before him.

Jonah went to the chair and sat in it. He kept his eyes on the bed until sleep closed them.

«««—»»»

Late the following morning Mary hit Prairie Creek State Park. When she was about halfway through she came around a bad bend in the road and a huge man in a white cassock stepped out from behind a shrub, a long stick extended before him at the height of Mary's head. Before Mary could do anything the stick collided with her forehead and everything went black.

«««—»»»

When she came to she dimly realized she was draped over someone's shoulder, being carried somewhere. She opened her eyes a crack and saw leaf-strewn ground moving beneath her. She saw the end of a white cassock and then she slipped back into unconsciousness.

«««—»»»

When she rejoined the world for a second time the first thing that greeted her was the sound of desperate pleading.

"No, no! *Please!*" a man was shouting. "Please, *NO!*"

She was lying on the ground. And there was a smell of something like rotten meat. She opened her eyes.

"Don't move."

She looked up to see a woman standing over her. In the woman's hand was Mary's gun which she was pointing directly at her. The woman was wearing a white cassock like the man who had knocked her from the bike. Mary turned her head in the direction of the pleading. She saw the terrified figure of a naked man, his arms being held by two men in cassocks. Facing the naked man was a long-haired similarly cassocked man, a blood-stained knife in his hand. There were splashes of blood on his cassock. Flanking him at either side were two more robed figures, a man and a woman. Both were pointing guns at the naked man. Behind them was a titan of a tree. Mary could see the source of the foul smell. A sizeable portion of the tree's trunk at person-level was covered in blood, most of it dried, some fresh. Flies buzzed about the large red blotch. On the ground at one side of the tree lay the naked body of a teenage boy, his limbs splayed haphazardly. His mouth was slightly open as were his eyes which stared softly at some point in the trees above him. A wide blood trail led from his slashed neck to his groin. His legs were coated in red. At either side of his genitalia there were also knife-wounds. Not far from his resting place stood three more cassocked figures observing the current proceedings.

"Please!" the naked man implored, crying now. "I'm *begging* you! *PLEASE!*"

The knife-man turned and faced the tree. He stretched his arms out at his sides. Her wits beginning to return to her Mary figured she was witnessing some sort of demented cult ritual.

"Great Iluvatar," the knife-wielder said over the naked man's hysterical supplications. "Supreme lord of the grove. Please accept our second offering of this day to you…"

Mary saw that the naked man was urinating, his legs trembling in terror.

"…may you draw strength from it as we draw strength from you on this the ninety-fifth day of the new time."

The knife-wielder bowed his head at the tree, all the other cassocked-figures doing likewise. Then he turned and stepped toward his intended victim.

"*NO!*" the naked man hollered. "*NO!*"

The knife arced once, twice.

The sacrifice's head flashed up toward the sky, his face a rictus of agony.

"*AAAHHHH!*" he roared, twin fonts of blood pumping rhythmically from his severed femoral arteries. "*AAAAHH—*"

The blade whipped across his throat and his second cry was cut short, abruptly becoming a strangled, gasping sound. A crimson flood rushed from the huge gash down along his body. The knife and gun-wielders moved sideways and the men holding the quivering, hemorrhaging victim dragged the body quickly to the tree. Two of the observers standing by the body of the dead boy rushed forward to help and the four-person team pressed the naked form against the tree trunk.

A gunshot sounded and the woman standing over Mary flew backward and collapsed to the ground. Two more shots rang out in quick succession and the two other gun-wielding cassocks went down. The quad pressing the naked man against the trunk abruptly abandoned their duty and stepped back from the tree. The blood-drenched sacrifice tumbled limply to the ground convulsing in his final death-spasms, the crimson jets from his femoral arteries now not much more than feeble spurts.

Mary saw a man approaching, a gun in his hands. He moved calmly and efficiently, a business-like look in his eyes. There was a rustling sound and the man's gaze flashed to his right where Mary saw a male cassocked figure fleeing the scene as fast as he could run. Nearby movement caught the corner of her eye and she looked up to see one of the cult members, a female, bending to pick one of the fallen guns from the ground. A shot rang out and the woman flew to the ground.

"Nobody moves," the new arrival ordered, drawing slowly closer, his eyes fixed on the cassocks.

Mary heard what sounded like a branch breaking and in the distance saw the fleeing cult member still racing away through the trees.

The gunman had obviously decided he was not a threat. Her gaze returning to her immediate vicinity Mary saw that the naked man was still, his sufferings at an end.

"You."

The gunman was pointing at her, his eyes still upon the cassocks.

"Collect the guns."

She began to rise to her feet. When she was semi-erect she hissed through clenched teeth as a bolt of pain flashed at the front of her skull.

"You ok?" she heard the gunman ask as she put a hand to her forehead. She flinched. There was a large bruise there courtesy of the crazy shithead who had clubbed her from her bike.

"Yeah," she said, and got moving. She retrieved her own gun first, returning it to its place in the waistband of her jeans. She then picked up the cassocks' weapons and walked toward the gunman with them, one in each hand.

"Put them in my bag," he said without looking at her.

Mary went to the bag on the man's back and put the guns inside. A wave of dizziness hit her and she staggered backward a little before regaining her footing.

"We're leaving now," the gunman said to the cassocks. "If anybody attempts to come after us, you're dead."

The cassocks regarded him silently.

"Go."

There was a rough trail behind the gunman and Mary began walking quickly on it. She could hear the gunman following her. On their way to the road she had two more dizzy spells which caused her to fall on both occasions. The gunman helped her to her feet each time. When they got to the road he looked up ahead to his left.

"That your bike?"

Mary looked in the direction of his gaze.

"Yeah."

Her bike was a little way up ahead on the opposite side of the road. It lay on its side at the base of a tree.

"Come on."

Her companion began jogging toward the fallen vehicle, Mary following after him.

"Quick," the gunman said when they arrived at the bike. "See if it starts." He turned and faced the woods they'd emerged from, scanning the trees. "I wanna' put some distance between us and those nutjobs."

You and me both, Mary thought. She felt strange, almost ethereal. Shock, she supposed. She still could hardly believe what she'd seen in the woods. Had the insane slaughter *really* happened? Well, the pounding in her forehead told her it had been real. And there were blood droplets on her jeans that hadn't been there earlier. She supposed they'd come from the woman who'd been guarding her when her rescuer had shot her.

Mary erected the bike. Apart from two dents on the exhaust pipe and a few tears on the seat the only other damage appeared to be scratches. One of the saddlebags had come free—it lay open on its side halfway down an incline on her right, its contents spilled about.

She turned the key in the bike's ignition and the engine caught. She turned to see the gunman walking toward her. She cocked her head in the direction of the stray saddlebag.

"I'm going to pick up this stuff-."

"Yeah, go on," he interrupted. "Make it quick."

She scooted down the incline and began gathering up the scattered food cans and water bottles. When she thought she had everything returned to the bag she scanned around to make sure she'd left nothing behind.

"Come on!" her companion called.

Spotting a bag of peanuts at the edge of a nearby stream she ran to it. She bent and picked the bag up and paused halfway through the act of standing up. At the other side of the stream were the shriveled remains of a child, a few strips of mostly-decayed flesh clinging to the small skeleton. Below the ribcage was an assortment of random items—a plastic pen cover, an elastic band, two batteries and some stones.

"Come *on*!" the gunman re-iterated, more urgency in his tone this time. "We gotta' *go*!"

Mary turned and went back up the slope. She returned the peanuts to the saddlebag. Continuing on her way up the slope, saddlebag in hand, she saw that the gunman was on the driver's seat of the bike. He was scanning the woods across the road. He turned to face her as she arrived at his side. She staggered as a spell of lightheadedness hit her. He reached out and grabbed her arm to prevent her from falling.

"Gimme the bag," he said when she was steady again.

She handed the saddlebag to him.

He tied the saddlebag into position quickly, glancing across the road occasionally as he did so. She saw that his own bag was on the ground. When he had the saddlebag secured he nodded at the passenger seat.

"Climb on."

She got on the bike. He lifted his bag from the ground.

"I need you to carry this."

He held the bag behind her and she put her arms through the loops. It was heavy but not too weighty.

"Hold on to me tightly in case you get dizzy again," he said. "I don't want you falling off."

She wrapped her arms around his waist and they pulled out onto the road.

《《《—》》》

A few minutes after they'd crossed the Klamath River Mary saw a rest area with some picnic tables and she asked her companion to pull over. Her head was killing her and she needed to take some pills for it. He obliged.

She sat at one of the tables chewing on some Excedrin, one hand supporting her pounding skull. Not only was her forehead thumping but the blow she had received seemed to have woken up the injuries that Jonah had inflicted upon her. Her cheek and temple were now aching in sync with the latest addition to the party.

"Hey."

She looked sideways and saw a bottle of water in the man's extended hand. She took it and drank, washing the Excedrin down. She closed her eyes and put her hand to her head again.

"You feeling really bad?"

She nodded slowly.

"Lie down for a while."

She exhaled loudly through her nose. That sounded like a good idea. She drank a little more water and then she laid down on the bench, her knees raised on its meagre length. She closed her eyes and waited for the Excedrin to kick in. She listened to the man as he alternated between walking about, opening food wrappers and clicking guns. Eventually her pains began to soften and she opened her eyes.

Her companion was leaning against the bike, peeling an orange. She studied him properly for the first time. He was of average height with short hair and a well-muscled physique. He had a short scar on his right cheek. She could see part of a tattoo on his forearm beyond the end of his sleeve. He looked young, in his mid-twenties at the most.

"Thanks for saving my life."

"You're welcome," he replied without looking up from the orange. After he removed the last bit of peel he began walking toward her, splitting the orange in two as he approached.

"Here."

Mary sat up and took the half-orange from his outstretched hand. "Thanks," she said. She pulled off a section of the orange and put it in her mouth.

"The head a bit better?"

Chewing, she nodded.

"You hurt yourself when you fell off the bike?"

"I didn't fall. One of those freaks knocked me off of it with a club." She looked up at him, pointing at her forehead.

"Fuck."

"Does it look bad?"

"Not now. But I won't lie to you. It won't look pretty tomorrow." His eyes dropped a little. "You've really been in the wars, haven't you? What happened your face?"

She lowered her head. "Don't ask."

A silence descended between them. The man's open hand entered Mary's field of vision.

"Gary Streth. Pleased to meet you."

She took his hand and they shook.

"Mary Leydon. Nice to meet you, Gary."

He studied her, a thoughtful expression on his face.

"You're a movie actress, aren't you?"

"I used to be."

"You were in a film a couple of years ago set on a submarine…"

"The War Beneath."

"Ah, yeah."

"What did you think of it?"

"I thought it was good."

"Good."

"I went to see it with a couple of submarine sailors actually."

"What did they think of it?"

"They spent most of the movie saying how crappy it was that the Navy didn't have more women that looked like you."

Mary chuckled and ate another piece of her orange.

"You handled it well back there," she said.

When she got no response she looked up, her eyes coming to rest on the half-concealed tattoo on his arm. Now that Gary was closer she could see a knife blade and boat oar emerging at forty five degree angles from what looked like the jaw of a skull.

"That an army tattoo?"

He pulled his sleeve up a little bit to reveal the remainder of the tattoo. It was indeed a skull, with black orbs for eyes and wings protruding from both sides of it.

"Recon Marine," he said.

Silence descended again as they picked at their oranges.

"I didn't see you on the road," Mary said.

"I was in the woods getting some water from a stream. When I heard you crash I ran to the scene. I must have got there in thirty seconds and when I saw no one I thought it was a bit weird. I was thinking you hardly got to your feet and started walking *that* quickly. Then I saw that path leading from the road and…I don't know, I…just got a bad feeling. I followed it and well…I was right."

Neither of them said anything for a while.

"What the hell *were* they?" Mary asked.

Gary shook his head a little.

"Some sort of crazy fucked-up cult I guess. Nothing like the end of the world to bring these freaks out of the woodwork."

Mary let her eyes fall to the ground. And then like a hammer, it hit her.

I came within minutes of being stripped and slashed to death.

While a horrible heat swelled inside her images flashed at speed in her head. She saw herself being held before the long-haired knife-man, his eyes empty of charity or mercy…her face contorted in agony after her femoral arteries had been opened…being flung against the stinking, red-daubed tree trunk, her own blood now being added to the life-fluid of past victims…her dead, crimson-streaked body lying on the ground by those of the teenage boy and the man who had been offered up before her…

Her heart was racing and her hands trembled uncontrollably. Feeling sick, she breathed deeply.

"You ok?" Gary asked.

"No, I…" She trailed off, unable to say any more.

"It's delayed reaction. It'll pass. Lie down again for a while."

She did as he suggested and gazed up at the cloud-wisped sky, waiting for the horrible feeling of dread to leave her. Eventually her heart began to slow and the nausea lifted but it was a long time before her hands stopped shaking.

«««—»»»

Gary had been serving in Pakistan at the time of the outbreak. As the disease had intensified and the authorities had begun to speculate that Mouther was an act of terror, he'd been drafted into a high-level intel unit, operating in the most dangerous corners of Pakistan's tribal areas. His team had spent two months pressing and squeezing and had come up with nothing. At that point, with the situation on home soil beginning to implode he was shipped to L.A. to help with law enforcement there. At that stage he'd still been in contact with his wife Celia and daughter Maggie who had fled north to Canada before the Canadians had initiated their deadly Operation Seal House all along the border. A few weeks later the phones had gone down and a little after that the internet. He hadn't spoken to or heard from his family in nearly two months. He'd stayed in L.A. until there had been nothing left to police. After that he and the few remaining peacekeepers had gone their separate ways in the hope of finding their loved ones still alive. Gary was now headed for Kamloops in British Colombia which was where Celia and Maggie had been the last time he'd heard from them.

"So," he said. "What's *your* story?"

Gazing at the slowly rising hill across the road, Mary exhaled loudly. She was glad he had asked her. She realized she needed to share her tale with someone. She'd hardly scratched the surface of it back in Buttonwillow with Gerald.

"Some of this…" she began, "…is going to be kind of hard to believe."

"Lady, if someone had told me six months ago that the world was about to end, I wouldn't have believed it," Gary said. "So…try me."

"Ok."

《《——》》

After she finished he remained silent for what seemed like an age.

"That *is* quite a story," he eventually said. Then in a gentle, respectful tone he added "I'm sorry about your husband and child."

"Thank you."

He snorted, shaking his head in disbelief.

"Christ. One of our own." He paused. "One of our own. Seven billion people." His face softened a little. "And the reason I don't know if my wife and kid are-."

Gary cleared his throat and blinked the toughness back into his expression.

"And he did it all for you."

"Yeah," Mary said bleakly. "I'm sorry."

"*Fuck* that. You've got nothing to be sorry about. This guy's a sick puppy. The world's full of them, and I've seen *so* many of them. Guess one of them was bound to bring the house down eventually. It's a miracle we actually lasted this long."

He went silent for a few seconds, his eyes going to the trees behind the picnic table. He looked back at Mary again.

"And when you find him you're going to put him away."

"Yeah."

Gary nodded slowly.

"I'll be your wingman. Keep you safe on the way. And when it's done, you come with me to Canada. Help me find my family."

Mary nodded. "Deal."

A faint grin rose in Gary's features. It was a nice grin Mary couldn't help but notice, and she imagined it had won him a lot of female attention over the years.

He extended his hand. "Shake on it."

Mary took his hand and they shook.

"So," he said. "Where's the asshole now?"

Mary took out the tracker.

《《——》》》

On the outskirts of Brookings they came across a Harley Davidson lying in the middle of the road. With Mary feeling capable of driving again Gary mounted the Harley and they continued on, Gary leading the way. Mary liked having him ahead of her. It made her feel safe. She hadn't felt protected since before Lowell had gotten sick and she hadn't realized how much she missed that feeling. She was an old-fashioned girl. It was good to have a man around again.

《《《——》》》

That evening as they sat down to eat in Gold Beach Mary looked at the tracker.

"Well?" Gary asked in between bites of canned tuna.

"He's in Waldport."

"How long do you think it'll be before he stops?"

"A couple of days max. He won't be able to hold out much longer. He needs to see me."

After eating they went to their bedrooms. As Mary waited for sleep to come it proved difficult to keep what had happened in the woods from her mind. Eventually exhaustion won the day and painted the images black.

《《《——》》》

She dreamed that she woke in the middle of the night and went to the bathroom. When she went back to the bedroom she opened the door to find a group of cassocked figures staring at her from the far side of the bed, their expressionless faces bathed in moonlight. Standing in the middle of them was the knife-man, blade in hand, his robe streaked with blood.

She started awake and lifted herself upright against the headboard. Shaking, her heart pounding in her chest, she looked frantically around the room. It was too dark to see anything. She almost fell upon exiting the bed and ran for the door. When she was outside the room she banged the door shut and stood back from it. Her breath coming in quick, long gasps she stared at the doorknob, waiting in terror for it to start turning. Eventually rationality came to the fore and her fear abated.

She stared at the knob for a few more seconds before turning toward Gary's room. She quietly opened the door and went inside. She closed the door and climbed into bed alongside him. She heard him shift slightly.

"Hey," he said in a sleep-filled voice.

"Hey. Is it ok if I stay here for the night?"

"Sure. You ok?"

"Yeah. Just had some bad dreams. Sorry I woke you."

"'S ok."

He said no more. She listened to his breathing grow more rhythmic. She found herself remembering the nights lying next to Lowell back in Hollywood in the early weeks of the virus. He would always fall asleep before her while she lay awake, staring at the ceiling, worrying. She would stroke her stomach, fearful for the child growing inside her, the fear growing in tandem with her baby.

She laid her hand on her belly where there was nothing now, the life having been torn from there by Jonah Gates. Rage filled her and she clasped her t-shirt tightly in her grasp. To calm herself she focused on Gary's breathing again. Its peaceful repetition dissolved her anger, giving her solace. Eventually sleep came.

Chapter Fifteen

In the morning they found bathing suits in the drawers and went for a swim in the ocean. The waves were big, the water cold and invigorating. She dived beneath a wave and felt its shockwave against her legs as it crashed behind her. It was interesting, the way the ocean carried on about its business, not bothered by the fate that had recently befallen the human race. It would go on hammering away at the land, disciplined and uncaring.

When they got back to the house they saw that Jonah had left Waldport and was headed inland. They had breakfast and got on the road.

«««—»»»

In the evening they stopped at Corvallis, a couple of miles from the interstate. Jonah had joined the interstate that morning and it looked like he hadn't had any serious congestion problems on it as the arrow on the tracker screen now pointed at Mount Vista, about fifteen miles north of Portland.

After eating they went upstairs. Mary didn't go to a room of her own, she simply followed Gary into his and he acted as though he had expected it. It happened quite naturally. In bed she snuggled up against his shoulder and placed her arm on his chest, savoring his warmth. He gently stroked her arm for a while and then he turned toward her and kissed her. The kisses grew hungry quickly and they undressed. The feeling of him inside her was beautiful, made all the more exquisite by its momentary washing away of the hell of the previous few months.

Afterward, it went like the previous night. His breathing lulled her to sleep once more.

«««—»»»

When she woke in the morning she found herself alone in the room. She dressed and went downstairs. She entered the kitchen to find Gary with his back to her, a hand resting on either side of the sink. His head hung low on his shoulders.

"Gary?"

He didn't respond or move.

"Gary?" she asked as she moved toward him. "You ok?"

She arrived beside him. His eyes were wet.

"That skeleton in the woods the other day," he said, not raising his head. "The kid."

So he had seen it.

"L.A. was tearing itself apart when my unit arrived from Pakistan. Looting, killing, raping…chaos. We were drafted in to boost the morale of local law enforcement, keep them from throwing in the towel. Me and my boys were the tough guys. We'd seen some awful things in Pakistan…we'd *done* some awful things there…we were supposed to be the rock in the defense. Nothing was supposed to faze us. And the violence didn't. We were able for that." He paused. "What we weren't able for was the kids. Seeing the effects of the virus in them. Seeing them drifting around with their empty eyes and sweaty faces…licking their toys instead of playing with them…seeing them in the playgrounds biting the swings and the merry-go-rounds…One day in Inglewood we had a roadblock up to stop these guys who were coming our way in a truck. The truck was full of women they'd snatched up off of the street. As the truck was coming toward us we told them to stop but they just kept on going. We opened fire and killed the two guys in the cab. When the truck finally stopped three more guys jumped out of the back and started shooting at us. We killed them too. We could hear the girls in the back of the truck trying to scream through the gags in their mouths." He paused again. "And none of it *got* to me. But what will never leave me…what will haunt me to my dying day…was this little girl standing on the sidewalk. She wasn't looking at the bodies on the street or at the truck. She had a bicycle chain draped around her neck like a necklace. Her t-shirt was smeared with oil from it. There was oil on her face too. She was running her tongue slowly along the chain links. Every now and then she'd bite down on it."

A knot of desolation tightened in Mary's gut. She closed her eyes briefly before opening them again.

Gary took a deep breath and continued.

"I saw my first child killing about a week after I arrived in the city. A mother and her daughter were out on the balcony of their apartment. The girl had a small dog in her arms. She was licking its ear over and over. Her mother was watching, crying. She took the dog from her daughter and put it on the ground. Then she lifted her daughter out over the balcony and let go."

Mary put a hand to her mouth to stifle an involuntary cry.

"We saw more and more killings as the time went by. Most of the time the parents would kill themselves too. Our numbers started to thin. Guys just couldn't take seeing that kinda' stuff. They just…disappeared in the quiet. Left without telling anyone. A couple committed suicide."

Mary saw Gary's lip begin to tremble.

"Killing your own offspring is the most unnatural thing in the world," he said. "But God help me…I…I think they were right! I think that if I'd seen Maggie getting sick…I'd have done it too."

He looked up at her, his chin shaking, his eyes full of tears.

Mary went to him and took him in her arms.

《《——》》

They had a straightforward run on the interstate until they were approaching downtown Portland. The congestion was nothing like what Mary had experienced on the Golden Gate but it slowed them nonetheless. It started to rain lightly as they approached the Willamette River. By the time they'd crossed the Marquam Bridge it was teeming down.

They were passing between a semi and a pickup when three men in military fatigues stepped out from in front of the semi's cab, blocking their path. Two of the men were pointing handguns in their direction while one had a shotgun.

"Get offa' the bikes and put your hands in the air," one of them, a tall thin man with red hair, ordered.

Mary and Gary killed their engines and did as they'd been told.

"I'm in the service," Gary said.

"Oh?" the redhead asked, a look of sarcastic interest on his face.

"Yeah. Recon Marine."

"Good for you," the redhead said. "Hank, take our...*colleague's* gun and his backpack."

The shotgun-carrying man went to Gary and took his gun from its holster.

"Let your arms down," Hank said. "Slowly. And don't try anything."

Gary lowered his arms and Hank removed the backpack. Hank walked back to his earlier position beside the redhead, deposited the backpack on the ground and trained his shotgun on Gary once more.

"Jeff," the redhead said, "disarm this—" he ran his eyes up and down along Mary's frame "—*fine* lady." The redhead looked back at Gary again wearing a slit-eyed, challenging grin.

The man who had his gun pointed at Mary smiled nastily at her. "My *pleasure*," he said in an ugly tone and went to her. He took her gun from her waistband and put it in his own.

"I'm going to frisk her," he said, his eyes fixed on Mary's, his unpleasant grin returning to his features. "She looks like she could be a sneaky one."

"Enjoy yourself!" the redhead said.

"Oh, I will," Jeff said in a low voice full of intent.

He bent and began patting both sides of Mary's right leg from her foot up. When he came to her crotch he probed around roughly against the denim of her jeans until he found what he was looking for. He pressed his index and middle finger hard against it. Mary ground her teeth in pain and disgust. Jeff's dreadful grin widened.

"Am I going to enjoy sticking my dick in *this*," he said, his eyes locked on Mary's.

"Now, now Jeff," the redhead said, smiling. "Don't be getting too enthusiastic with our new lady friend!"

"Yeah," Hank said. "Plenty time for that later."

What happened next took place in seconds.

A small knife appeared in the redhead's throat. His left hand flew to the blade. His eyes wide and his mouth open, he staggered backward against the back of a van. His gun fired harmlessly into the sky. Mary looked across at Gary. She saw him dive between two cars as a deafening shot rang out from Hank's shotgun.

Mary took it as her cue to act. In a flash she grabbed her gun from Jeff's pants and shot him in the chest. He flew backward against an SUV and tumbled lifelessly to the ground. She pointed her gun at Hank just in time to see him turning his shotgun toward her. She fired twice and he collapsed to the road.

She looked at the redhead. He was still alive but wouldn't be for long. He was on the ground, his back against the van he had fallen against. His fingers were trembling on the rain-drenched ground at either side of him. His rapidly-blinking eyes were staring at some point back the way Mary and Gary had come. Blood pulsed in thin jets from his severed carotid artery, the knife still implanted in the wound.

Mary's eyes flashed to Gary. A hot ball of dread flared in her gut when she saw him lying unmoving on the ground.

"Gary!"

She received no response.

She ran to him. He was on his back, a hand on his side just beneath his chest. His fingers were bloody against a gunshot wound. His eyes were gazing weakly at the sky. Mary ran to his backpack and frantically opened the pocket that he kept some basic medical supplies in. She took out a bandage roll and scissors. She opened out a long section of roll and cut it. She balled up the section she'd cut and ran back to Gary. She knelt beside him.

"Gary, we need to stop the bleeding so I'm going to press down with this, ok? It might hurt a bit."

She took his hand from the wound and pressed down with the wad of bandages. There was a lot of blood. He let off a terrible moan that made her flinch inwardly. She saw that there was some blood beneath him. She took his hand and pressed it on the bandages.

"I need you to keep pressure on this Gary, ok? I need to lift you up a little to get a look at your back."

He moaned.

She put her hands underneath him and lifted. Her heart sank when she saw the blood pouring from the chestnut-sized exit wound in his back. Demoralized, she laid him back down on the red asphalt. His eyes already looked weaker and his face was pale. She got to her feet and went to the backpack again. She cut off a larger wad of bandages.

When she got back to him she stood looking down. Gary's hand had fallen from his chest and now lay unmoving at his side. His chest was still. Mary got down on her knees and put a hand to his face. It was cold. She gently closed his eyes before closing her own. She cried for a while, hardly feeling the rain hammering down on her.

She took off her jacket and covered Gary's face with it. She rose and went to his backpack. She put it on and got on her bike. She started the engine and got moving.

«««—»»»

She woke in the morning with a sore throat, no doubt after the drowning she'd endured the previous evening. She looked at the tracker. Jonah was north of Seattle, on the move already. She had some breakfast and left Portland.

«««—»»»

She felt the first tremor when she was negotiating her way through congestion a few miles south of SeaTac. Having lived in L.A. for nearly nine years and being used to its moody ground she thought nothing of it.

The second one struck when she could see the spires of Downtown Seattle in the distance. It was stronger than the first and caused the few vehicles on the road around her to vibrate. She stopped the bike at more or less the same time that the shaking stopped. She waited a while, the engine idling, her feet planted firmly on the ground on both sides of the bike. Eventually she drove on.

A few minutes later the third one hit. It was worryingly strong, causing a truck a little way in front of her to sway alarmingly. When it stopped she was very relieved, her heart pounding and her hands trembling on the handlebars. She was just about to drive on when the shaking started again, powerful and sustained this time. Cracks appeared in the asphalt and in the concrete divider at the center of the interstate. The truck tipped over with a deafening crash. Cracks appeared on the guardrail to her right.

She stepped on the gas. The part of the interstate she was on was elevated on supports and she didn't want to be there if the supports gave. She saw an off ramp and took it. When she reached the bottom of it she found herself on a road with industrial buildings on either side of it. She stopped in the middle of the road, thinking it the safest place to be. She watched as bits of the buildings around her caved in and their windows shattered.

Eventually the earthquake stopped. An eerie silence followed. Movement caught the corner of her eye and she looked up to see a huge slab of the interstate guardrail heading for the ground. It crashed onto the road below it with a loud DHOOM.

She could hear things moving in the distance ahead of her, in the bay direction. What sounded like large things. A lot of clattering and groaning metal. A soft breeze began to blow against her face. A knot tightened in her stomach. There was something wrong with this breeze she knew, something ominous in its suddenness. And then the wind's maker revealed itself.

A wall of water was surging along the road toward her. In its midst was every manner of item: cars, boats, timber, iron, bits of buildings. With the speed it was approaching at Mary doubted she could outrun the tsunami. She turned and drove back up the off ramp. It was in a bad state, with cracks and gaps everywhere on the asphalt. The guardrails were badly cracked too. Her progress up along it was labored.

The breeze was cold and strong now. The noise of the wave was growing louder as it neared, a rising rumbling thunder. The off ramp was shaking dully. For a brief moment she wondered was it an aftershock but she knew it wasn't. It was the signature of the approaching juggernaut. As she maneuvered around two mini-crevasses in the asphalt Mary could feel panic threatening to engulf her. With the shape the off ramp was in she doubted it would survive the wave's impact.

She reached the interstate. Two seconds later the tsunami roared beneath her. The off ramp disintegrated and was swept away in the galloping deluge. Mary drove on, moving as fast as she could along the gapped and fissured surface. She didn't know how badly damaged the interstate supports had been in the earthquake and if they'd be able to withstand the force of the flood for long. She wanted to get onto solid ground as soon as possible, the higher the better.

About a mile further on, with the buffer of the Downtown towers between her and the bay she felt safe enough to stop. She looked back the way she'd come. There was a gap in the interstate at one side of which a large ragged slab of asphalt hung at an angle from the road just over the rushing torrent. The water was almost at the top of the supporting columns. Boats and cars bobbed about against the guardrail on the bay side. She heard a faint bang as a shipping container struck the guardrail. A few seconds later a section of the interstate on the far side of the gap gave up the ghost and parted company with the rest, falling slowly sideways under the water.

And then she noticed it. The lack of noise. Human noise. No warning sirens, no alarms, no roaring or crying or the sound of engines scrambling for safety. The irony of it all. Seattle had been expecting an earthquake for years and it had waited until now to strike, a disaster in a dead city. She drove on.

«««—»»»

She lay in bed shivering. She felt bad, her sore throat having worsened during the day. She sneezed. She missed Gary terribly and wished his reassuring warmth were beside her in the cold bed. The day and a half on the road since his death had been hard going. At times she'd yearned for his company in the solitude.

It had all happened so fast. One minute he'd been beside her in the rain and then a few minutes later she'd been continuing on her way along the freeway through the congestion on her own. And he'd saved her again. And who knew, maybe it had been from a fate even worse than death this time. She didn't want to think about what the three soldiers had had intended for her.

Yes Gary had been a good man alright. Strong, fearless, kind. The direct opposite of the monster who was responsible for his death. She'd checked the tracker before getting into bed. Jonah was in Vancouver. Their little conversation in Sausalito had been five days previous. She figured he'd stop moving any day now.

The sooner the better. She had a little present that she'd taken from a corpse outside SeaTac, not long before the first earthquake tremor. And she was looking forward to giving it to him.

Chapter Sixteen

She woke early the following morning, her cold still with her but mercifully no worse than the previous night. The first few miles of her journey were grim. The tsunami had inundated the land north of Seattle too. Boats of all shapes and size were scattered about in waterlogged fields and roads. In a scene that wouldn't have looked astray in a surrealist painting she saw a small fishing trawler perched perfectly atop an upside-down sedan. She came across a few boats on the freeway, even a mini-yacht. Her progress was hampered by all manner of other objects including trees, chunks of masonry and the occasional large dead animal. Mercifully the freeway itself had survived the calamity relatively intact. Pieces of it were missing here and there but no sections of it had been eliminated like she'd seen back in Seattle.

There was a macabre side to the catastrophe. Everywhere, in the fields and roads and lying in the shallow ponds and lakes left behind by the wave there were leathery skeletons, the last remnants of flesh on them being picked at by crows.

«««—»»»

She stopped for some food outside Everett. The land around her was dry, the areal extent of the disaster having expired a few miles behind her. She checked the tracker. The arrow was still pointing at Vancouver. She let out a long breath. So today would be the day. Good. She took a drink of water and moved on.

«««—»»»

She'd expected the border to be bad, very bad even, but nothing could have prepared her for the scale of what she came across. Gary had told her that the Canadian Operation Seal House had been fairly furious but Mary hadn't been expecting the scale of Armageddon she came across between the town of Blaine and Canadian soil. Abandoned, crashed and burnt out military vehicles lay interspersed with all manner of civilian transportation. There were jeeps, APCs, army trucks, tanks, and helicopters, their rotor blades creaking forlornly in the sea breeze. The tide was out on the beach to her left revealing a grim spectacle. She saw the remains of two fighter jets there, their crippled forms festooned with seaweed. Around the deep holes in the sand which she presumed were bomb craters were hundreds of skeletons. As there were all around her now. She was in the midst of a charnel house.

With her way ahead blocked by destruction she turned and went back into Blaine. She made her way across town to the road that trucks had to use to enter Canada. There the same scenes of carnage greeted her. There was a wooded area to the left of the road and she decided to try this. She drove onto the grass and proceeded cautiously, not wanting to get stuck. With the ground proving solid beneath her she sped up a little as she headed for the trees. Upon entering the wood she slowed down again. It was dark and horrible, with carcasses everywhere. All manner of weaponry lay scattered about. After a while she saw light beginning to grow stronger between the distant trees. She was relieved at the prospect of emerging from this murky battleground.

She emerged from the trees onto soil that was bare except for tufts of grass here and there. She stopped the bike. On the earthen strip on either side of her were uprooted and half-uprooted trees. Some of them had very little foliage on them and some were little more than trunks. The reason for the disturbance lay directly before her. She drove forward a little. A few feet from its edge she stopped, the bike's engine idling beneath her. She gazed at the vast bomb crater. All around it, like a corona, the earthen strip she was on continued. She guessed the hole was a hundred meters in circumference at least. She estimated that its depth to the surface of the water it contained was probably a hundred feet and more. Little wavelets rippled on the surface of the mini-lake far below her. Toward the far side of the trough the tail of a helicopter peeked above the water. A bird was standing on one of its rotor blades.

After a while Mary got moving. She drove slowly all the way around the crater and then she re-entered the trees at the far side.

«««—»»»

The rest of the journey to Vancouver was uneventful. When she reached the city's outskirts she looked at the tracker. He was in Stanley Park. She sneezed twice and swallowed. Her throat felt a little sorer than it had been earlier in the morning. She put away the tracker and drove on.

«««—»»»

The arrow was pointing right at the tip of the park, at the Prospect Point viewing area. She parked her bike by a tourist cafe at the beginning of the trail that led out to the viewing area. She took her gun from her jeans and put it in one of the saddlebags. She began walking along the trail. She called out before she saw him, her arms raised in the air.

"Jonah! It's me. I'm not armed."

She slowed her walk.

He appeared in the viewing area, his gun pointed at her. He kept it trained on her for a little while before eventually lowering it and putting it away.

She put her hands down and stopped before him. His face bore a contrite expression.

"I'm sorry for what I did to you back in Sausalito."

"It's ok. I said some terrible things. I'm sorry too."

He nodded, a faint smile on his lips.

"What happened your forehead?"

"Just some trouble on the road."

Jonah remained silent as though he were expecting some further elaboration. When none was forthcoming he spoke again.

"I met a guy this morning and he told me there'd been an earthquake in Seattle. A bad one."

"Yeah. I was right in the middle of it. It was pretty scary."

"It's great to see you safe and sound."

Mary smiled.

"Fate, I guess."

"I guess."

They gazed at each other, their eyes locked. He broke contact first, turning his head to the left.

"It's beautiful, isn't it?"

It certainly was. They were looking out over Burrard Inlet, with North Vancouver facing them from across the water. Behind the tall buildings at shore level, lovely wooded residential areas rose gently upward into the North Slope Mountains. Mary wondered how many people were dead over there, murdered by the man before her, nothing but bones now in their own homes.

Jonah began walking toward the edge of the viewing area.

"I'm staying in a house over there," he said.

She walked to him and stopped by his side, the two of them looking across the inlet.

"It's correct name is Unity."

She looked across at him.

"The virus," he continued, still facing straight ahead. "I originally designed it for terrorists. They called it Retribution. The world called it—" his face wrinkled a little in distaste, "—*Mouther*. But its real name...*my* name for it...was Unity. I called it that because that was what it *was*, Mary. A means of bringing us together. And of wiping away the old world."

He turned to face her.

"I couldn't bear to think that he had you. That you were his completely. I had to do it. And you *know* that it's worked out for the best. You *know* we were always meant for each other."

When she responded she did so in a quiet, earnest tone.

"Yes. I know that now."

She moved closer to him, her eyes fixed on his. She put her hands around his neck and gently pulled his head down toward hers. Their lips met and they began to kiss. He moved closer to her until their bodies were touching. He put his hands on her back and pulled her closer still. He was in heaven! He had waited so long for this moment.

Something was wrong. There was only one hand on the back of his neck.

He opened his eyes and looked down to see her right hand emerge from behind her back holding a knife. He grabbed her forearm just as she thrust the knife toward his stomach. The blade stopped about an inch from his body and vibrated in the air as they struggled, she pushing forward, he doing the opposite.

"AA*AAAAHHHH*!!!!!" she roared as he began to gain the upper hand, the blade moving slowly backward.

With her other hand she made a grab for his gun. He clamped his hand down on hers as she went to pull the gun from its holster. He brought his knee up into her stomach.

"Wuuh!" she gasped and slouched over.

He pushed her away from him, too hard. She careened backward, her foot catching against a tree root. She fell and her momentum carried her over the edge of the steep slope at the front of the unguarded viewing area. He raced forward. He watched as she rolled down the slope, colliding with the occasional grassy rock before eventually coming to rest on an embankment about thirty feet below.

He watched as she lay still on her side. He dimly registered the rain as it began to fall. Eventually he saw a leg move. He took out his gun and pointed it downward. He put his finger on the trigger. The seconds passed and his hand holding the gun began to shake. He turned and walked away quickly.

《《—》》

Three-quarters of the way up the slope a rock she was holding onto came free from the earth and tumbled away beside her. She began to slide downward. She clawed desperately at the slope for purchase. When she finally stopped moving she looked upward and saw she'd lost five or six feet at least. Her hands were burning and bleeding after the mad scramble against stones and rocks. She was exhausted and soaked to the skin and the rain showed no sign of letting up. She was seized by a coughing fit. When it finally passed she rested her forehead against the earth, waiting to get her breath back. She felt slightly sick. She closed her eyes and immediately wished she hadn't.

In the blackness she saw herself kissing Jonah and she could almost feel his arousal against her. It was too much. She turned her head sideways and vomited weakly. She placed her forehead against the slope again, feeling the trickles of water flowing down along her face. She felt close to despair. She'd come so close to finishing it. So close. But instead she'd ended up a bruised wreck at the bottom of a cliff and the bastard was still alive. There was a large rock on the embankment below her. She'd come close to crashing into it after her fall. It would be so easy now to just lean back and let herself go. Her head would hit the rock and the impact would surely kill her. And that would be it, no more pain.

She gritted her teeth and started climbing again.

«««—»»»

Standing in her underwear she studied the wreckage in the mirror before her—the pale face around the heavily-bagged eyes, the bruised forehead and cheek. And then the injuries from the fall: torn and bruised right shoulder, bruises on both sets of ribs, torn and bruised right hip, bruised left thigh and calf. And not forgetting her raw palms and fingers.

She sneezed. She blew out the candles beneath the mirror and limped into bed.

«««—»»»

She woke in the middle of the night with a pounding headache. She put two Excedrin in her mouth and washed them down with some water. She grimaced when she swallowed, her throat feeling terribly sore. She wrapped the duvet tightly around her and went back to sleep.

«««—»»»

A coughing fit woke her at dawn. Her head was roasting and her eyes felt woefully tender. Her body was freezing. She got out of bed and went to the next room, shivering uncontrollably as she walked. She took the blankets and duvet from the bed there and returned to her own room. She spread the extra bedclothes on top of her own duvet and climbed back into bed.

«««—»»»

She opened her eyes. She stared dully at the dark shape before her with the thin line of light running around it. What was it? Had she died? Was she looking at something...otherworldly? Then she realized she was looking at a curtain. The light around it was the light of day. She looked to her left at the half-open bathroom door and she remembered where she was.

She turned her head to the bedside locker. The two bottles of water on it were empty. She could remember drinking the first but not the second. She was very thirsty. She pushed the bedclothes back, a job that took some effort what with there being so much material on top of her. She got to her feet slowly. She felt...woolly. Strangely distant from her body, as though she were remote-controlling it from somewhere else. She pulled one of the duvets from the bed and wrapped it around her. She shuffled from the room and began heading down the hallway toward the living room, where she'd left the bike. A few times the duvet caught under her feet almost causing her to fall. Her head was on fire. She knew her temperature was well over a hundred.

In the living room she took a water bottle from one of the saddlebags and drank it back. She took two more bottles from the bag and went back to the bedroom with them. She returned to the living room for the two remaining bottles but no sooner had she taken them from the bag than she began to feel woozy, her legs beginning to quiver beneath her. She went to leave the room but only made it just beyond the doorway. Yellow lights began to swim before her, obscuring her vision. She fainted.

«‹‹—››»

What was that hissing sound?

She listened to it for a while. It sounded like someone was cooking. Frying. Then she heard whistling. It was the melody of *Bad Moon Rising*. Her heart lifted. Lowell! Lowell was here and he was cooking her breakfast! He cooked the meanest fry anyone could taste. She got out from under the duvet and struggled to her feet. She saw through the living room window that the sun was sinking and thought it a little odd that Lowell was frying in the evening. He only fried in the morning. And she couldn't *smell* anything either. She reached the kitchen doorway.

There was no one at the stove. There was a frying pan on one of the burners but it contained nothing—only dust. She realized the whistling had stopped. There was a bottle of water at her feet. Dimly acknowledging that her fever had just caused her to hallucinate she sat down beside the water bottle and rested her back against the wall. She was very thirsty. She opened the bottle and drank half of it before stopping. She saw the other bottle she'd taken from the bag lying a little way down the hallway. She crawled to it and picked it up. She crawled back to the duvet and got under it again. The cool timber of the floor felt blissful against her fiery cheek. She'd lie there for a few minutes and then she'd get up and head back to bed.

«‹‹—››»

The sound of something hitting the floor caused her to pull the duvet sideways out of her field of vision. A glass vial was rolling to rest by her feet. A pool of black fluid lay on the floor at its mouth. She could see a pair of shoes beyond the vial. She looked up and saw that their owner was Jonah. He was dressed in a white lab coat and he was looking at her. His eyes dropped to the floor and she followed them.

She watched in terror as the black fluid rose up from the floor and morphed into a huge, horrible spider that ran up onto her duvet. She screamed as the abomination sped along the duvet toward her face. She swatted madly at it and hurled the duvet from her. She scrambled backward up against the wall and gazed at the duvet, her heart pounding, waiting for the dreadful creature to spring over it or burrow out from underneath it. The seconds ticked by and nothing happened. She realized that Jonah was gone.

She picked the two water bottles from the floor and stood up. She headed toward the bedroom, keeping her eye on the duvet as she made her way past it. She could not bring herself to pick it up.

«««—»»»

When she woke early the following morning she felt a little better, her fever having broken during the night. She didn't feel hungry but she forced herself to eat a light breakfast. Her last meal (an afternoon snack would be more accurate) had been nearly two days previous.

Afterward she fetched the tracker. She let off a double sneeze as she went to study the screen. This was followed by a horrible, phlegm-filled coughing episode which left her tender throat feeling raw and brought tears to her eyes. Her legs being devoid of any real strength she sat down on the edge of the bed. There would be no driving today.

Jonah was a hundred and seventy five miles east of her in a small town called Princeton.

«««—»»»

The arrow stopped moving in the evening at Grand Forks, three hundred and twenty miles from her. A big gap to close. And she very much doubted he'd be stopping any more. Reality had surely hit home with him by now.

«««—»»»

And yet by afternoon the following day the arrow hadn't moved. Later when she looked at the tracker after taking shelter for the night she kept her eyes on the screen for a long time. He was *still* in Grand Forks.

Exhausted she climbed into bed. With her flu still having some hold on her it had been a tough day on the bike. She'd had to take a lot of breaks. At one stage a vicious coughing fit had blindsided her while she'd been driving and she'd come damn close to crashing.

She closed her eyes and took a deep breath. What *was* Jonah up to? Surely the deluded, desperate wretch wasn't ready to try again? No. She couldn't believe he was.

This is it. He's making a stand.

Yes, this was more believable. He was waiting for her alright but now he had the same intentions for her as she had for him. He wanted done with the chase. As did she. Tomorrow they would have closure either way.

«««—»»»

Grand Forks appeared in the distance before her late in the afternoon. Not wanting to be a sitting duck for him on the bike she parked the Honda around the back of a shed near the town's welcome sign and started walking.

When she reached the far end of the town she stopped in the middle of the road and looked to her left at a small blue bungalow. The tracker was telling her that he was inside the house. She put the tracker into her pocket and walked toward the bungalow, her finger poised by her gun's trigger.

When she turned the knob of the front door she found it unlocked. She opened it quietly and crept inside. The living room was on her right and she checked this first. His bike was there. She went back out into the hallway and continued on toward an open door on her right. She smelled him before she heard him. An unpleasant, fleshy odor.

"Hello, Mary."

She raised the gun before her and pushed the door inward. He was standing at the other end of the kitchen, by the sink. In his right hand was a cane which he was using to support himself. His face was terribly pale and there was a sheen of sweat on his skin. She entered the kitchen, keeping her gun trained on him as she moved. She sniffed. The smell was stronger now.

"Bad, isn't it?" Jonah asked. "I tried to cut it out three days ago. The chip. Turns out Soranor had it planted nice and deep. I didn't get to it. The pain was too much."

"Good," Mary said.

Jonah paused before continuing.

"Turns out I was better at opening my leg up than I was at patching it back together. The wound's infected. I'm dying. Blood poisoning. So you can finish it now or just…walk away. Either way, you're getting what you want."

They gazed at each other in silence, the seconds ticking by. A wave of frustration began to grow in Mary as she stared down the barrel of her gun at the man she had pursued for thousands of miles and tried unsuccessfully to kill three times. Her moment had finally come and… her finger wouldn't pull the trigger. Even after all he had done to her she couldn't do it. She could not take the life of a sick, defenseless… dying human being.

"Do it," he said.

She blinked. The gun didn't fire.

"Drop your weapon!" a voice commanded.

Startled, Mary looked to her left to see a man with a middle-eastern complexion standing beyond the kitchen door in the hallway. He was pointing a machine gun at her. Mary let her gun fall to the ground.

"Move back against the wall."

Mary did as she was told. Keeping his gun on her the man entered the kitchen. He diverted his gaze to Jonah for a moment before returning it to her. Mary was wondering was she about to die when a second man entered the kitchen, a handgun at his side. He studied her briefly before turning in Jonah's direction.

"I told you I would come for you, Doctor," Zarrani said.

He raised his gun and fired.

Jonah flew backward, colliding with the presses behind him. He tumbled to the ground where he lay clutching his chest, his breath coming in shallow gasps.

Zarrani walked to his side. He pointed the gun at Jonah's head and fired.

Jonah lay still.

Mary watched the man turn and walk back the way he had come. He turned his stern eyes toward her briefly. Then he was gone out the door. The man standing before Mary remained where he was for a second or two longer before turning and leaving.

She remained rooted to where she stood for a while, staring at the empty doorway. Eventually she looked to the top of the kitchen. A pool of blood was gathering around Jonah's head. His eyes were staring at the ceiling, no colder than when they'd been alive. She picked her gun up from the floor and went to leave. In the hallway she stopped. She blinked as a picture of Gerald Verlayne appeared in her mind. In it she saw the old man sitting on his porch, all alone in a dead, dust-swept McKittrick.

She remembered his last words to her.

Put one in him for me.

She turned and went back into the kitchen. She walked to where Jonah lay and pointed her gun between his eyes. She fired. Then she turned and left.

Epilogue
Four months later

ary pulled the last bit of weeds from the side of Lowell's grave and knelt back to study her work. She looked from Lowell's grave to Esther's. Yes, both were nice and tidy. She rose to her feet and looked out over the wall. She studied the sun setting on the horizon for a few seconds and then she shifted her gaze to the basin below her.

The southern and central portion of the city was still a grey and black expanse but she thought the dismal miasma was growing a tiny bit smaller with each passing day. There was a colossal clean-up job taking place down there, which she was part of.

On the night she'd arrived back in the city four months earlier she'd seen the orange sky over the mountains in Burbank. From a lookout on Mulholland Drive she'd gazed at the inferno soaring into the dark sky in the distance. As she'd watched it a man had driven by and stopped to ask her was she going down to help the effort to block the fire. She'd said yeah and had followed after him. The blocking effort had been concentrated along West Century Boulevard. Hundreds of people had been piling all manner of incombustible material against a wall of sand, gravel, and dirt that had been constructed in the path of the approaching blaze which had just crossed the Glenn Anderson freeway. Even though it had been nearly a mile away, the heat from the fire, powered by the oil refineries it had consumed, had been intense. To the immense relief of the defenders rain had fallen at dawn and weakened the imminent conflagration but it had still crossed the hastily-constructed barrier. Disheartened, the defenders had begun to scramble together a new wall on Florence Avenue. And then in the afternoon luck had smiled. With the fire gaining in strength as it had approached Manchester Avenue the skies had darkened and a prolonged deluge had fallen. By the time the rain had stopped it had weakened the fire so much that the defenders had easily been able to snuff out what had remained burning. When the smoke had cleared the full scale of the disaster had been revealed. In the three weeks Mary had been away fifty square miles of the city had been burned. Torrance, Gardena, Compton, Lakewood, Carson and swathes of Long Beach had been lost.

Mary gazed at the earth-moving equipment driving and swiveling in the distance, the long metallic arms clawing rubble from the ground. The city was slowly recovering. Every day more people arrived from the surrounding areas. They were even coming from the surrounding states and Mexico. New faces kept appearing in her neighborhood; unfamiliar vehicles kept popping up in driveways. One evening she'd gone for a drive around Beverly Hills. The front gate of Martin Barbara's house, who had directed her in *The War Beneath* had been open and on the front lawn she'd seen two young couples drinking and dancing to some music. In the front garden of a huge property on Ladera Drive she'd seen children racing around after each other while at the top of the garden a man and woman had been standing at a barbecue grill. In the driveway had been a pretty beatup RV. The man and woman had called out to her and invited Mary to eat with them and she'd accepted. The burgers and sausages had been canned but Mary hadn't had cooked meat in so long that the food's blandness had seemed glorious to her. She'd stayed chatting with them for a while, watching the kids as they'd played, smiling occasionally at their life and enthusiasm.

Life.

She let her eyes drop to her stomach and put a hand on it, letting it rest there. A few seconds later she felt a kick. In five months' time she would be bringing Gary Streth's baby into this barely-alive world. A knot of concern tightened in her gut as she pondered the future that lay ahead for their child. It would be very hard, being born into a crippled world. She lifted her gaze again to the colossal expanse of ash in the distance, focusing on the machinery scattered about sporadically in its midst.

She found herself remembering the many times she'd stood right where she was, her arm around Lowell, gazing at the city in all its glory. She wiped a tear from her eye. Would the child in her womb ever see that spectacular sight, the black scab before her now erased and replaced once more with teeming life?

Yes, she thought. One day it would.

A past prize-winner at Listowel Writers Week, John Leahy has a number of online publishing credits to his name. *CROGIAN*, his first novel, was published by Necro Publications in 2012. When not writing he spends his time teaching music, performing in piano bars, working out and keeping abreast of current affairs. John lives in Killarney, Ireland.

CPSIA information can be obtained
at www.ICGtesting.com
Printed in the USA
LVHW041754050919
630060LV00016B/1239